# Dragon Seeker

Anne Forbes

# Dragon Seeker

 Kelpies

Kelpies is an imprint of Floris Books

First published in 2011 by Floris Books

The publisher acknowledges subsidy from
Creative Scotland towards the publication
of this volume.

British Library CIP Data available
ISBN 978-086315-808-7
Printed in Great Britain
by CPI Cox and Wyman, Reading

*To Margaret, Mary and Robert Scougall*

Other books in the Dragonfire series:

# Contents

# Prologue

Gasping for breath, the little dragon landed heavily on the grassy slope and collapsed weakly, his gleaming red scales smeared with earth and leaves. Relief swept through him as he realized just how lucky he'd been to spot the hill, for it had loomed suddenly in the distance like a beacon of hope amid the swirling morning mist.

The mist, however, was thinning fast and, looking round anxiously, he sought a place to hide; a cave or some sort of shelter that would save him from the swords and lances of the soldiers. It was, he knew, a forlorn hope as, wherever he'd hidden on his long flight from the South, they'd somehow always managed to find him.

Drawing on the last of his strength, he crawled into a shallow space between two outcrops of rock. It offered little protection against the death that he knew was near and, with a sigh, he wished now that he'd paid a bit more attention to his mother's words. *Stay close to home,* she'd always warned. *Don't stray far.* But, of course, he hadn't listened. Young and headstrong, he hadn't believed her tales of men in shining armour who killed dragons for sport. What man, after all,

could match the magic strength and power of a
dragon?

He hadn't, however, reckoned on the ruthless
cleverness of the soldiers who had hounded him
over the countryside, allowing him no time to rest
by day or by night. And now the end had come.
He was exhausted and knew that he could go no
further. He was going to die in this strange place,
far from home and no one would ever know where
or how he had perished.

There was a sudden shout and the chilling blast
of a hunting horn. The dragon's heart sank. The
soldiers had spotted him. This truly was the end.
He folded his wings over his ears to shut out its
dreadful call. Again it rang out; a strange inhuman
sound that froze the blood in his veins.

Tears spilled down his cheeks as he looked round
hopelessly for help. Nearby, a rugged grey castle,
set on top of a black mass of rock, loomed against
the morning sky and, from the cluster of houses
crowding its base, he could see men and women
running over the fields towards him. Roughly
clad, they were nothing like the fine soldiers who
had chased him over moor and hill; flags waving,
armour gleaming, swords shining. Moving in from
the left, he could see *them* already, marching in
ordered columns with their leader riding in front,
his black flag embossed with a golden sword.

The soldiers fanned out round the base of the
hill, waving their swords threateningly at the
townspeople who now thronged the lower slopes
in ever increasing numbers. Minutes passed and
it was only when some sort of order had been

established that the knight cantered forward, the black plume on his helmet fluttering in the breeze. All eyes were focused on him when, with a wide gesture, he set his right hand against the golden hilt of his sword. A dreadful silence fell as he slowly drew it from its scabbard and held it aloft.

Everyone watching knew immediately that it was no ordinary sword. The soldiers who had, in the past, witnessed the deaths of many dragons, were silent but a troubled, uneasy growl rose from the ranks of the townspeople who stiffened with fear at the blinding blaze of magic that radiated from its blade.

"Come, dragon," the knight shouted, urging his horse forward. "Come, dragon, so that my sword may drink your blood. Have you not heard of Dragonslayer? It has come for *you*!"

The dragon had, indeed, heard of Dragonslayer. He trembled. This, then, was the terrible sword that all dragons feared. No wonder the soldiers had always been able to find him. The sword would have led them to him, wherever he had hidden. Dragonslayer! The magic sword whose blade could pierce the scales of dragons. This then was Sir Pendar, the Black Knight, the famous Dragon Seeker!

Sir Pendar, for his part, looked at the dragon almost petulantly. It really was too bad, he thought irritably. He'd *so* wanted his fiftieth dragon to be a great beast; a huge, fire-breathing monster that he could boast of in the halls of kings and of princes. And what did he get? This miserable, half-grown specimen that probably couldn't breathe a

candle's worth of fire! He pressed his lips together
in annoyance. Killing it was really hardly worth
his while. Nevertheless, he thought, as he heaved
a sigh, a dragon was, after all, a dragon. Urging
his horse forward, he straightened in the saddle,
brandished his sword and prepared to charge.

Helpless against the magic that drew him
inexorably towards the blazing sword, the dragon
rose to his feet, his claws digging into the earth
as he prepared to meet the enemy; for even young
dragons knew that death had to be faced bravely.
Shaking with fear, he gathered the remains of his
courage and moved forward awkwardly across
the rough ground to meet the Black Knight and
Dragonslayer, his terrible sword.

Sir Pendar's eyes glistened as he urged his horse
to the gallop.

With all eyes on the charging knight, it's hardly
surprising that none of those watching witnessed
the arrival of yet more actors in the unfolding
drama. Perched on a rocky bluff above the dragon,
they appeared out of nowhere. Gorgeously dressed
in velvets and furs, they were magicians of great
power who, more than a little taken aback at what
was happening on their own doorstep, had decided
to take a hand in the matter.

It wasn't often that they chose to interfere in
the world of men but dragons are magic creatures
and they guessed that it must have been this that
had drawn the creature to them. They'd tut-tutted
a bit at first, for they were very old, but given that
the whole affair had taken them by surprise, were
determined to do their best. The dragon had come

to them for help and this must certainly be given. And, as they, too, had heard of Dragonslayer, they very quickly decided that here was an ideal opportunity to remove the sword, once and for all, from the clutches of the world of men.

So it was that even as the horseman rode at full speed towards the dragon, one of the magicians stepped forward and, lifting his arm, sent a streak of light flashing from his fingers. The result of the hex was only obvious when the horse careered headlong into the invisible barrier that had risen between it and the dragon and, not unsurprisingly, crashed to the ground. Its rider, too, fell heavily and before the startled soldiers could move to help their master, the horse, hooves flailing wildly, rolled over him. Thus, Sir Pendar, with a cry of anguish, met his end.

No one was more surprised by this turn of events that the dragon himself who stood rooted to the spot, unable to believe that he had been spared. Vaguely, he wondered why the soldiers and the townspeople were backing off and making no move to assist the knight or gather the reins of the sweating, shivering horse, which had, by this time, struggled unsteadily to its feet. It was only when he turned his head and saw the wonderfully dressed individuals making their way towards him that he understood. Magicians! Like the townspeople, he recognized them for what they were and immediately sank to his knees. They had saved him.

The eldest of the magicians stepped forward and, lifting both of his hands for silence, addressed the

fearful crowd. "Hear me, people of Eidyn," he said
in a stern voice that rang over the hillside, "and do
as I command! Bury the knight, Sir Pendar. Bury
him deep in the rock of your castle yonder and
place his sword and his horn by his side. I, Lord
Alarid, command you so to do!"

He surveyed them grimly as they muttered and
murmured among themselves. At any other time,
he might have worried that the sword would be
fought over but, given the powerful hex in his
words, knew that there would be no squabbling.
They would follow his instructions to the letter.

Before the soldiers could move towards their
stricken master, however, the magician turned
from them towards the hill. Again, a flash of
light flew from his fingers and, to gasps of
amazement, the bluff of rock split apart in a
sharp crack of sound. This was followed by a
petrified silence as the huge, carved door that
had been revealed, swung slowly and majestically
open. More, however, was to come for, from the
doorway, small faery folk appeared. Full of
excitement, they ran to the dragon and welcomed
him warmly.

The kneeling dragon struggled confusedly to his
feet as they clustered round. After the perils of
his journey, he was quite overcome. His wonderful
eyes lost their look of fearful dread and started
to glow as he saw the kindness in the faces of the
little people who were urging him to come with
them into the safety of the hill.

He drew a quivering breath as, heart swelling
with relief, he realized that a new life lay before

him. With no hesitation whatsoever, he turned his back on the outside world and, escorted by the magicians and the faery folk, stepped forward through the massive doorway, into the hill.

# 1. Lord Jezail of Ashgar

I doubt if you will find Ashgar on any map of Central Europe, for it is a tiny, mountainous country that nestles, almost unnoticed, between its more important neighbours. It has few towns and although cars are not unknown, most people still use horse-drawn carriages or ride on horseback, the roads in many places being little more than rutted tracks. Deer, wild boar and wolves roam the countryside but apart from hunters, few people venture deep into its forests as old tales speak of dwarves, dragons and other strange creatures that lurk in dark places among the trees.

Neither did the country folk, themselves, encourage visitors. A surly, silent lot, they were happy enough to sell their farm produce at market-stalls in towns and villages, but they kept their affairs to themselves and made no mention of the growing number of wolves that roamed the countryside, descending on their farms at night to steal their chickens; nor did they tell of the of the evil black crows that watched the highways and byways for curious strangers. Neither did they speak of the mountains of the north where dragons lived, nor of the lands to the east where powerful magicians dwelt in dark castles.

Magicians such as the great Lord Jezail, whose turreted citadel dominated the narrow streets and quaint, red-roofed houses of Stara Zargana; a little country town that was old even in ancient times. Separated from the houses by a curved, rocky bridge that reared high over a fast-flowing mountain stream, no one visited it willingly. Rumours of strange happenings within its walls had, over the years, made its citizens wary. Wary, I might add, but not surprised for, although no one talked of it openly, it had long been known that the citadel was a magic building. Indeed, it was whispered that in days of old, when Lord Jezail's father ruled the eastern province, it gleamed in shades of white and cream; slim, slender and elegantly beautiful against its majestic background of forests and mountain peaks. As evil had crept into Lord Jezail's heart, however, so the colour of the Citadel had gradually changed. Now it rose, black and threatening over the town and few people looked at it without a shudder of fear.

High in the topmost tower of this, his great citadel, Lord Jezail stood silently by a slit window that gave a clear view over the distant, tree-clad slopes of the mountains that lay to the east of the town. His face was unusually worried. Where *was* the man? *Why* hadn't he come? Idly, he fingered the chain of the heavy, gold medallion that hung round his neck. Inscribed with ancient runes, he had inherited it from his father and its magic was strong. His talisman, too, was powerful and he

smiled in satisfaction as the sunlight glinted on
the silver band that clasped his wrist.

Idly, he thought of his forthcoming journey and
excitement glistened in his dark eyes for, if what
he had been told was true, then he might soon
be able to add the fabulous *Book of Spells* to his
collection. His spirits lifted at the thought for with
such a book in his library he would command the
respect of every magician in the world!

Such visions of future fame and glory, however,
soon faded as, once more, he lifted his eyes to
scan the mountain passes. Tapping his fingers
impatiently on the smooth, stone window-sill,
he could barely conceal his impatience. Where
was the man? What was keeping him? Winter
had already given way to spring and the passes
through the mountains had long been open to the
peoples of the east, yet his crows had *still* brought
no news of him.

A slight draught told him that a door had opened
and he turned to see Count Vassili enter the room.
His aide, dark-haired and handsome, adjusted the
neck of his ruffled shirt and straightened his black
velvet robes before bowing low before Lord Jezail.
His mind, however, was working swiftly as he'd
been quick to spot the frown on his master's face.
"You're tired, Milord," he murmured. "Come and
sit down. I'll have tea sent to you at once."

"*Tea!*" Lord Jezail muttered. "It's not *tea* that
I need to make me feel better!" But he left the
window without argument and sank gratefully
into the pile of cushions that lined his ornate, gilt
chair.

Eyeing his master thoughtfully, the count rang a bell, knowing that the servants would arrive within minutes, bringing tea, sandwiches and the little sesame seed cakes that his master so adored.

"The mountain passes have been open for weeks now," Lord Jezail grumbled. "He should have been here long ago!"

The count lifted his eyebrows as he poured water into a tall glass. So *that* was what was bothering him. "You're expecting the Khan of Barazan?" he queried. "You didn't tell me!"

"He said he would come after the snows had melted in the mountains!" Lord Jezail said grumpily as the count reached for a pillbox. "He's bringing me more medicine," he continued, aware of the surprise in his aide's voice.

"But we are well stocked with your dragon pills, Milord," Vassili frowned, shaking one from its box as he spoke. "We've enough to last you well into the autumn," he added, offering it to his master with the glass of water. The count's face was bland but inwardly he felt a touch of concern. During the few years he'd been with his master, he'd seen him in many moods but lately he'd noticed a strange lethargy that puzzled him for, although an elderly man, he'd always been quite active. Vaguely he wondered if it was anything to do with the silver talisman that his master wore round his wrist. It was a talisman that didn't really belong to him and, as he well knew, such magic tokens had their own way of showing their displeasure. Could it be the *talisman* that was making the old man sick?

"Dragons' blood's all very well," Lord Jezail snorted, swallowing the pill distastefully, "but quite honestly these pills aren't really doing me much good. The Khan thinks I've become too used to them and the last time he was here, he promised to bring me potions made from dragons' bile." He frowned irritably as he gave the glass back to the count. "I only hope he arrives with it before we leave for Scotland," he muttered.

Vassili's lips set in a straight line. He was a lot less enthusiastic than his master about the proposed visit to Scotland and had already made his feelings plain. As for *dragons' bile!* He cringed at the thought. That was *all* he needed! Just *wait* until he saw the Khan of Barazan. He'd have more than a few words to say to him on the subject! Nevertheless, he frowned as he glimpsed the flash of silver on his master's wrist and wished with all his heart that he'd never brought the talisman back to Ashgar.

It had all started many years ago, when Lord Jezail had given the silver clasp as a gift to his daughter, Merial. When she'd grown up and married a human, however, he'd cast her off entirely and, as far as the count knew, had neither seen nor spoken to her since. It wasn't, therefore, surprising that on her death, Lady Merial hadn't returned the talisman to her father, nor given it to the witches who had cared for her when she'd arrived friendless in Scotland; she'd left it instead to a human child, her niece by marriage, Clara MacLean.

Knowing that many people craved its power, her father included, Lady Merial had hidden the talisman, leaving Clara a riddle as a clue to its hiding place. Lord Jezail, furious and determined to get the talisman back, had then sent Count Vassili to Scotland to find it. At the thought, the count's lips twisted in a wry smile for, despite the problems he'd faced, he'd enjoyed his stay in Scotland. Convinced that the talisman had been hidden somewhere in Netherfield, Clara's school, he'd taken a post there as a German master and during the course of the term had grown to like both Clara and her brother, Neil. His loyalty, however, had always been to his master and, although he'd have much preferred Clara to keep the talisman, he knew where his duty lay and had taken it back with him to Ashgar.

Even then, he mused sourly, things hadn't turned out quite as he'd thought. Envisaging some sort of praise for a job well done, his lips tightened as he remembered how, when he'd returned to the citadel, Lord Jezail had casually slipped the talisman on his wrist with barely a word of thanks. No praise or recognition of all the dangers he'd been through! Nothing!

Knowing Lord Jezail as he did, the count almost shrugged. It was, after all, a fairly typical reaction and, he supposed, to be expected; for by the time he'd returned to Ashgar, his master had heard that the fabled *Book of Spells* had been found and had been so full of excitement that he couldn't think of anything else! Some said it was the witches who had started the rumour but the fact remained that word had quickly spread throughout the world of magic that the

MacArthurs, the faery folk who lived in the depths of Arthur's Seat in Edinburgh, had somehow managed to lay their hands on it.

The news was enough to send Jezail into raptures. The *Book of Spells* had been found; and, quite naturally, *he* wanted it! Indeed, the thought had occupied his mind ever since!

Of course, Vassili thought, looking back on the matter, he should never have said anything about Clara; but the minute his master had mentioned the *Book of Spells*, he knew that it had been Clara who had found it. The spell she'd used to summon daemons (in the middle of the school concert, for goodness sake) had been uttered in the words of ancient magic. And she had obviously known the spell by heart, for she'd said it confidently, without hesitation. He wished now that he'd kept his mouth shut; for it was *that* particular piece of information that had given Lord Jezail his *big idea*. He knew perfectly well that there was little chance of his being able to steal the *Book of Spells* from the MacArthurs — there was, after all, their dragon to contend with — but if this child had memorized them...

"I know what you're thinking," Lord Jezail growled suddenly from the depths of his chair, "but kidnapping this girl is the only way I can get my hands on the spells. She knows them all off by heart. You told me so, yourself."

The count looked at him warily. Did his feelings show as much as that? If Lord Jezail could read his thoughts with such accuracy, he'd certainly have to be a lot more careful. It wouldn't do for him to discover the *real* reason for his presence in the citadel.

Lord Jezail smiled sourly at the count's expression of dismay. "After all," he pointed out, "it won't take her all that long to write the spells down, will it? She wouldn't be my prisoner for long and ..."

A gentle tap on the door announced the arrival of a servant who entered with a tray piled high with cakes and sandwiches. Vassili watched as he set the table and then made haste to serve his master.

Forgetting the Book of Spells, Lord Jezail drew his chair closer to the table. "It's ridiculous, really, when you think of it," he groused, his eyes falling on the little box of dragon pills. "Here am I, one of the greatest Dragon Seekers of all time, and *look* at me! Reduced to this! Waiting — waiting, like a servant, for the Khan to arrive! If he doesn't come, I've a good mind to go out and kill a dragon myself!"

"Well, it would be exciting to say the least, Milord, but I can't say I recommend it," the count's eyes twinkled as he lifted a plate of sandwiches from the table. "You were a lot younger in those days, for a start," he pointed out, "*and* a lot fitter. But your deeds, you know, aren't forgotten. Everyone remembers the great beasts that you slew."

"Hmmph!" Lord Jezail sounded disgruntled but Vassili's rare words of praise pleased him, nevertheless. He straightened in his chair, smiling slightly as he reached for a sandwich. "Those were the days, Vassili!" he said dreamily. "Stalking dragons, trailing them through the forests and over the mountains, losing them sometimes when they flew off to that dratted valley ..."

The count sighed. He knew what was coming next. He'd heard it all *so* many times before. Yet, if all the old tales his father had told him were true, then Lord Jezail had, indeed, been a great Dragon Seeker in days of old. So much so that the remaining dragons in the area had eventually taken refuge in a deep, desolate valley, which they had guarded fiercely ever since.

"It's monstrous!" his master muttered. "That valley's *full* of dragons and yet *I* have to rely on the Khan for my pills!" He leant forward to choose another sandwich. *"And* pay a fortune for them!" he added, sourly.

Vassili shrugged. "Well, there's not a lot we can do about it, Milord," he said, a trifle ruefully as he poured his master's tea," unless, of course," he added teasingly," you're really serious about visiting the Valley of the Dragons!"

Jezail looked suddenly grim. "If I weren't so weak, I'd go tomorrow!" he snapped.

Vassili looked at him sharply, startled at the sudden strength of his tone.

"When I said that the Khan charged a fortune for his dragon pills, I meant it," his master said bitterly. "Every time he comes, he charges me double. Says they've become scarce! And I do *need* the pills, Vassili! My will might be strong but my body, these days, is old and weak. The dragon pills give me strength! And," his voice became fretful, "what will happen when his supplies run out? Tell me that, Vassili? If you rule out the Valley of the Dragons, then tell me: where is he going to find more dragons in this day and age?"

The count looked at his master thoughtfully; for Lord Jezail certainly had a point. "I don't know," he was forced to admit. "Times have changed, haven't they? I mean ..."

"They used to be ten a penny in the old days," Lord Jezail said tiredly. "Well, maybe not quite," he was forced to admit, "but there were a lot of them around."

Vassili nodded, remembering stories of one particularly ferocious dragon that had roamed the countryside round his father's castle at Trollsberg. "It couldn't have been much fun having them prowling round the place," he said, "but as for killing one ... well," he looked at his master in grudging admiration, "I wouldn't like to face up to a dragon myself!"

"Having a good sword helped," the magician answered. "It had to be sharp, of course!"

"May I ask how many dragons you killed?" Vassili asked, genuinely interested.

"Twenty-three," Lord Jezail said proudly, his good humour restored. "You wouldn't think so, looking at me now, but I was reckoned one of the best Dragon Seekers of my day! Of course, twenty-three wasn't the record. That was held by the English knight, Sir Pendar."

"You can hardly compare yourself to him, though," Vassili objected, holding out a plate. "*He* had a magic sword, after all! *You* didn't! *His* job was easy by comparison!"

"That's true," Lord Jezail mused, helping himself to a piece of cake. "He killed forty-nine dragons if the old stories are true."

"And died trying to kill Arthur!"

"Yes, Arthur was to have been his fiftieth kill," Jezail agreed. "You know the story, then?"

The count nodded. "Well, sort of. I know that the Lords of the North rescued Arthur and that he's lived with the MacArthurs in Arthur's Seat ever since ..."

"Mmmm," Lord Jezail bit into the slice of cake. "Sir Pendar's buried in Edinburgh, too — in the castle rock. Did you know that?"

"No, I didn't," Vassili looked surprised. "In the rock, itself?" he frowned. "How on earth did the townspeople manage that?"

"They didn't," Lord Jezail answered. "The Lords of the North hexed his tomb out of the rock and guided the people to it. Once he'd been laid to rest with his sword, horn and flag by his side, they closed the tomb by magic. At least, so the story goes."

"So he's still there," Vassili mused, "after all these years? With his sword and all?"

"As far as I know," Lord Jezail nodded, putting the last piece of cake in his mouth and waving his hand to indicate that he'd finished eating.

Vassili rose to his feet to summon the servant and, in so doing, missed the strange expression that crossed his master's face.

Dragonslayer, Lord Jezail thought, a sudden wave of excitement shooting through him. Why hadn't he thought of it before? Dragonslayer; the magic sword that could pierce the scales of dragons!

As Vassili had just so conveniently pointed out, it was still there ... in Edinburgh!

Gripping his hands together to calm his racing mind, he was careful to keep a straight face. Vassili must never suspect. He knew the count. If he got so much as a tiny hint of the scheme that had suddenly flashed through his mind, he'd start putting all sorts of obstacles and objections in the way.

But ... to *own* Dragonslayer! To become a *Dragon Seeker* once more! The thought was really quite breathtaking and, he realized excitedly, certainly more than possible; for he wouldn't need his old strength to wield such a wonderful sword. Dragonslayer would slice into a dragon as easily as a knife slides through butter. And, as they were going to Scotland anyway, they could certainly include Edinburgh in their travels. If he failed — well, he wouldn't be any worse off, but if he were to succeed ...

Thoughts of Dragonslayer filled his mind for the rest of the day. Opening the tomb, he thought, might present problems, especially if it had been closed by magic ... but, on the other hand, maybe not.

So it was that when night fell and lamps were lit in the town, he stood once again at the high window of the citadel. This time, however, his eyes were blind to the twinkling lights of Stara Zargana or the high peaks of the mountains standing stiffly against the darkening sky; for his mind was full of swords, dragons, magic ... and the earthquake that might make all of his dreams come true.

# 2. Earthquake

"Hey, Clara," Neil shouted excitedly, "tell Mum and Dad to come and look at the telly! There's been an earthquake in Edinburgh and they're showing it now!"

Clara called her parents and rushed to the TV set in the living room where the announcer talked them through the earthquake that had devastated Edinburgh and, more to the point, rocked the great castle that loomed, in all its majesty, over the city centre.

"My goodness," Mrs MacLean said worriedly as they watched," just look at the expressions on people's faces!"

In the mobile phone footage, everyone on Princes Street was looking up in alarm at the sudden noise; a fearful, growling roar that sounded as though several jumbo jets were about to land on top of them! Some stared anxiously over the broad stretch of Princes Street Gardens towards the castle, thinking perhaps, that its guns had fired an unexpected salvo, but it was only when the ground started to shake and the pavement swayed beneath their feet that the truth dawned. It was an earthquake! Startled faces paled with fear as realization dawned that the dreadful roar was the voice of the earth itself.

They watched in awe as the TV screen showed cars braking frantically, shrieking to a halt as the road in front of them took on a life of its own. Horns blared as buses collided, their terrified passengers struggling to get out. Shoppers and assistants alike fled from stores and fought their way through the tumble of people struggling to keep their balance on the pavement before they, too, were caught up in the heaving, rippling roller coaster that was Princes Street.

Stumbling across the road to the relative safety of Princes Street Gardens, they clung to the railings to keep their balance and watched, powerless, as the heaving earth continued to shake even the largest buildings.

"Look at that!" Clara gasped, pointing to the screen as several pillars fronting the art gallery bulged dangerously.

The cameras focused again on the garden side of Princes Street where a woman was screeching like a banshee! "The castle!" she was screaming, her face contorted with disbelief. "Look at the castle! It's falling down!"

Fortunately, this proved to be a bit of an exaggeration for it wasn't actually the castle that was falling but the part of the rock that lay below the esplanade. Clara gasped. It was like watching a film in slow motion for, in front of their disbelieving eyes, a huge part of the rocky slope bulged slowly outwards and then sheered away in an explosion of sound, sending a thundering avalanche tumbling

down into the gardens and onto the railway line
below.

"Thank goodness there were no trains running,"
John MacLean said, as the video footage finished
and the camera homed in on the castle itself,
revealing the deep scar that had been carved out
of its rock before panning down to the tumble of
stone and earth that covered the railway line." If
that load of rock had hit the carriages, they would
have been flattened!"

The announcer was saying much the same thing
as the camera showed Princes Street where yellow-
jacketed workers had already started clean-up
operations. "Princes Street," he said, "seems to
have been badly hit, as you can see. A complete
disaster zone! We are hearing, however, that
the rest of the city seems to have escaped major
damage. In fact, the earthquake only seems to
have affected Central Edinburgh." He glanced
casually at his monitor. "We're expecting a report
on its magnitude any minute now. I'll give it to you
as soon as it comes in."

"I wonder if it shook Arthur's Seat?" Mrs
MacLean frowned, thinking of the great hill,
shaped like a sleeping dragon, that dominated the
Edinburgh skyline. "I hope the MacArthurs are
alright!"

"I'd forgotten about them!" Neil gasped, for
Arthur's Seat was home to their friends; small
faery folk called the MacArthurs.

Before they'd moved from Edinburgh to the
Borders, Neil's father had been the Park Ranger
on Arthur's Seat and both he and his sister,

Clara, had not only played with the MacArthurs as small children, but had also met the enormous dragon that lived with them in the hill. Despite the fact that they now lived miles away, they'd nevertheless continued to be involved in many of their adventures. Sitting up anxiously, Neil looked at the TV, hoping it would show more of the city, but the camera had changed direction and was now moving over the deep cracks, piles of rubble and twisted tramlines that littered Princes Street.

"Maybe we could go up to Edinburgh at the weekend?" Clara suggested. "I'm a bit worried about the MacArthurs. Could we, Mum? I mean, once we're there we can call our magic carpets and go into the hill."

Neil nodded enthusiastically. "Yes, let's do that," he said. "It's ages since we saw the MacArthurs!"

"And Arthur!" Clara smiled, thinking of the great red dragon that lived in the hill.

Mrs MacLean looked at her husband who nodded thoughtfully. "I don't see why not," he said unconcernedly. "You can tell them we were asking for them ... and that we hope the earthquake didn't do any damage."

"If it did," Clara laughed, "they'd just use magic to fix it."

Clara didn't know it, but at that particular moment, Lord Jezail was thinking much the same thing. Should he use his magic to mend Sir Pendar's tomb?

He frowned in annoyance as sunlight, streaming

in through a jagged gap in the outer wall, revealed a ceiling that tilted alarmingly and stone walls full of deep cracks. How *could* he have made such an error of judgement? The hex he'd cast had been too strong by far. Indeed, he'd been lucky that the tomb hadn't slipped down the side of the castle rock with the rockslide!

Taking a deep breath to steady his quivering nerves, he stepped back and took another searching look round the interior of the small stone chamber, his sharp eyes missing nothing as they darted here and there. A black flag with a golden sword in its centre listed crazily against one wall and, underneath its dusty folds, stood a huge coffin. Cut out of solid rock, it dominated the room. The heavy stone slab that had obviously been its lid, lay shattered on the floor, witness to the strength of the mighty earthquake he'd hexed up.

Reverently, he approached the coffin and peered inside. Would it be there, he asked himself anxiously? Would the sword be there?

At first, he was too taken aback to notice it, for although Sir Pendar lay in great splendour, his shining armour encased the white bones of his skeleton. His skull grinned up at him from the depths of his helmet; his bones showed clearly through the joints in his armour and his horn lay by his side. It was then that a burst of joy filled the magician's heart — for the skeleton's hand clutched a sword across its chest in a bony grasp. Dragonslayer! There was no doubt about it! He feasted his eyes on its broad, embossed blade and fingered the delicate curve of the carved dragon that decorated its hilt. Dragonslayer! It was his for the taking!

His hand shook as he reached into the coffin to take the sword but Sir Pendar's grasp was unyielding. He pulled at the sword but it didn't move. Not an inch.

The magician's face turned ugly. He hadn't come all this way to find the sword and leave without it!

Seeing his face, the sword trembled within itself. The earthquake, totally unexpected, had frightened the wits out of it but when the lid of the coffin had slid off and crashed to the floor, a great well of happiness had surged through it. There was light: it could see!

Dragons layer's happiness, however, dimmed when the magician bent over the coffin, his face evil and triumphant. It had already sensed the presence of magic and the feeling was confirmed the minute Lord Jezail put his hand on its hilt.

The sword thought rapidly as a myriad of possibilities flashed through its mind. It would, quite naturally, have much preferred to have been found by a human; preferably some simple soul like Sir Pendar who had done *what* he was told, *when* he was told. Magicians, however, were a very different kettle of fish and the sword was wary. It was as Lord Jezail pulled again at the hilt that the sword gauged the depths of the magician's power and was overtaken by doubt; for this was a powerful magician, indeed.

The sword sighed. It was the same story all over again! All its life, it had been hampered by the fact that it couldn't move around on its own. It needed to belong to someone who would care for it, carry it around and obey its wishes. But a magician? It hesitated for a few seconds more, weighing up the possibilities — and then relaxed its grip, deciding that belonging to a magician might, after all, have its advantages.

The magician pulled again, this time with all his strength — and promptly fell over backwards as the sword slid easily from Sir Pendar's grasp. Staggering to his feet, he looked at it greedily. He felt its power and, holding it by its hilt, waved it triumphantly in the air so that the sunlight sparked off its shining blade.

It was then that a voice spoke to him.

He spun round, his eyes darting into every nook and cranny, but it was only when the voice spoke again that he realized that it came from the sword in his hand.

"Who are you?" the sword demanded. "What is your name?"

Lord Jezail froze. Hurriedly, he changed his grasp and held the blade of the sword flat across the palms of both hands and bowed to it, his mind in turmoil. It had never entered his head that Dragonslayer might have this kind of magic and he wasn't at all sure if he was happy about it.

"My name is Lord Jezail ... Lord Jezail of Ashgar," he stammered.

"Ashgar?" The sword slowly changed colour and glowed with a golden hue as the information registered. "Ashgar ..." it repeated in a different tone. "Where there is a valley of dragons?"

"Yes," Lord Jezail answered, breathing a sigh of relief.

He had sensed the sword's initial hesitation but mention of the Valley of the Dragons had done much to allay its fears.

Excitement flared through the sword at the very thought of the valley that had been famous even in the days of Sir Pendar. "We will go there," it announced. "But not yet! First of all, I would like to bid farewell to my knight, Sir Pendar. Please hold me over his body, if you will!"

Lord Jezail raised his eyebrows. An order, he thought. Nicely put, but an order nevertheless.

Obediently, he moved forward and, as he held Dragonslayer over the body of the knight, felt a beam of magic shiver from the blade of the sword. Gasping in surprise, he looked down to see that, once again, Sir Pendar clasped a sword between his bony fingers. A sword that was identical to the one he held in his hand.

"We cannot leave a knight without his sword," Dragonslayer pointed out, sensing the magician's surprise. "Sir Pendar was a good man and served me well. He deserves no less."

Lord Jezail bowed in agreement but his mind was racing frantically. This wasn't at all what he had expected. A magic sword, yes; a magic sword whose blade could pierce the scales of dragons, yes; but a sword that could talk, give orders and throw spells ... this wasn't what he'd had in mind at all!

# 3. Secret tunnels

"For goodness sake, don't take any risks, Johnson," Colonel Jamieson spoke briskly as the first of the two soldiers who'd volunteered to suss out the earthquake damage, dangled his legs over the wide split that had opened in the floor of one of the castle's dungeons. "And that goes for you, too, Mason," he added, turning to the other man who was still being roped up.

It was the deepest of all the dungeons and, until then, everyone had assumed that the bedrock of the castle lay underneath it. The opening in the rock, however, had caused more than a few raised eyebrows among the team of engineers, for the strong current of fresh air that blew from it, indicated that there was a lot more than rock under their feet.

Ian Johnson looked into the hole in the ground, assessing the possibilities. The opening, fortunately, was wide enough to give him plenty of room to manoeuvre but sloped steeply sideways into the depths.

"We'll watch out, Sir. Don't worry!" Stuart Mason grinned confidently, as he made a final adjustment to his harness.

Ian lowered himself carefully into the hole and, hanging on to the rope with one hand, shone his torch downwards, hoping to see how deep the shaft actually was. The incline made it impossible to judge, however, and as the voices from above grew fainter, he was grateful for the comforting sense of security the rope provided. Eventually, he came to the bottom of the shaft and, feet now planted firmly on solid ground, he relaxed and took stock of his surroundings. Shining the beam of the torch this way and that, he was surprised to discover that this was no crack caused by the earthquake; he was in a tunnel ... a tunnel that had been cut out of solid rock.

Ian frowned. Like every other soldier in the regiment, he knew about the underground tunnels that ran from the castle to the High Street and beyond. They were well documented, appearing on many of the old maps in the archives. He'd peered into a few of them himself but hadn't fancied exploring them, knowing that over the years they'd become unstable; rockfalls making many of them actively dangerous. However, none of them, to his knowledge, had been cut out of solid rock — nor were they anywhere near as deep as this.

The silence around him was deathly and his torch, although powerful, only lit up part of the tunnel before the beam petered out into the darkness. The air, however, was fresh and turning the beam up the shaft, he pulled three times on the rope; the signal for Stuart to join him.

Stuart arrived several minutes later in a scatter of small stones, and was equally impressed. He

looked at Ian and whistled in amazement. "Well,
well," he said, his eyebrows raised, "somebody's
taken a lot of trouble to carve out this tunnel — a
whole lot of trouble!"

"That's what I thought," Ian nodded, unhooking
his rope from his harness. "Let's see where it
leads! There's plenty of fresh air coming through."

Pulses racing, they shone the torch round the
walls and set off, moving along swiftly and easily.
They hadn't, however, gone all that far when the
tunnel stopped abruptly, blocked by a mass of
earth and shards of rock. Not only that, a wide
crack split the wall of the tunnel on one side.

"The wall seems to have opened up here," Ian
breathed, shining his torch into the wide cleft that
stretched from floor to ceiling. Cautiously, he
stuck his head inside. "Hey, hang on a minute,"
he whispered, "this is where the fresh air's
coming from. It's blowing through here!" He
edged further in. "And I can see daylight!" he
added. "Come on," he gestured, "there's plenty
of room. It gets wide enough to walk through.
Might as well have a look!"

Stuart switched off his torch as daylight
streamed in and then cannoned into Ian who'd
come to an abrupt halt in front of him. "What's
up?" he muttered, before falling silent as they
both took in the fantastic sight that lay before
them. The cleft opened out into a small room
that, like the tunnel, seemed to have been carved
out of the rock itself. Lit by the stream of sunlight
that poured through a gash in its outer wall,
they saw a scene that took them straight back

in time. Dimly remembered childhood stories
of knights in armour and romantic castles flew
through their minds as they gaped in wonder
at the huge black flag with the golden sword in
its centre that hung, lopsidedly, above a coffin;
a stone coffin. Its lid had obviously come off
during the earthquake as its shattered remains
were scattered across the floor, but that wasn't
what held their attention for, from where they
were standing, they could see that the coffin
contained a body.

"Wow!" Ian breathed, excitement flowing
through him like a river. "What's this, then?"

"A knight by the look of things," Stuart answered
as they picked their way over the rock-strewn floor
to peer inside, for the coffin contained the skeleton
of a man in armour.

Ian frowned and looked round. It seemed a
strange sort of burial.

"Whoever put him here, laid his sword and his
horn beside him," Stuart muttered, moving closer,
his eyes taking in the grinning skull that looked
pathetically small inside the crumbling helmet.
He took a step backwards. "That must be his
standard!" he muttered, looking up at the black
flag that hung on the wall above the alcove. "The
sword on it looks like the one he was buried with.
Look at the detail on the hilt. There's a dragon
curving round it. And see here, the same design's
on the mouthpiece of the horn."

Ian nodded. *"What a find!"* he whispered,
turning to examine the rest of the stone chamber.
"We're going to hit the headlines with this! Can

you imagine the excitement it's going to cause! Archaeologists are going to have a field day!"

"You can say that again," Stuart agreed, and as Ian peered at Princes Street through the massive crack in the wall, he reached out to pick up the horn gingerly. "The horn seems solid enough," he remarked, turning it over in his hands. Ian looked round at his words and before he could do anything to stop him, Stuart wiped the mouthpiece of the horn on his sleeve and blew with all his might.

Ian put his hands over his ears at the sound and even Stuart looked shaken.

"You shouldn't have touched it," Ian snapped in exasperation. "Honestly, Stuart, with a find like this, it's really important that everything is left as it was found!"

As they stared at one another angrily there was a sharp crack of sound and a sudden flash of light that made them cower.

"What was that?" Ian gazed round apprehensively.

"I don't know but I suggest we get out of here," Stuart's voice was urgent. "We don't want the roof falling in on us!"

Ian nodded. "Put the horn back first, for goodness sake," he said, his mouth stern. "I still can't believe you actually blew it!"

Stuart stepped forward and placed the horn carefully beside the knight. "There," he said, totally unrepentant. "I've put it back exactly where it was. No one will ever know that I touched it!"

In this, however, Stuart was as wrong as it is possible to be; for the blast of the horn had rung out loud and clear, in every corner of the world of magic. It was heard by magicians, hobgoblins, trolls, giants and dragons ... and they all knew what it meant!

# 4. Voice of the horn

"Thank goodness there wasn't much damage, Father," Lady Ellan said, settling comfortably in her chair as she glanced round the cavernous heights of the Great Hall that lay in the depths of Arthur's Seat.

Her husband, Lord Rothlan, nodded. "We thought it might be a lot worse," he admitted.

"It's just as well that earthquakes don't happen often in this part of the world," the MacArthur observed sourly from the cushioned depths of his throne-like chair. "Gave us quite a shock, I can tell you."

The great, red dragon that lay curled by his side, looked at him affectionately and stretched lazily. He was very fond of the MacArthurs, the magic people who lived inside Arthur's Seat, especially Archie, who sat comfortably in the crook of his arm.

"Some of the passages that lead down to the store rooms have collapsed," Archie said, "but Hamish and Jaikie say that they won't take long to clear."

Arthur blew a tiny puff of smoke and Archie turned to look at him warningly. He knew the signs. Arthur, delighted to see the MacArthur's daughter, Lady Ellan, and her husband Lord Rothlan, who had just arrived through the magic mirror from their estate at Jarishan, was just itching to breathe a few welcoming clouds to show how pleased he was to see them. As this generally set everyone coughing and spluttering, it wasn't exactly a popular pastime, however, and Archie was just about to say "no" very firmly indeed, when the dreadful, eerie blast of a horn rang through the Great Hall.

Everyone froze in their chairs. Arthur gave a terrible dragon scream. His body convulsed as he buried his head in his wings, desperately trying to shut out the sound. Never again had he thought to hear that piercing blast. Its memory had gradually faded with the passing of the years and it no longer sounded in his dreams but now the old fear swept over him again; Sir Pendar's horn!

Archie threw his arms round the trembling dragon, trying to comfort him while the MacArthur and Lord Rothlan looked at one another in horror and amazement. "Pendar's horn!"

Lord Rothlan snapped. "How on earth ...?"

Hamish and Jaikie rushed into the hall and, like Archie, went to comfort the dragon who was still shivering violently as old memories clouded his mind. Sir Pendar's horn ...

The hobgoblins in Morven looked at one another in disbelief as the sound of the horn swept through the mountain. It was so long since they'd last heard it that at first they hardly recognized it.

Then, as memories returned, the tiny nodules on their heads started to sprout long, anxious tendrils and their goat-like little faces puckered anxiously. Sir Pendar's horn!

With one accord they headed for the curving flight of steps that led to the blue and silver halls of their masters, the Lords of the North. Creeping upwards on tiny hooves, they peered at the curve of silver thrones that dominated the Great Hall. The lords would surely know what was going on.

In this, they were not mistaken. The Lords of the North, old and wizened with age, had been dozing comfortably in their chairs after a good lunch. Now wide awake, they knew exactly what the blast signified.

Lord Dorian blinked irritably and looked at Lord Alarid, his eyebrows raised. "I thought you hexed that wretched tomb ages ago, Alarid," he remarked sourly.

"I did," Lord Alarid snapped, an anxious frown creasing his forehead.

"The earthquake?" Lord Alban suggested, glancing round the semi-circle of gorgeously robed magicians. "It hit Edinburgh pretty hard and I understand there was some damage to the castle. You never know, it might have opened the tomb ..."

The Lords of the North exchanged thoughtful glances and, rising to their feet, moved instinctively towards an oval table of beaten silver where a shining crystal ball rested on an ebony stand. Lord Alarid passed a hand over it and, as the lords crowded round, breathed in sharply as he saw two soldiers standing in the ruins of Pendar's tomb. One of them was holding the horn!

As the eye of the crystal moved over Sir Pendar's coffin, Lord Dorian stiffened. "Never mind the horn, Alarid," he said, grasping the velvet sleeve of his robe, "hex the sword! Hex it now! *Now!*" he repeated, as Lord Alarid wavered. "For goodness sake, Alarid, stop dithering! *We* won't be the only ones to have heard the horn!"

Hastily, Lord Alarid spoke the words of a powerful hex and as he watched the soldiers swing round at the sudden crack of sound, breathed more easily. The hex was in place.

"Someone else is watching through a crystal," Lord Alban pointed out as the crystal registered the presence of magic.

"The MacArthurs, perhaps, or Lord Rothlan?" Lord Alarid hazarded a guess.

Lord Dorian's eyes narrowed as he bit back a sharp retort. "Possibly," he said icily, "but personally, I wouldn't be surprised if we haven't just stopped Lord Jezail in his tracks. He must have heard the horn and now he's seen the sword!"

There was a moment's silence as his words registered. They all knew that Lord Jezail craved power. And Dragonslayer was enormously powerful!

"One way or another," Lord Dorian continued, "there's going to be trouble over this! Think about it, Alarid! He managed to get the talisman last year and I wouldn't be at all surprised if he isn't working on some sort of scheme to steal the *Book of Spells!* He flung out his hand dramatically towards the crystal where the startled soldiers were looking fearfully round the tomb. "And now, this!"

Lord Alarid frowned in annoyance. "Relax, Dorian," he said shortly. "Dragonslayer will never again slay a dragon. Not with *that* particular hex in place!"

Lord Dorian, however, wasn't convinced. "That's all very well," he stated firmly, "but *Jezail* doesn't know that, does he? Believe me; he'll move heaven and earth to get his hands on that sword! Don't forget that he was a Dragon Seeker of old!"

There was a long silence as the magicians considered the matter.

"You know, I think I agree with Dorian," Lord Alban said thoughtfully. "Jezail was always ambitious, remember, and if he sees half a chance of getting his hands on Dragonslayer, he'll take it! And you never know, Alarid ... his magic is such that he might well be able to reverse your spell!"

The Lords frowned worriedly and Lord Alarid's face grew stern at the thought of the terrible power of the sword that had killed many of the world of magic's most precious creatures.

# 5. Dragon tears

The minute their magic carpets soared into the MacArthur's Great Hall in the depths of Arthur's Seat, Neil and Clara knew that they had been right to come. They'd been at home playing Nintendo when they'd heard the dreadful sound of the horn and had known instinctively that something had happened in the world of magic. Something dreadful!

Neil, peering over the edge of his magic carpet, looked across at Clara and pointed at Arthur, for the huge red dragon was curled in a huddled heap, his wings covering his head. Everyone, it seemed, was trying to comfort him for he was surrounded on all sides by a crowd of MacArthurs.

Indeed, so concerned were the MacArthurs about their dragon that it was only Amgarad, Lord Rothlan's great eagle, who noticed the carpets soaring in across the vastness of the cavern. He flapped into the air as they lost height and Clara waved to him delightedly as he circled round them. It was only when they landed, however, that Lady Ellan, the MacArthur's daughter, turned to see what was happening. She came across swiftly and hugged them tightly. "It's *so* nice to see you," she said, "but you've chosen a bad time to visit, I'm afraid!"

Amgarad, his great wings beating the air, swooped down to land on Clara's shoulder and she winced slightly as his claws dug deep into her jacket. Neil looked on admiringly as the bird settled its wings and started to pull gently at Clara's long brown hair with its frighteningly curved beak.

"What's the matter with Arthur, Lady Ellan?" Neil asked. "He's not ill, is he?"

Several heads turned at the sound of his voice. The MacArthur, himself, looked up as did Lady Ellan's husband, Lord Rothlan, who was deep in conversation with Sir James Erskine, the owner of a local distillery. After several adventures involving a variety of goblins, monsters and magicians, he too had become familiar with the MacArthur's world, wore a firestone and had his own magic carpet.

The eagle answered, shifting on his claws. "The voice of the horn frightened him," he said. "Did you hear it too?"

Clara nodded, her eyes apprehensive. "We thought it was a horn," she said. "It sounded ... I can't describe it ... it made my blood freeze!"

It was then that Sir James walked over and shook their hands warmly. "Hello, you two," he said with a smile.

"Hello, Sir James," Neil's expression relaxed and he grinned. "We heard that you'd been in the States for a while. Are you back for good?"

"No, this is a flying visit, I'm afraid," Sir James replied. "I still have business to finish off when I get back to New York."

"That sounds impressive," Clara said, looking up at him. "Did the MacArthur tell you that we've moved house?"

Sir James nodded. "Yes, he did. So, how are you enjoying living in the Borders?"

"Well," Neil said after some consideration, "we still miss Edinburgh but the country's nice as well. It's different. We're taking riding lessons and stuff like that ..."

"And we've made lots of friends at school," Clara added.

Sir James raised his eyebrows. "Aren't you missing something out?" he queried, hiding a smile. "The MacArthur's just been telling me about a whole lot of witches and a certain *Book of Spells*?"

Neil grinned and told him briefly how they'd flown to the witches' castle in the middle of the night, crept inside and stolen the precious book from their library.

Clara, however, frowned; for their set-to with the witches hadn't been at all the light-hearted adventure that Neil was painting. Stealing the fabulous *Book of Spells* from the witches' castle had been one of the most frightening events in her life and, as she now realized, the consequences were still with her. Thinking back to the time when she'd had the book hidden in her room at school, she now reckoned that it had *wanted* her to learn the spells. It was a magic book with its own power; and the spells, written in the language of old magic, had somehow imprinted themselves in her brain. How she *wished* they'd never stolen it!

It was then that Lady Ellan interrupted their conversation and, putting an arm round Clara, gestured to the dragon who had folded his wings back and was being cosseted by the little people. "Come and say hello to Arthur," she whispered. "He's very upset and frightened at the moment. I'll explain things to you later."

Neil followed her over to where Arthur lay and patted the dragon awkwardly but Clara flung her arms round his neck and laid her cheek against his scaly head, murmuring words of comfort as a shudder ran through the length of his body. "Don't worry, Arthur," she whispered, "we'll all look after you! You know that!" The dragon gave a long sigh and his wonderful eyes opened for a few seconds before closing again. It was enough. She knew he was happy to see them.

Archie, one of a little group of MacArthurs, looked at them seriously. "He'll be alright," he whispered. "He just needs a bit of time to get over the shock."

Jaikie nodded at them reassuringly. "He's much better than he was. Don't you think so, Hamish?"

"Is it because of the horn we heard?" Neil whispered as they moved towards the dais where the MacArthur was arranging the pile of cushions on his ornate chair. Hamish nodded briefly as they sorted themselves out. Lord Rothlan and Lady Ellan opted to share a divan but everyone else pulled up chairs, stools or cushions.

Lady Ellan, who had overheard Neil's remark, looked round the little group with a slight smile. "You must all have been wearing your firestones to have heard the horn," she observed.

"May we ask whose it was?" Sir James asked, looking from her to the MacArthur. "It made my hair stand on end!"

"Aye, and so it might!" the MacArthur began in a grim voice. "It's a story that goes back hundreds of years to the time when Arthur came to the hill." There was a murmur of surprise at this as, until then, no one had really given much thought as to how Arthur had come to live in Arthur's Seat. "The horn you heard," he continued, "belonged to a knight called Sir Pendar who had a sword called Dragonslayer. The name," he said sourly, "speaks for itself — for Dragonslayer is a magic sword with an overpowering desire to find and kill dragons."

"Yes," Lord Rothlan mused. "Poor Sir Pendar! I've often felt sorry for him!"

*"Poor Sir Pendar?"* repeated Neil questioningly.

Rothlan nodded. "Just think about it, Neil. The sword's natural instinct is to find and kill dragons," he explained. "Once he laid his hand on Dragonslayer, I doubt if Sir Pendar had much of a say in his choice of career. The sword's magic would have taken him over completely and driven him on to kill more and more dragons. Mind you," he added thoughtfully, "he probably did very well out of it, too ..."

"How do you mean?" Clara sounded puzzled.

Lord Rothlan turned to look at her. "Dragons are, as you know, magic creatures, Clara, and, like everything else, magic has its price. Apothecaries ..." he stopped as he saw Neil frown over the word, "I suppose you'd call them chemists or pharmacists, nowadays," he explained. "Well, they used to follow knights like Sir Pendar round the country. Wherever *he* went, *they* went and once he'd killed his dragon, they'd pay him for its body. Then they'd drain its blood, remove its tongue and collect its scales and things. Not its flesh, for dragon's meat is poisonous to humans."

"Its *tongue*?" echoed Neil.

Lady Ellan nodded. "In those days, people believed that if you possessed a dragon's tongue, no one would be able to poison you. Kings and princes paid a fortune to own one."

Clara gave a horrified gasp at this and looked across at Arthur, hoping that he couldn't hear what was being said. The MacArthur, following her glance, lowered his voice and went on to tell them what had happened on that fateful day, long ago — but it was only when they heard of Sir Pendar's burial in the castle rock that they understood Arthur's fear at the sound of the horn. No wonder he was afraid! It meant that Dragonslayer had been found and was free to work its magic again.

"The minute we heard the horn," Lady Ellan said, "we looked in the crystal and saw what had happened. The earthquake had cracked open the tomb and some soldiers were there from the castle. We think they were probably investigating the earthquake damage and had stumbled on the tomb by accident. From what they were saying, it was obvious that they had just found it."

"It was one of the soldiers who blew the horn," Lord Rothlan added.

The MacArthur nodded. "Fortunately, Lord

Alarid, too, used his crystal and saw what had happened. He hexed the sword immediately," he continued, "and put a protective shield round it so that it can't be used against dragons."

At this, they all turned and looked at Arthur.

"But Arthur — well, you can see for yourself. It's brought back all his old nightmares!"

Sir James frowned. "The newspapers are full of the discovery," he said slowly, "but there's a lot they're not telling us. Colonel Jamieson obviously doesn't want people scrambling up the rock face to get in from the outside. The artefacts will be valuable."

"What do you think he'll do with them?" Clara asked.

"Put them on display, I should think," Sir James answered.

"And the skeleton?" Neil asked.

Sir James looked serious. "Sir Pendar himself? Well, I read in the *Scotsman* this morning that he's going to be given a proper burial in the castle. They're going to make a big thing of it, by the sound of things."

"It's the sword we're really worried about," the MacArthur said frankly. "We're afraid that Lord Jezail may try to steal it. He'd like nothing better than to own Dragonslayer."

At the mention of Lord Jezail's name, Sir James looked at the MacArthur sharply. Even Neil and Clara sat up and took notice for, from what they'd heard in the past, he was definitely not a magician to be trifled with. Neil's eyes gleamed with excitement but Clara felt her stomach sink.

"Lord Jezail!" Sir James repeated, startled. "In that case," he said slowly, "I think it might be a good idea to pay Colonel Jamieson a visit. I'll go up to the castle tomorrow morning and find out what's going on."

"I was hoping you'd say that," the MacArthur smiled gratefully. "We need to know exactly what they're planning to do with the sword."

"No problem," Sir James assured him. "I'm sure Jamieson'll tell me what he has in mind. I got to know him quite well when I gave the commentary at the Tattoo ... as you all doubtlessly remember!" he added with a knowing grin.

Neil and Clara laughed at the memory but Lady Ellan blushed and Lord Rothlan chuckled at this reminder of the time when they had both been enemies.

"If this sword is as dangerous as you say it is," he continued, looking at the MacArthur, "then the least I can do is make sure it's properly guarded!"

# 6. Festival fever

"We've hardly stopped since the tomb was discovered," Colonel Jamieson admitted, leaning back in his chair. "You've no idea the amount of interest there's been. I think every antiquarian society in the world's accessed the website we've set up ..."

"It's good of you to see me, in that case," Sir James smiled. "Sheer curiosity on my part, I confess ..."

The colonel grinned understandingly. "We've had experts into examine it," he said, "and they reckon it was made around the time of King Arthur." Rising from his desk, he ushered Sir James towards a glass-topped table that held the sword and the horn. "From around 500 AD, I'm told." He unlocked the lid and lifted the sword reverently from its bed of dark blue velvet. Holding it across the palms of both hands, he showed it to Sir James. "Here, have a closer look."

Sir James took the sword carefully, exclaiming at its weight as he examined it closely. It had, indeed, been beautifully made; the blade gleamed and the fire-breathing dragon that curled round the hilt had certainly been delicately carved. Nevertheless, he felt more than slightly disappointed. Knowing that it was a magic sword, he'd have expected some reaction from his firestone — but there was nothing; no wave of excitement, no buzz of recognition. He frowned slightly. Maybe, he thought, it was because of the hex that Lord Alarid had put around it.

Colonel Jamieson's voice broke into his thoughts. "We're thinking of displaying it in the castle, along with the horn, the flag and the suit of armour," he said, replacing the sword on its bed of velvet. "It's a magnificent find!"

"Yes, one way or another, the earthquake's caused quite a stir," Sir James observed.

"In more ways than one," the colonel agreed, "and quite frankly we're planning to make the most of the King Arthur theme this year in the hope that it'll draw lots of visitors to the castle. We're expecting a flood of tourists."

"What about the tomb, itself?" Sir James queried.

"We'll probably open it up eventually," the colonel nodded, his face brightening, "So far the engineers' reports have been positive. Most of the tunnels under the castle are notoriously unstable but this one, remember, was cut out of the rock. If we could have it cleared by the start of the Festival, it would really draw the crowds. I mean, going along a secret passage to a buried tomb ..."

"Quite something," agreed Sir James.

"Quite a money-spinner," corrected the colonel. "And I'm not being mercenary," he added, seeing Sir James's look of surprise. "You've no idea how much it costs to maintain the castle buildings at the best of times. Astronomical, I assure you. The earthquake gave the buildings a good shaking — you'll have heard that we've had to cancel the Tattoo because of it. The esplanade is badly cracked."

"What about a different venue?" suggested Sir James ."There's always the Meadows."

"We thought of that, but a circus is already booked to appear there. A pity, as the Meadows would be ideal; plenty of room for the crowds," the colonel remarked absent-mindedly. Then he stiffened and whirled round. "I've got it!" he said excitely. "James, I've just had a brainwave! It all ties in."

"Ties in with what?" Sir James looked blank.

"With the sword and the horn ... and the knight! We'll have a tournament ... a real mediaeval tournament with people in costume!"

"A tournament?" Sir James sounded wary.

"We could have it on Arthur's Seat with Holyrood Palace in the background. You know the sort of thing! Knights in shining armour, with lances, knocking one another off horses ..."

Sir James's eyes sharpened at the mention of Arthur's Seat. He wasn't sure what the MacArthur would say to that but as there was no stopping the Colonel, he nodded his head. "It's a good idea and original as well. We've never had anything like that at the Festival before."

"Mmmm," the colonel said, his mind already working out the details, "it's a pity you have to go back to the States or I'd have asked you to do the commentary. You couldn't put it off, could you?"

Sir James shook his head. "I've a business deal to wrap up,' he said ruefully, "otherwise I'd have been delighted to take it on. It's a fabulous idea. And you're right! There's a whole host of things you could tie in with it!"

Colonel Jamieson nodded, enthusiasm flooding through him once more as the scale of the idea hit him. "True," he agreed, as he started to pace the room excitedly. "We could have mediaeval banquets with venison and hog roasts. People dressed in costume; a funfair; pedlars selling scarves and trinkets; fortune-tellers; jesters in costume — it would be fantastic! And actually, if we moved the circus to Arthur's Seat we could still go ahead with the Tattoo in the Meadows. What do you think?"

"I think it's a great idea," approved Sir James, warming to the theme, "and you're right, it links everything together; the knight and the sword."

"We've had masses of publicity about the knight and the tomb already," the colonel said excitedly, "but this will really draw the crowds. A tournament! I can't think *why* I didn't think of it before!"

# 7. Plots and plans

"Read the article again," demanded the sword.

Count Vassili looked up at Dragonslayer with raised eyebrows and, taking a deep breath, glanced across at Lord Jezail to see if he agreed.

He'd been totally flabbergasted when his master had appeared with the sword in his hand and utterly furious that he hadn't discussed it with him beforehand. This, more than anything else, made him uneasy for, in the past, Lord Jezail had always shared his plans and ideas with him. This time there had been nothing and he wasn't at all happy at the thought of losing his confidence. He shuddered slightly. If Lord Jezail could go ahead and do this without breathing a word to him, what would he get up to next?

All in all, he sighed, the whole trip was proving more than a bit of a nightmare. The easiest part had been setting up their headquarters, here, in the ruins of an isolated old Border keep, a few miles from the MacLean's house on the outskirts of Coldstream.

It hadn't taken long to make it comfortable; a few hexes here and there had transformed the barren ruin into a very comfortable residence. Tapestries covered the bare walls, carpets covered the stone flagstones that paved the floor, comfortable armchairs were dotted here and there and the huge open chimney now housed a roaring fire that kept the chill at bay.

The sword, at its own request, had been fixed to the wall above the fireplace and from there it issued its commands. Vassili sighed but said nothing, knowing that his master, too, had his doubts about Dragonslayer. One minute he was triumphant at having found it and the next, seething with temper at its demands. Always eccentric, he was proving more difficult to manage by the day.

Jezail frowned at the sword's words and looked across at the count. "Oh, for goodness sake, do what it says and read it again," he snapped, his voice sharp with ill-concealed anger.

Picking up the *Scotsman,* the count folded it to the page where the tournament was advertised in bold letters. He was wishing now that he'd never mentioned it, but the sword had been in such a bad temper over the past few days that he'd thought the news of the proposed tournament might cheer it up. He'd also read the bit about Sir Pendar's tomb; the excitement it had caused and how visitors were pouring into Edinburgh from all over the world to see it.

As it happened, the sword hadn't been really all that impressed. It knew, of course, that the sword the soldiers had found in Sir Pendar's tomb was the replica it, itself, had conjured up and shrugged, totally uninterested to hear that it was now on display in Edinburgh Castle. Vassili's mention of the tournament, however, was something else! Memories of days long ago flooded through its mind: Old England, where knights lived in castles and troubadours and jesters entertained at court; lovely ladies in beautiful dresses; the thud of horses' hooves on the turf; the clash of swords and the shine of armour. Those were the days!

"By the way," Lord Jezail said, stretching his legs lazily in front of the fire, "where is this tournament going to be held?"

It was then that Count Vassili uttered what proved to be fateful words. "On the slopes of Arthur's Seat!" he said casually.

The sword said nothing for quite a few seconds and then glowed an exquisite shade of gold as the full meaning of his words hit home. The tournament, it thought, revelling in a mixture of deep contentment, flaring excitement and mouth-watering anticipation, was going to be held on the slopes of *Arthur's Seat!*

How long, how very long, had it waited, cooped up in that wretched tomb, for just such an opportunity as this? How often had it dreamt of finishing off that pathetic excuse for a dragon? And on Arthur's Seat, itself! He would be close, so close to the dragon! Close enough to draw it out of its lair and then ... and then ...

"We will take part in the tournament," the sword said in a voice that brooked no argument.

Lord Jezail and Vassili exchanged glances.

"You know Sir Pendar's story!" the sword almost snapped. "The dragon was mine and I was deprived of my prey! But this time," it gloated, "there will

be no mistake. I will draw it out of Arthur's Seat
and it will face me again; for you, Lord Jezail, will
be holding me in your hand and I will make sure
that I pierce its heart! Besides which," it added in
a more business-like tone, "it will be good practice
for you when we get to your Valley of the Dragons!"

Lord Jezail's face changed at the sword's words.
Frail as he was, he leapt to his feet, quite consumed
with excitement. "Wonderful," he agreed, his face
shining. "A sort of practice run! Just the thing!"

Vassili blinked and swallowed hard. "Master," he
implored, trying to keep his voice steady, "please
don't be too hasty. You know perfectly well that the
Lords of the North will never let anything happen
to Arthur and ... and well, you haven't been in
the best of health lately, have you? I mean, riding
in a tournament ..." His voice petered out as the
enormity of the situation hit him.

"The high and mighty Lords of the North know
nothing of what happened in Edinburgh," Lord
Jezail replied dismissively, resuming his seat.
"*They* think that Dragonslayer is in Edinburgh
Castle and, by this time, I bet they'll have put a
hex on it that would stop an army in its tracks!
No, Vassili, the sword is right." He rubbed his
hands together and a triumphant smile curled
his lips. "It'll be fantastic! We'll certainly give the
newspapers something to write about!" He bowed
low to the sword. "Between us, we'll kill a real
dragon!"

"And Clara?" the count asked, hoping to divert
his thoughts from the tournament. "What about
her? Aren't you going to kidnap her anymore?"

"Yes, yes, of course we are. The tournament isn't taking place for a while yet. We've plenty of time to kidnap Clara. In fact," and here he looked up at the sword, "we were talking about it last night and Dragonslayer has come up with a wonderful idea."

Count Vassili's heart sank. "What, exactly, did Dragonslayer 'come up with', Milord?"

"Well, it's a long time since it's been able to use its magic and it thought of conjuring up a Gra'el!" he finished excitedly.

"A Gra'el?" Astonishment mingled with a look of extreme disgust flashed across Vassili's face; for Gra'els were the vultures of the world of magic. Scavenging on the flesh of dead dragons, they were huge, black, ugly birds with long necks and cruel, curved beaks. "You can't possibly use a Gra'el to kidnap Clara," he said forcefully. "Not a Gra'el! There are lots of other ways! I mean ..."

Lord Jezail leapt to his feet, looking furious. "You forget yourself, Count Vassili," he snarled angrily. "Kindly leave us! Now! At once!"

The sword hissed softly with pleasure. It knew that the count hated it and smiled inwardly. How wonderful it would be to call up a Gra'el again; for one of its greatest pleasures had been the sight of the dreadful bird, beak agape, swooping hungrily over the carcasses of dead dragons.

The count, rather white about the lips, bowed low to the magician and to the sword and left the room, his mind in turmoil as his growing suspicions suddenly became certainties. It was the sword's doing! Lord Jezail had many faults but he knew his master of old. In days gone by, he'd never have dreamt of calling up such a monster to catch a child!

The maid saw him as he passed the kitchen door. "Count Vassili," she asked nervously seeing the grim set of his lips, "is the master alright? I mean, he hasn't been ill again, has he?"

"Lord Jezail's fine," he answered sourly. "I'm just a bit fed up at the moment."

"The sword?" she queried.

He nodded grimly. "I'm sorry to have dragged you into all this, Maria," he said wearily. "Things aren't turning out quite the way I expected!"

"Isn't the girl coming?" she asked in surprise.

"She'll be here soon, by the sound of things," he replied, forcing a smile. "Clara's a nice girl," he added. "If ... if, by any chance, I'm not around, you must look after her well. Do you understand?"

"But ... why wouldn't you be here?" she looked alarmed. "I don't want to be alone with the master," she whispered. "He ... frightens me with his bad temper."

"I'm not going anywhere, Maria," he assured her. "I just wanted you to know in case ... well, in case anything happens."

She smiled and nodded, only partly reassured. It had seemed like a great adventure when the count had asked her to travel with them to Scotland to look after a young girl. Now she was starting to wish she hadn't agreed to it. Count Vassili, too, was nervous and that worried her more than anything.

# 8. The Gra'el

The country road that ran between stretches of woodland and fields of ripening wheat was deserted apart from two children in riding kit who walked along casually, enjoying the summer sun. Wild flowers waved in a gentle breeze and the hedgerows on either side were covered in a sprinkling of wild roses.

Neil stopped suddenly in the shade of some trees and glanced around. Ever since they'd left Blackriggs Farm where they'd been riding, he and Clara had been deep in conversation, talking non-stop about the sword, the tournament and the MacArthurs. Now, for some reason, he felt uneasy.

"What's the matter, Neil?" Clara asked idly, following his glance back along the long stretch of winding road that dipped and curved between woods and fields. It would have been hard to imagine a more peaceful scene. The cornfields, swaying gently in the breeze, seemed to stretch for miles under a sky of azure blue.

"Something funny's going on," Neil said, shaking his head. "Don't you feel it?"

Clara looked suddenly anxious. "Now that you mention it," she whispered, "yes, I do!"

"Magic ..." Neil said, his voice trailing off.

"Look, Neil! Over there! Do you think it could be them?" Clara said uneasily as a movement in the sky caught her eye.

Neil screwed up his eyes against the sun. "Earth witches — and a full coven, at that," he remarked, counting six witches on either side of their leader.

"You're right," Clara said, counting them. "Thirteen! That's a bit unusual, isn't it?"

Neil nodded, for the earth witches, whose underground castle was nearby, usually travelled across the countryside in twos or threes. He could tell they were earth witches. They were all dressed in black; black dresses, black cloaks and black squishy hats that ended in drooping points. They were, actually, the least attractive of all the witches, their faces bold, strong and cruel. Even the wind witches were better looking, their features elegant and refined and their dresses a shimmering rustle of grey silk. Of them all, however, the snow witches were the most beautiful. White skinned and raven-haired, their dresses were gorgeous robes of chiffon and ivory brocade.

Both children stopped to look at the earth witches as they soared over the fields towards them in a perfect V formation. Well, almost, Clara grinned slightly, for the last witch, a lot smaller than the others, was way out of line.

At the last moment, they curved downwards and, wheeling with mathematical precision, landed gently in the road beside them — apart, that is, from the littlest witch at the end who, fortunately unseen by the others, lost her balance and fell into the ditch.

Clara looked at them nervously for of all the magic people they knew, the witches were in a class of their own and weren't their friends. Maritza, Queen of the Earth Witches, dismounted from her broomstick and stared at them through eyes as black as night. Clara's heart sank and she moved closer to Neil for she knew that the queen hadn't forgiven her for stealing the *Book of Spells* from her castle under Witches' Wood.

Maritza, however, her eyes darting here and there, seemed to have other things on her mind for she, too, was looking round uneasily, as were the rest of the coven. Clara relaxed thankfully. Maybe they might be able to explain what was going on, for it was pretty obvious that something strange was happening.

"Bow!" breathed Neil into her ear. As she and Neil bent low to the Queen of the Earth Witches, Maritza's face relaxed slightly. At least they knew how to behave, she thought approvingly, and inclined her head in acknowledgement.

Neil had no idea how to address a witch but decided that a bit of flattery wouldn't come amiss. Both he and Clara knew that the Lords of the North had forbidden the witches to harm them but, nevertheless, he could well imagine their fury when they had discovered that their precious *Book of Spells* had disappeared. Better, he thought, to keep relations on a good footing. "What's going on, Milady?" he asked, gesturing worriedly.

Maritza scanned the land and the sky and shook her head slowly. "There's definitely magic around somewhere," she said. "I can feel it. Strong magic!" she said, suddenly alarmed. Her witches felt it, too, and lifted lightly off the ground, ready to take off.

"Come," she said harshly, "you'd better come with us. Harriet, take the boy and Clara, you come with me. Quickly, sit on my broomstick and I will take you to safety!"

The thought of flying on a broomstick with the Queen of the Witches was too much for Clara. She took a frightened step backwards, her eyes suspicious. Was all this a trap set up by the witches to capture her? "No," she said, her mouth suddenly dry, "no, no, I won't."

"Stupid girl," Maritza said coldly. "I mean you no harm!"

Clara looked at her doubtfully and it was as she hesitated that an enormous shadow fell over them.

Neil glanced upwards, his eyes widening in horror as he saw a monstrous black bird swooping down on them from the sky, its talons outstretched to grab Clara. Instinctively, he pushed her violently towards Maritza who, seeing the bird and aware of the danger, unceremoniously hauled an astonished Clara across the front of her broomstick and, kicking her heels down hard on the road, took off in a steep, screaming curve into the sky. Harriet wasn't far behind her either! She grabbed Neil with strong arms, lifted him off the road and didn't hang around. Zig-zagging frantically, she followed her mistress into the air with the rest of the coven scattering wildly as the bird, deprived of its prey, let out a venomous squawk of anger and, great wings flapping, soared after them.

It was then that the little witch at the back of the coven redeemed herself in the eyes of her mistress. She swung the handle of her broomstick determinedly upwards and, hanging on grimly, shot up vertically like a bullet out of a gun and hit the monstrous bird from below with such force that it gave a fearsome, agonized cry, doubled up in agony and, forgetting in the heat of the moment that while flying it is advisable to keep ones wings flapping, dropped like a stone. Neil grinned as he watched it flopping around frantically as it tried to stay airborne. The witches, however, didn't stop to gloat. Now in tight formation, they sped off, glad to have a head start on the awful creature.

What kind of a bird was it, Neil wondered, peering back over the witch's shoulder. It was certainly nothing like *anything* he'd ever seen before and he certainly hadn't heard it as it swooped down. It had been its shadow that had given it away. Thank goodness, he thought, that the witches had been around; for the more he looked at it, the more frightened he became. Its long neck curved, snake-like, to end in a head dominated by a huge, curved beak, its black wings flapped silently and its massive feathers were like whole handfuls of ... *furry caterpillars,* he thought; soft, black, ugly, squidgy caterpillars.

The bird, however, hadn't given up. Despite looking decidedly the worse for wear, its great wings, nevertheless, carried it swiftly through the

air and again it tried to dive-bomb them. Maritza
and Harriet swerved crazily here and there over
the sky while Clara shut her eyes, held on tightly
to the broomstick and, like Neil, tried not to feel
sick.

The rest of the witches, abandoning their tight
formation, now did their best to spoil the bird's
aim, flying in front of it, under it, over it and
generally doing anything in their power to slow it
down. The countryside below was familiar to them
and they had quickly gathered that Maritza was
leading them to the safety of the children's house.
It was still some way away, however, and she was
going to need as much time as she could get if
she was going to get there safely. Every second
counted!

Kitor and Cassia, two black crows, who had
been waiting in the MacLean's garden for Neil and
Clara to return from their riding lesson, almost
fell out of their tree when they saw the witches
and the huge black bird flying towards them. Kitor
squawked in horror, hardly able to believe his eyes.
Witches, in all-out battle with a huge black bird!
It was the size of a small aeroplane, for goodness
sake!

Unlike Neil, Clara and the witches, the crows
knew exactly what the bird was. Not that they'd
ever seen one before but their parents had heard
tell of it in ages past and told them enough about it
to freeze their blood. "A Gra'el," Kitor said, almost
falling out of the tree.

The witches now changed their tactics and, as
they neared the house, flew as close to the ground

as they dared. Kitor nodded approvingly as this made it harder for the bird to swoop on them. It was only as the battle drew nearer that the crows looked at one another in amazement and squawked in disbelief. Neil and Clara! Riding with the witches on their broomsticks!

This rather threw Kitor. Indeed, for a few seconds he didn't quite know what to think for he had helped Neil and Clara steal the witches' *Book of Spells* and knew only too well that the two children weren't exactly flavour of the month with Maritza. Nevertheless, she and her witches were certainly trying to save them from the clutches of the ghastly bird. It was still on the attack and Kitor saw problems looming. Once the witches landed, they'd be even more vulnerable. The bird would make mincemeat of them!

Quickly, he flew to the house and, wings flapping madly, pressed his heavy beak hard and persistently against the bell while Cassia squawked loudly to attract Mrs MacLean's attention.

Wiping her hands on a tea towel as she came running from the kitchen, Mrs MacLean wondered what was going on and threw the door wide open.

"Witches," Kitor said urgently, as he and Cassia swooped in and perched on her shoulder in a flurry of feathers. "They're coming here! They've got Neil and Clara!"

Mrs MacLean's eyes widened as she looked out of the door and saw a whole horde of witches speeding towards her across the lawn with a great, black bird swooping in behind them. Stepping hurriedly backwards, she flattened herself against the wall as Maritza shot through the front door at high speed with the rest of her coven behind her.

"Shut the door, Mum," Neil screamed as he flew past. Mrs MacLean leapt forward, watching with a pounding heart as the last witch, trailing perilously behind the others, zig-zagged in with inches to spare as the bird tried to catch her in its claws. It was a close-run thing. Cloak flapping and hat askew, the little witch more or less skated across the black and white tiles of the floor, her broomstick a nervous wreck.

The minute she streaked through, Mrs MacLean slammed the heavy door shut. She made it in the nick of time, but only just, and they drew back in horror as the full weight of the bird hit the door with a ghastly, resounding thud. Deprived of its prey, they could hear it clawing at the wood with screams of rage.

Neil ran to the little window in the cloakroom and watched as the bird, realizing that it couldn't get into the house, shimmered suddenly and gradually faded to nothing.

"What," Mrs MacLean said weakly, as the dreadful noise stopped, "what on earth was *that?*"

# 9. Witches for tea

John MacLean shook his head and smiled somewhat wryly at the MacArthur. "I knew something had happened the minute I arrived home. My front door, for a start — solid oak, mind you — was almost scratched to pieces, the front hall was full of broomsticks and Janet was entertaining a houseful of witches!"

Neil and Clara looked at one another and smiled for their father's face had been a picture of horror and disbelief when he'd walked in, demanding to know what was going on — and then, mouth open, had stopped dead in his tracks as he realized that his living room was full of witches!

They were everywhere, crowding the settees, perched on the arms of chairs and crouched on the cushions. Not only was the room full of witches, but they were being served tea in what he recognized as his wife's best china; china that was never used except on very special occasions. He couldn't believe it! Janet, who loathed witches, was fussing over them busily like a mother hen over a brood of chicks!

"I think you'd better have some tea, Dad," Neil

said swiftly, shoving a cup into his hands. "We're ... we're all a bit shaken up, actually ..."

It was only when Maritza, the Queen of the Earth Witches, rose to her feet and bowed rather shakily, that their father realized that the witches were more than a bit upset; which was no more than the truth, for they, more than the children, understood the very narrow escape they'd just had and still couldn't believe that it had happened at all. A Gra'el! It was unheard of!

Clara, still looking white, was hugging Katy, the thin little witch who had been last in the line, and very lucky to have made it through the front door at all. She was sobbing her heart out and trembling like a leaf while the other witches talked in low tones, shaking their heads and gulping down hot, sweet tea greedily as his wife made the rounds with a fresh pot, topping up empty cups and spooning sugar in vast amounts.

"What happened?" he asked abruptly.

Everyone immediately flooded into speech, his wife and children included!

"Here, Dad, have a seat," Neil said, carrying in one of the chairs from the hall, "and I'll tell you what happened."

There was a silence broken only by the hiccupping sobs of the littlest witch as he told his father how they had been attacked by a huge black bird, how the witches had taken them on their broomsticks and how Kitor and Cassia had saved them by ringing the front door bell.

"It's true, John," Mrs MacLean nodded. "The bell kept ringing and ringing and when I opened the door, the witches flew in with that fearful, monstrous bird behind them."

"It almost caught me," the littlest witch whispered, tears streaming down her face.

Clara pulled more tissues from the box on a side table and helped her mop up. She'd never, ever, have thought she'd feel sorry for the witches but this was certainly a different side to them. Their bold, strong faces were worried and their confidence seemed to have vanished. Even Maritza looked undecided about what to do next.

"More tea, Maritza?" Mrs MacLean asked.

"Thank you, Janet," Maritza nodded, holding out her cup almost absent-mindedly. Ever since they'd arrived, her mind had been racing frantically. Was the Gra'el still outside, waiting for them to leave? She didn't know and the more she thought about it, the more she realized that this was something she couldn't cope with on her own. Her witches relied on her to keep them safe and as she sipped the sweet brew, she came to a decision. Carefully laying her cup and saucer on a side table, she called her witches to order. "I think that Wanda and Samantha," she said, speaking in the language of the witches, "must be told about this."

There was a murmur of agreement at her words and her face was grave as she looked at them all in turn. "I propose that we summon them immediately. Gra'els can only be called up by magic and very strong magic at that! I don't need to tell you how lucky we were to escape! Next time," she paused, "we might not be so fortunate!"

Her black eyes swept the room as the witches looked at one another in something like awe. To summon the Witch Queens so abruptly was not a decision to be taken lightly. Indeed, there was a subdued mutter of apprehension at the very thought. They all, however, knew that there was nothing else to be done and as Maritza stood up, slowly raising her arms in front of her, the witches, too, rose to their feet in a rustle of black silk.

The MacLeans, who of course, hadn't understood a word of what she'd said, looked at one another somewhat anxiously as a deadly silence fell. Suddenly, the homely atmosphere of the old house was replaced by a feeling, the like of which they had never felt before; for the witches' magic was powerful and as old as time itself. Clara gasped and felt her blood run cold as Maritza invoked a spell in a torrent of weird, harsh sounds.

"Wow!" Neil said softly as Maritza lowered her arms and bowed to the witches. "How cool was that!"

Much to Clara's relief, the atmosphere immediately returned to normal, the witches sat down again and, reaching once more for their teacups, chattered excitedly. No longer upset at the thought of their encounter with the Gra'el, they were bright-eyed and excited, their glances drifting expectantly towards the door that led into the hall.

Maritza swept across to the MacLeans, frowning worriedly as she saw their somewhat nervous expressions. "I'm really sorry about the spell," she apologized, "but we're not powerful enough to deal with the Gra'el our own. I hope you don't mind but I've had to call for help!" She ran a hand dramatically through her hair. "Please bear with me, Janet! My nerves," she confessed, "are in absolute shreds!"

Two minutes later, Kitor fluttered from his perch on top of one of the bookcases and, flapping down onto Neil's shoulder, whispered into his ear. Neil looked towards the windows. "Kitor says it's snowing," he announced.

"So it is," Janet MacLean looked up in surprise, "and the wind seems to be picking up, too!"

"Wanda and Samantha," Maritza said with satisfaction. Everyone knew who she meant — even the MacLeans!

"Shall I let them in, Dad?" Neil asked, looking at his father doubtfully. Samantha, he knew, was Queen of the Snow Witches and Wanda, Queen of the Wind Witches. He'd had dealings with them both in the past and hadn't been at all impressed. And now they were outside, circling the house ...

"Of course," he mother interrupted, "at once, Neil!"

Neil looked warily at his mother. He knew how she hated the witches and hadn't really understood her change of heart.

Still he hesitated. "Go on," she urged, more or less pushing him towards the door. "Don't keep them waiting! They saved your life, didn't they?"

Knowing that the witches would be on broomsticks, Neil opened the door wide and, sure enough, in they swooped. The Queen of the Wind Witches entered first, sweeping into the hall on

the heels of a howling gale, followed closely by
the Queen of the Snow Witches, who arrived in a
flurry of snowflakes.

Neil closed the door hurriedly, wondering if
he should put the central heating on, for the
temperature in the house had, quite suddenly,
gone down like a lift!

Wanda and Samantha parked their broomsticks
by the hall table and raised their eyebrows as
they looked at the mess of shivering broomsticks
that lay, any old how, across the hall floor. The
significance wasn't lost on them and, indeed,
nothing could have told them more clearly the
seriousness of the situation for the broomsticks
had obviously been so traumatized that they'd
lain where they were thrown. Trouble was most
certainly afoot!

Neil bowed to each of the witches in turn and,
gesturing towards the living room door, followed
them in.

Wanda and Samantha strode in regally and Clara
hid a grin as they, too, stopped dead in amazement
at the sight of an entire coven of earth witches
drinking tea in the MacLean's living room. The
earth witches hung on to their cups and saucers,
rose to their feet and curtseyed deeply.

Maritza, too, curtseyed respectfully as Samantha
and Wanda looked at her blankly.

"What's going on?" Wanda demanded.

"Why did you summon us?" Samantha asked,
looking totally bewildered.

Neil brought in more chairs from the hall as
Maritza introduced Mr and Mrs MacLean to the

newcomers and Clara slipped off to the kitchen to put another kettle on to boil. The cup of tea that Mrs MacLean had originally offered the witches had multiplied to four or five cups at least and, given the way things were going, might stretch to four or five cups more ...

The meeting was quite lengthy but as the witches spoke in their own language, the MacLeans didn't understand a word of what was said although they did gather that Wanda and Samantha weren't too keen on Maritza's suggestions. Eventually, however, there was a nodding of heads and Maritza turned with a relieved smile to John MacLean.

"It is settled," she announced, "we will do our best to protect Clara from danger."

Mrs MacLean looked at her sharply. "Protect Clara?" she questioned. "But what ... what about Neil?"

"Oh, we'll keep an eye on him as well," Maritza nodded, "but it was Clara the bird wanted. She's the one that's in danger."

John MacLean looked at his wife in alarm and made to argue but Neil held up his hand and said quietly. "The Queen of the Earth Witches is right, Dad. The bird wanted Clara. *I'm* sure of it, too!"

"Well," the MacArthur said, once they'd finished telling him all that had happened, "if anyone else had told me a tale like this, I'd never have believed it for second!"

Archie, too, looked alarmed and Arthur flapped his dragon wings anxiously.

Never have believed what?" John MacLean asked.

"That Clara was attacked by a Gra'el. It isn't a bird that can be called up lightly, you know."

"What exactly *are* Gra'els?" Neil asked. "I know they're birds, but ..."

At his words, a grumbling roar gathered in Arthur's throat and he blew an angry cloud of smoke that set them all spluttering.

"Gra'els," the MacArthur continued when they'd stopped coughing and waving their hands about to disperse the cloud of sparkling smoke, "are vile birds, a bit like vultures. They can only be conjured up by magic and in the old days were used to pick clean the bones of dead dragons — once the apothecaries had finished their task, that is. Dragon flesh is poisonous to humans, you see; which is why magicians used them as scavengers."

"But," Clara looked mystified, "apart from Arthur, there are no dragons in the world today, are there?"

"There are, actually," Archie said, breaking into the conversation. "There's a whole valley full of dragons in Ashgar."

Neil looked at him in surprise. "In Ashgar!" he repeated, "then it *could* have been Lord Jezail who called up the Gra'el," he said, looking worriedly at Clara. "If what you've told us about the sword is true then I bet he came the moment he saw it in the tomb! He wants the sword and ..." he paused, his brow wrinkling as he tried to puzzle things out, "... now it looks as though he wants Clara, too. Otherwise, why would he send the Gra'el to capture her?"

The MacArthur looked thoughtful. "The only other thing that Jezail would want is the *Book of Spells*," he frowned. "That's why I gave it to the Lords of the North for safe keeping. He might be able to get into the Arthur's Seat but he'd never get into Morven. Not in a million years!"

Neil turned pale. "But, that's it, then," he whispered, looking anxiously at his father. "That's why he wants Clara. She knows all the spells off by heart."

Clara's heart sank. She knew instinctively that Neil was right. It was the spells that Lord Jezail wanted ...

There was a sudden silence as they all looked at Clara.

"The witches said they'd look after me," she said in a small voice.

"I'm sure they will," the MacArthur said grimly, "and it was good of them to offer, but if Lord Jezail *is* here then I think you're going to need more than witches to protect you, Clara. The Lords of the North will have to be told of this!"

"Has Prince Kalman returned yet?" John MacLean asked.

The MacArthur nodded. "Yes, he and his father got back yesterday."

There was a murmur of delight from the children. Since the prince had returned to Morven, they had seen him many times and, indeed, they held a special place in his affections for he was very conscious that Neil and Clara had saved his life; Clara by giving him her firestone to wear when he was on the brink of death and Neil by working out that, unbeknownst to anyone, Lord Jezail had hexed him. When they'd heard this, the Lords of the North had been quick to lift the dreadful hex that had left him near death and now, once more, his easy, charming self, the prince had become firm friends with Neil and Clara.

"They were in Turkey with the Sultan when the horn sounded," the MacArthur continued, "and decided to cut short their stay. The Sultan came back with them and now they're busy trying to find Lord Jezail."

"Have they had any luck?" John MacLean asked.

The MacArthur shook his head. "They're working round the clock," he assured him, "but so far the crystal hasn't picked up on the slightest whisper of magic. Lord Jezail is hiding himself well."

# 10. Circus days

"Well, you can go and have a quick look round, I suppose," Mrs MacLean said, looking at her watch. "I'll be about an hour at the hairdresser's, maybe a bit longer if she's really busy. You've got your mobiles on you, haven't you?"

Neil and Clara nodded. They'd intended to do a bit of shopping while they were in Kelso but on the way in had spotted a series of brightly-coloured posters pinned to trees announcing the arrival of the circus; the same circus that was due to appear in Edinburgh for the Festival the following week. Although they'd no intention of going to see the show, the fairground looked like a lot of fun.

Kelso was, in fact, heaving with people; men and women, old and young, many with young children in tow, were heading for the broad, grassy banks of the river where fluttering flags atop the circus tents, flew in the breeze.

The circus was busy and the fairground remarkably big. It seemed to have everything — from swings and roundabouts, a helter-skelter and a coconut shy to a ghost train, a fortune-teller's tent, dodgems and, of course, the Big Top itself.

Clara relaxed as the tinkling music of the fairground raised her spirits. It wasn't long before they were totally absorbed in the sights and sounds of the circus as they wended their way among the various stalls and booths. Clowns on stilts, a fire-eater and jugglers mixed with the sellers of ice cream, popcorn and candy floss, all of whom seemed to be doing a roaring trade given the number of families out for the day armed with pushchairs and hordes of children.

"Tell your fortune?" A pretty young girl, her dark hair tied up in a colourful gypsy scarf, beckoned to them as they passed. "Tell your fortune, Milady?"

Clara laughed and hesitated. "My pocket money's nearly all gone," she confessed.

"I'll do it for your pretty face," the gypsy girl smiled, grasping her hand and pulling her forward. "Business is slow, you see," she whispered. "Folks are shy when it comes to fortune- tellers but others will come if they see you sitting in front of my crystal ball with a smile on your face."

Clara looked doubtful but she'd always wanted to have her fortune told and although she didn't believe in it ...

"Go on," Neil said, looking at the crystal ball with a grin, "I won't be far away. I just want to have a quick look at that rifle range over there."

Clara sat down on the somewhat rickety chair and pulled it in towards the little table that held the crystal ball. It rested on a black cloth, spangled in the silver and gold signs of the zodiac. She waved as Neil moved off and, looking at the crystal ball with interest, hid a smile. It looked exactly like the MacArthur's, even down to the swirling mist that clouded it.

"Just put your hands on the ball, Milady, and we'll see what it shows us."

Clara put her hands round the crystal and sensed its magic at once, for it tingled straight through her. Her mind screamed danger and she wanted to get up and find Neil but, by then, it was too late to cry out, too late to run away, too late to let go; the crystal had her in its power and it was only as she turned round, trying to free herself, that she saw the strangely distorted face of the gypsy and realized with a gasp of horror that somehow she had been hexed into the crystal and that the gypsy girl was looking at her from the outside. Huge fingers grasped the ball, clouding her view as she was tossed around in the crystal's interior ... then everything became suddenly dark.

Neil turned round before he reached the rifle range as it suddenly crossed his mind that it really wasn't a good idea to leave Clara on her own. He turned round and blinked. He was quite sure that he'd walked in a fairly straight line towards the rifle range and yet there was no sign of the fortune-teller or her tent. Nor of Clara! He looked round frantically and a terrible fear gripped him as he realized that she'd disappeared.

He looked up and saw two of the wind witches hovering helplessly above the stalls. They didn't know what to do. It wasn't their fault, he thought. It was his! How could he have been so careless! Hands shaking, he got out his mobile phone. His mum and dad had to know about this and, he thought, Sir James as well. He'd tell him to go straight to the hill to tell the MacArthur what had happened.

He'd barely started scrolling down, however, when someone bumped into him and knocked the phone from his hands. As he bent to grab it, a foot kicked it hard and sent it spinning across the ground. He looked up to see two heavily built, rather swarthy men beside him and one gave him another shove.

"Hey! What did you do that for?" a young man shouted at them. He'd seen what had happened and, understandably, thought that they were trying to steal Neil's phone. Glowering furiously at them, he bent and picked it up. Built like a rugby player, he was quite willing to take them on and at his ferocious glare, the two men backed off quickly and melted away. Heads had turned and a bit of a crowd had started to gather — the last thing that Lord Jezail wanted.

"Wait until the fuss has died down," Lord Jezail said quietly, speaking through the mouth of the man he'd merged with. "Then we'll get him!"

Vassili nodded wearily. He hadn't been keen on the idea of kidnapping Neil; especially when he found out that Jezail intended to use him to force Clara to write down the spells! When they did eventually return to Stara Zargana, he thought, he was most definitely going to leave the magician and return to his father's castle at Trollsberg. He was fairly sure that the book he'd been looking for in Jezail's library wasn't there ... if the magician had ever had it in the first place, which he now doubted. Yet his father had been so sure that Jezail had stolen it ...

Thinking that the two men were nothing more than petty thieves, Neil looked at the man gratefully as he gave him back his mobile. "Thanks a lot," he said.

"No problem," came the answer. "Just watch out, mate!"

Neil nodded but once the man had gone and he started to dial again, he saw the same two

men in the crowd and knew they were still after him. Were they really just thieves, he wondered, or were they out to kidnap him, too?

Stuffing his phone into his pocket, he darted round the side of some stalls and then realized it had been a stupid move. There was hardly anyone around and he could hear the sound of running feet behind him. Fear lent him wings and, jumping over guy ropes and dodging among the stacks of empty cartons that lay behind the stalls, he swerved towards the rear of the circus tent where rows of animal cages were lined up.

Tigers growled, a lion roared and just as he thought he might make it through the row of cages to the safety of the crowds, he found he was in a dead end.

Neil paled. He was trapped! There was no escape! The men knew it, too, for they paused and then, smiling triumphantly, moved forward to grab him.

The witches, however, hadn't forgotten their promise to keep an eye on Neil and Clara and had been watching the chase. Clara's disappearance had freaked them out but they'd kept their heads. Although they hadn't been able to do anything against such powerful magic, they were more than capable of rescuing Neil. So it was that, grey robes flapping, the wind witches swooped in on a gust of wind, grabbed him by the arms and soared exultantly skywards. The Lords of the North were going to be more than pleased with them!

# 11. Prisoner in the tower

The sword looked down from its place above the mantelpiece and frowned at the still figure of the girl. "She's very young, isn't she," it said suspiciously, "and she doesn't seem to have much magic in her ..."

Lord Jezail sensed its disapproval. "Don't worry, she won't be here for long," he said reassuringly, casting a rather anxious glance at Count Vassili as the sword gleamed with an angry reddish tinge. "All she has to do is write down the spells I told you about and then she'll be free to go."

"The sooner the better," the sword muttered irritably, thoroughly fed up at Jezail's insistence that the girl had to be captured before they returned to Ashgar. More and more, it rued the day that it had given itself into the magician's hands. "So far you've done nothing but made a mess of everything!" it pointed out with ruthless candour, thinking of the Gra'el's fury at its useless mission. "And why are we staying here, in the country, miles from anywhere? I want to be in Edinburgh. That's where the action is! I want to find out more about the tournament." And at the thought of the tournament, its colour changed to a golden glow.

"I'm just as anxious as you are," the magician said truthfully, reaching out to touch its hilt. The sword's magic sent a surge of excitement through him. His face changed and his spirits rose. All of a sudden he felt six feet tall, brave and courageous! He could see himself holding the sword in his hand, facing the dragon on the slopes of Arthur's Seat! The feeling was so strong that he almost felt like leaving Clara there and then and hastening back to Edinburgh that very evening.

Aware that Count Vassili was watching him strangely, he turned away, hiding his feelings under a cloak of impatience as he looked down at Clara. "Isn't she awake *yet*?" he demanded.

Almost as though she heard him, Clara blinked and struggled shakily to her feet. Where was she? The darkness was clearing from her mind and, as her eyes fell on the glowing crystal ball that lay on the table beside her, memories of the circus flooded her thoughts. She shivered and instinctively looked round for the young gypsy girl.

A hand took her elbow gently. "Just relax, Clara," a voice said reassuringly. "The dizziness will pass. You'll feel better in a minute or two."

"Count Vassili ... what are *you* doing here?" She looked at him in blank surprise, recognizing the distinctive voice at once. "Where am I?"

"You're quite safe, Clara," he assured her. "Nobody is going to harm you."

Gazing round, her eyes widened as they took in the rough stone walls and high slit windows of some sort of tower. Surely she was in one of the old Border keeps! Scattered here and there throughout the countryside, they had, in the past, guarded the neighbourhood from the raids of the infamous Border Reivers. She'd gone round one on a school trip not many months before and relief flooded through her as she realized that she was probably quite close to home.

"I told you she'd be alright, Vassili," a soft voice spoke from behind her.

Clara whirled round to meet the shrewd black eyes of a richly dressed old man whose mane of dark hair flowed round his shoulders. So elegant and expensive were the cut of his robes that he could quite easily have been mistaken for one of the Lords of the North.

"Excellency," Count Vassili bowed low, "may I present Miss Clara MacLean."

Clara gave a somewhat shaky curtsey. She guessed what was coming next for the old man had the same deep-set eyes and beak of a nose as her aunt. The likeness was unmistakeable.

"Clara, this is His Excellency, Lord Jezail of Ashgar."

Clara looked at him in awestruck wonder and not a little apprehension. Anyone who could put dreadful hexes on people, as he'd done with Prince Casimir and Prince Kalman, was certainly to be feared. Glancing at the count, she relaxed slightly as he nodded encouragingly. His presence was a comfort, for he had been her German teacher at Netherfield and she knew instinctively that he wouldn't let anyone harm her. She took a deep breath and her gaze, when she met Jezail's eyes, was steady enough. "You," she said, "are my Auntie Muriel's father."

It didn't take the count's indrawn breath to tell
Clara that she'd said the wrong thing although she
couldn't understand why. But it was, nevertheless,
the truth. Muriel had been her uncle's wife and
it was only after her accident that they'd learned
that her father was a magician.

To Vassili's amazement, however, the magician
showed no sign of anger. Instead he smiled kindly
and when he spoke, his voice was as smooth as
treacle. "We are, of course, related," he agreed.
"Perhaps you could look on me as some kind of ...
er, uncle," he continued.

Clara curtseyed again and Lord Jezail, seeing
Vassili's totally stunned expression, frowned
warningly at him over Clara's bent head.

It was then that Clara froze. The magician was
wearing her talisman! She clenched her hands
tightly for seeing it there, on his wrist, made her
feel quite odd.

She turned away and in doing so, caught Count
Vassili's eye. She knew that he'd noticed but she
didn't care; for although she was glad he was there,
she doubted if she could trust him. He had known
all along that her aunt had left the talisman to her
and yet he had stolen it and taken it to his master.

"Come and sit down, Clara," Lord Jezail gestured
to a chair near the fire.

She was, indeed, quite glad to sit down. It all
seemed like a dream, somehow; the magnificent
room, the warm fire that made her sleepy and
the incredible presence of Lord Jezail and Count
Vassili.

It was as she looked above the fireplace that she saw the sword. Sitting up abruptly, her expression changed to one of horror as her eyes travelled down the blade to the carved dragon that curled round its hilt. Dragonslayer! It must be! Sir Pendar's sword had made the front pages of all the newspapers and she was quite sure that this was it!

She looked at Lord Jezail questioningly. "The sword!" her voice was a whisper. "It's Dragonslayer, isn't it?" She glanced across at the count, who dropped his eyes and stayed silent. "Did ... did you steal it from Edinburgh Castle?" she continued hesitantly.

Lord Jezail smiled openly. "No," he said, shaking his head. "I didn't need to steal it. This, you see, is the *real* sword. The sword in the castle is a ... a replica. Is that the right word?" he looked at Vassili, his eyebrows raised.

Vassili nodded and rose stiffly to his feet. From his expression, Clara gathered immediately that he was none too pleased at what was going on.

Her thoughts raced and she felt a surge of alarm as she thought of Arthur and the Lords of the North. She had to tell them! She had to escape and tell them that Dragonslayer wasn't in the castle. It wasn't safe, as they thought — it was here, in the hands of Lord Jezail!

The sword looked down on Clara and sighed irritably. Altogether, things weren't turning out quite as it had hoped. Still, Jezail had promised him that the girl wouldn't be around for very long. Once she'd written down the spells he wanted, she'd be returned to her parents. And the sooner the better, it thought sulkily.

Unaware of the sword's displeasure, Clara looked round nervously to see that Lord Jezail had turned to talk to someone who had just entered the room ... a dark-haired young woman. She stiffened, feeling suddenly afraid. It was the same girl; the gypsy who had imprisoned her in the crystal. In her anxiety, she forgot all about the sword as memories of the fortune-teller's tent flooded through her once more! Her parents must be out of their minds with worry. And Neil! How must he be feeling? Suddenly, it was all too much to take in. A feeling of tiredness gripped her and she yawned widely, feeling suddenly exhausted.

"The child needs to rest," the girl sounded anxious as she approached Clara. "Come with me, Milady," she said. "What you need is a nice long sleep."

Clara's eyes searched the room. Where was the count? He wasn't there ... and then she saw him by the front door. He was pushing an enormous bolt into place and, making sure it was fast, turned and strode up to her. "Go with Maria, Clara," he said. "There's a bedroom upstairs and she will see to it that you have something to eat and drink."

"I am hungry," Clara admitted, suddenly discovering that she was, indeed, starving, "and thirsty ..."

"I'll bring up a tray with all your favourite food on it," Maria promised as she guided Clara to a narrow stone stairway that curved upwards from the main hall.

The bedroom made Clara gasp. Never had she seen anything more magnificent than this ornate room; it was immense — so much so that the huge four-poster bed hung with heavy brocade drapes, did not look the least bit out of place. It was wonderful, the soft carpets, the tapestries on the walls, the dim lamps and the sweet sense of incense that hung in the air; it all reminded her of a picture in a story book. *The Sleeping Princess,* perhaps ...

Maria broke into her thoughts. "There's a bathroom here," she said, opening an arched door, "and pyjamas on the bed."

"Thank you," Clara whispered. Maria looked at her for a second and then came over and slipped an arm round her shoulders. "Don't worry, Clara," she said comfortingly. "I'm sorry about putting you in the crystal ball but you know yourself that while you're in it, you know nothing and you feel nothing."

Clara nodded. It was true. She hadn't remembered that she'd been in a crystal at all until she'd seen it on the table and the memory had come flooding back.

"Now, you just sit down here and I'll be up in a second with your supper."

Clara ate, drank, bathed and brushed her teeth in a daze. She was so tired ...

The minute she lay down, snuggled between cool sheets and soft pillows, her eyes closed and she fell into a deep and dreamless sleep.

# 12. Networking

"Look! If I say I can't do it, it means that I *can't*!" Clara said shortly, as she scowled at Lord Jezail. Why, why, *why* wouldn't he believe her?

Vassili handed his master a glass of water and took a pill from a little box. "Take this, Milord," he said, "and you'll feel better."

The magician stretched out a quivering hand for the pill and, still breathing heavily after his outburst of rage, swallowed it and sank back in his chair.

"Lord Jezail hasn't been very well," Vassili explained, coldly. "You see, he's hoping that there might be spells in the book for ... for medicines that will help him regain his health. Surely it's not asking too much to ask you to write them down?"

"The spells have nothing to do with medicine," Clara said stubbornly. "It's not that kind of book."

"Look, can't you just write them down? He needs to be kept calm and, quite frankly, you're not helping him by being awkward!"

This, she thought, was more than a bit of an understatement as, at her refusal to put pen to paper, Lord Jezail had strode up and down in a towering rage before collapsing into his chair.

Clara glowered at him and sighed, for the morning had actually started quite well. She'd had breakfast in bed and when she'd come downstairs, streams of sunlight had been pouring through the high windows of the tower. Maria had obviously been busy, for the room smelt fresh and clean, the remains of the fire had been neatly swept away and a bundle of freshly chopped logs lay in the iron basket, ready to be lit. Lord Jezail and Count Vassili, who had obviously been waiting for her, looked up, smiling pleasantly.

From then on, however, things had gone from bad to worse and she lowered her eyes, unable to look at the count, who now stood stiffly by the side of his master's chair. She'd thought him her friend but he'd given her no help and, indeed, had sided with his master. Resting her head on the back of the chair, she let her eyes wander round the ornate room before returning somewhat hopelessly, to the sheet of paper and pen that lay before her on a small table.

"Why don't you try again?" Vassili suggested, his voice stern. "Maybe you could write out the spell that you used last year when you ... er, called up daemons in the middle of the school concert." Even now, he winced at the thought of them. "You must remember it, surely!"

Clara shrugged and said nothing.

"Don't forget that I was there, Clara,' he continued, his voice hardening. "I heard you. You said it as if you knew it off by heart. You didn't falter once!"

Clara picked up the pen and fiddled with it, her hand trembling slightly. Tears pricked her eyes.

How could she make them understand that the
words of the spell just weren't there? Sensing their
anger and feeling decidedly nervous, she closed her
eyes tightly and tried again to remember the hexes
in the witches' *Book of Spells*. Nothing happened.
"I told you," she said, looking upset, "I told you I
can't remember them."

Lord Jezail sat back in his padded armchair
and, with an effort, hid his frustration. He'd gone
to great lengths to capture the child and now she
either couldn't or *wouldn't* write down the spells
that he was quite convinced she knew. It was then
that he'd tried to bully her and thrown a temper
tantrum that had left him weak with exhaustion.

Clara, watching him anxiously, picked up on the
nasty glint in his eyes and shivered slightly. She
deliberately hadn't mentioned that she only knew
the spells when she was wearing the talisman in
the hope that they'd let her go but the viciousness
of his expression really frightened her. What if he
hexed her or something equally horrid? On the
other hand, she thought, hope rising in her heart,
once she had the talisman on her wrist, she might
possibly be able to escape ...

"Calm down, Clara," the count said quickly.
"Just relax and perhaps the words will come to
you."

"They won't come to me," she said in a small
voice. "Honestly ... they're just not there anymore.
I only ever knew them when I was wearing the
talisman."

Lord Jezail spoke a few words in German,
thinking, no doubt, that Clara wouldn't understand.

As the count had been her German teacher at Netherfield the previous year when they'd both been hunting for the talisman, Clara had more than a fair idea of what had been said. Lord Jezail had asked the count if he should let her wear the talisman! She lowered her eyes and thought fast.

"What do you think," Lord Jezail continued in German. "Is it worth the risk?"

Vassili looked at Clara warningly. He hadn't told Lord Jezail that she had understood their conversation and again she felt that he was very much on her side. Best to let him take charge, she thought. At least he'd keep her safe, for Lord Jezail was proving to be every bit as horrid as the MacArthur had said.

"Lord Jezail is going to let you wear the talisman, Clara," the count said, "to see if it will help you remember."

Lord Jezail pulled up the wide sleeves of his velvet robe and with long, white fingers, made to pull the talisman off his wrist and then hesitated at the thought of it leaving him. "No," he said, his eyes narrowing thoughtfully, "no, I won't let her wear it. It's too risky. She can touch it while it's on my wrist though. We'll see if that will make her remember the spells!"

Clara's heart sank, but the count nodded. It was, he thought, certainly worth a try. Helping his master out of his chair, he carried it across the carpet and placed it by the side of the little table so that Clara could touch the talisman on Jezail's wrist with her left hand and write with the other.

"Go on, try it," Vassili urged as Lord Jezail

laid his arm along the edge of the table and she stretched out a tentative hand.

It was only when she touched the talisman that Clara realized how much she'd missed it. Its magic flowed through her in a surging wave of happiness that told her, without doubt, that *she* was its rightful owner. Her aunt had left it to her and the talisman, itself, knew it. Suddenly feeling much more confident, she sat up straight in her chair and smiled at Lord Jezail. It was a strange smile that almost made him pull his arm off the table.

Count Vassili stiffened as his master crouched in his chair like an animal waiting to attack. "Can you write the spells now, Clara?" he asked hurriedly, unsure of his master's reaction.

"Yes," Clara nodded. "I know them now," she admitted, as fear gripped her. Unlike Vassili, who was standing to one side of his master's chair, she had seen the change in Lord Jezail's face and the flare of madness in his eyes. She just *had* to escape! But what could she do? The only hexes she knew were those from the *Book of Spells* and none of them would transport her out of this prison.

"Write," Jezail ground out, spittle forming in the corners of his mouth.

She glanced at the count as she picked up the pen and he nodded.

Pulling the table closer, she straightened the paper and started to write. The spells were all there in her mind and, using her best handwriting, she wrote slowly and carefully, seeing the words in her mind as though she were copying them off the whiteboard at school.

"What spell is that?" Jezail asked, leaning forward anxiously as she drew a line below it.

"I really don't know," Clara lied, "I can see only the words in my head but I don't know what they mean — or even what language they're in."

"Let me see the paper," he demanded.

She pushed it towards him and he bent over it greedily before looking up and handing it to Vassili.

"The language is the language of old magic," Vassili nodded, handing the paper back to Clara.

"How do I know she hasn't made a mistake?" Jezail queried. "She could have missed words out — or mixed them up!" he hissed.

"I wouldn't do that," Clara tried to keep her voice steady in the face of his anger.

"Master ..." Vassili said imploringly.

Clara gave a half smile. There was one sure way to prove that she hadn't cheated and he didn't half deserve it! Before they knew what she had in mind, she picked up the piece of paper, gripped the talisman on Jezail's arm firmly and read out the spell. The words and the magic flowed from her lips in a stream of sound that echoed softly round the old stone walls of the tower.

Vassili swore violently and whirled round, while Jezail wrenched his arm from Clara's grasp and, despite his frailty, leapt to his feet as a sparkling web of silver stars appeared out of nowhere, hovered in the air and then dropped over them both with alarming swiftness.

Still grasping the paper, Clara rose to her feet and backed away warily, wondering what she'd called up this time; for the sparkling net of stars seemed quite tame after the dreadful daemons of the school concert.

She watched apprehensively as the count and Lord Jezail started to struggle to free themselves. The stars in the net, however, were sharp and spiky and even as she watched, she saw blood running down the count's arm and, although his feet were free, Lord Jezail seemed to have most of the net looped in folds round his head. Vassili, at least, had had the presence of mind to throw his cloak over his head before the net descended. Then she realised that the net was tightening round the two magicians. Maria started to scream and, with a sinking heart, Clara knew that however much she hated Lord Jezail, she couldn't allow the count to be hurt.

Looking down at the paper, now crumpled and twisted in her hand, she hurriedly smoothed it out and started to read the spell backwards as quickly as she could, positively gabbling the last words. It was then that Maria stopped shrieking and ran forward to help her master as the silver net melted away. The spell, thank goodness, had been reversed.

Clara took her chance. As Maria hovered round the magicians, she flew across the room to the door. Grasping its round, iron handle, she twisted it sharply and hefted it open. Sunlight poured in and her heart lifted as she left the tower behind and ran up a slight incline towards a stand of trees. She was free!

Clara didn't feel the hex as it hit her in the back, nor was she aware of Maria carrying her back to the tower. It was, perhaps, just as well for Lord Jezail's face was a mask of fury as he watched her lay Clara gently on one of the sofas.

"Bring the crystal, Maria," he snapped.

Vassili looked worried, his lips set in a thin line, but he nodded to Maria as she glanced at him anxiously. There was nothing he could say or do. Jezail's fury was such that there was no reasoning with him. It had to be done. The only consolation, he supposed, was that Clara, herself, would know nothing about it. Nevertheless, he had to force himself to watch as Maria put both of Clara's hands round the crystal and then catch it as she disappeared inside.

Maria carried the crystal to the small side table and placed it gently on its stand. Inside she could see the child curled up, her eyes closed and her arms round her knees. She looked at Vassili a trifle grimly. "She'll be alright," she said. "I'll keep an eye on her, don't worry."

"Worry?" Lord Jezail's voice was venomous. "Isn't it time somebody worried about me?"

Vassili turned immediately to his master. He, himself, had got off lightly as the folds of his cloak had done much to protect him. His master, however, was a different case; there were deep scratches on his face and blood poured from a jagged wound on his head.

"Bring some hot water and a towel, Maria," he said as calmly as he could. "Lord Jezail will be fine. Head wounds always look worse than they are ..."

# 13. Of knights and knaves

"Well, it's all starting to take shape, Colonel," Sir James remarked, looking across at the green slopes that swept the base of Arthur's Seat. Or rather, what could be seen of them, for the park at that particular point in time was little more than a huge building site. It looked completely chaotic, as building sites do, but both men knew that there was method behind the madness. In front of them, pieces of a platform were being fitted together like a huge jigsaw puzzle and squads of workers in overalls and hard hats were busily supervising the erection of tiers of seating for the many spectators who had bought tickets for what was turning out to be the star attraction of the Edinburgh Festival; the Mediaeval Tournament.

Colonel Jamieson nodded. "Yes," he agreed, "it's coming together nicely. I think it'll be very successful."

Sir James eyed him sideways. "I heard on the grapevine that you've asked Cameron to give the commentary *and* that you've managed to get hold of some fantastic knights for the jousting ..."

The colonel nodded enthusiastically. "The black knight and the red knight! Peter and Simon —

two fantastic guys," he grinned. "Professional stuntmen, the pair of them! I don't know where they learned to ride but the way they handle the horses is a pleasure to watch."

"You'll have provided stabling for them?"

Jamieson nodded. "The stables are up and running. Had to be, actually, as there's an enormous amount of preparation involved. Peter and Simon have spent the last week getting the horses used to the mock battles. In fact," he said, "you're in luck. They're just taking the horses out now if you want to watch them at work."

Sir James looked on interestedly as two horsemen, sitting astride a black and a silver-grey horse, cantered across a grassy stretch of flat turf.

"They make a good team," the colonel smiled. "Actually, I can't believe we've been so lucky," he admitted. "Their knowledge of tournaments is really quite fantastic ... and the museum staff has been wonderful, too. They've come up with some wonderful illustrations of tents, pavilions, pennants, flags, armour and the like. Everything is going to look as authentic as possible. "And you should just *see* the horses' trappings! We've used black and gold for the black knight, of course."

"And the red knight?" queried Sir James.

"A red dragon on a silver background," the colonel said. "We took the emblem from an illustration in an old manuscript. They'll look fabulous, the pair of them."

"What about insurance?" Sir James queried. "I mean, surely the whole point of jousting is that somebody gets knocked off their horse ..."

"We're covered, of course," Jamieson nodded, "but so far there haven't been any injuries. These boys are real pros! Their bones could be made of rubber for all the knocks they've taken. They know how to fall, alright."

"And the armour? I mean, falling off a horse is one thing but if you're all togged out in armour ..."

"It isn't heavy at all," the colonel answered. It looks fantastic but, apart from the helmet and breastplate, the rest is just thin plastic — as light as a feather. Even the swords are made of rubber."

"It's a pity you couldn't use the sword from the castle," Sir James said daringly, wondering if Jamieson had any plans to use Dragonslayer to draw in the crowds.

His answer, however, put Sir James's mind at rest. The Colonel shot him a look that would have stopped an army in its tracks. "You must be joking, James!" he said witheringly. "For a start, it's far too valuable to be taken out of the castle and, anyway," he added sourly, "Health and Safety would never allow it. A naked blade? They'd have kittens!"

Sir James looked at him sympathetically.

"As it is, we've had to prove to them that every move made during the fights is pre-planned. It's like a piece of theatre, actually — the men know what they're doing down to the last blow!"

Sir James nodded absently, his attention drawn to the two horsemen who had been galloping towards one another. The sound of thundering hooves reached them but the horses didn't flinch as they passed each other at high speed.

"I can't wait to see the knights in their armour and the horses in their regalia," the colonel confessed as Peter and Simon dismounted and handed the horses' reins to two grooms

Catching a glint of red hair, Sir James laid his hand on the colonel's arm. "Don't I know that pair?" he asked.

"Probably," Colonel Jamieson replied. "The McKenzie twins. You can't miss them — not with hair like that! You probably came across them when you gave the commentary at the Tattoo."

Sir James nodded. "That's right! I remember now," he grinned. "Do they still answer to the same names?"

"Mac and Kenzie?" the colonel lifted his eyebrows. "Yes, they do. Heaven knows what their real names are!"

"Not that it matters," Sir James smiled. "If I remember rightly, nobody can tell them apart anyway!"

Colonel Jamieson's eyes followed the horses as they were led away. "They're a good pair," he smiled. "Normally, they'd be in charge of the stabling for the Tattoo but I decided to nick them for the tournament. They're efficient and know what they're doing! Nothing'll go wrong when they're in charge!"

"I'm sure it'll all go like clockwork!" Sir James said soothingly, sensing his underlying concerns at the million and one things that could go wrong, given the scale of the tournament.

"Well, I hope so. It's a big undertaking but so far everything seems to be slotting into place quite

nicely. There's the circus as well, don't forget' he
added, nodding to where the Big Top was being
put up, "and, of course, the fairground. Having it
beside us will really add to the atmosphere. I asked
them to give it a real mediaeval flavour, so there'll
be jesters, pedlars, minstrels and the like, mixing
with the crowds. All in costume!"

Sir James looked impressed. "It sounds
fantastic," he admitted, giving praise where it was
due. "You know, your idea of the tournament has
transformed the whole Festival, somehow. There's
a real air of excitement. People are talking about
nothing else. It's just a pity I have to go back to
the States next week," he shot him an apologetic
glance, "otherwise, I wouldn't have missed it for
the world."

"I'm sorry, too," the colonel said, pursing his lips
ruefully. "Cameron's good but you always seemed
to hit just the right note with the crowds."

"Cameron will be fine," Sir James said
reassuringly as they paused to look at the rearing
slopes of the hill and the impressive grey towers
of Holyrood Palace, "so stop worrying! After all,"
he added, "you've got everything going for you!
Just look at the scenery! Arthur's Seat is the ideal
venue. It's all going to be really *quite* spectacular!"

In this, Sir James was correct but even he had
no idea of just *how* spectacular the tournament
was going to be.

# 14. Threats and promises

"Honestly," Neil said, "I just turned round for a second and when I looked back, she'd disappeared ... and so had the gypsy girl, her tent and the crystal ball. It was like they'd never existed!"

Lord Rothlan frowned, while Lady Ellan, seated beside Mrs MacLean, pulled at the folds of her dress with nervous fingers. Clara! Kidnapped! Archie, Hamish and Jaikie looked at one another, totally appalled.

The MacArthur, gathering his fur-lined cloak around him, shifted uneasily in his great chair and didn't know quite what to say, for the hill had never seen a meeting like this before. Even the witch queens were present. Honoured at having been asked to attend, they sat straight and proud in tall chairs to the right of his throne-like chair. None of them had ever been invited to the MacArthur's halls before and their eyes were everywhere, absorbing the richness of the furnishings, the rolls of magic carpets stacked against the walls and the ancient hangings that swung gently in the heights of the cavern. What really held their attention, however, was the great red dragon that lay coiled beside Neil. Samantha,

Queen of the Snow Witches, clenched her hands
tightly for she'd had the misfortune to see Arthur
in action when he'd flown over her ice palace
breathing great bursts of fire and ... she hastily
put the thought from her mind, remembering that
they were now all on the same side. Clara had to
be found.

Arthur obviously felt the same. He uncoiled his
slender body and, stretching his length, flapped
his wings and blew an enormous cloud of sparkling
smoke. This sent everyone spluttering and choking
but for once Arthur was in no mood to apologize.
"Clara," he hissed in his dragon voice. "We must
rescue her at once!"

"We would,' Prince Kalman pointed out,
dispersing the smoke with a wave of his hand, "if
we knew where she was. You know that, Arthur!"

The dragon coiled himself in front of the
MacArthur's chair again and folded his wings,
his eyes flashing and his head rearing angrily. He
knew that the prince was right but nevertheless
wanted to do something — right away!

The MacArthur looked apologetically at the
MacLeans. "The witches have been helping us,"
he told them, bowing his head regally to the three
witches, "but although they've covered a vast
amount of country, they haven't picked up on any
strange magic."

Janet MacLean looked gratefully at the
witches, knowing that they'd spent many long
hours scouring the countryside for traces of her
daughter.

"And," the MacArthur continued, "the crystal

is useless. Clara has been deliberately hidden
from the world of magic. We've no idea where
she is."

"So what do we do?" John MacLean asked,
trying to sound reasonable despite his anxiety. He
knew they would do everything in their power to
help him for they were all as upset and worried as
he was.

Lady Ellan put an arm round Janet, trying to
comfort her as she started to sob. Although John
MacLean had himself well in hand, his wife, stiff
with fear at the thought of her daughter in the
hands of such a wicked magician, was heading
rapidly for a nervous breakdown. Gently, Lady
Ellan murmured the words of a hex and smiled
with relief as Mrs MacLean relaxed and, dabbing
her eyes with a tissue, managed a tentative smile.
"I'm sorry," she apologized. "I know she'll be
alright and that you're all doing your best."

Lord Rothlan rose to his feet and spoke
reassuringly. "Lord Jezail won't harm her, Janet,"
he said, seriously. "My guess is that Count Vassili
told him that she knew the *Book of Spells* off by
heart. We don't know for sure, of course, but that
could be the reason he kidnapped her."

Prince Kalman nodded in agreement. "Clara
was his last resort," he said thoughtfully. "He
might have been able to steal the book while it
was here, in the hill, even although Arthur was
guarding it," he said slowly, "but once you," and
here he bowed to the MacArthur, "once you gave it
to us to guard — well, that was it. There's no way
he could steal it from Morven."

"So, you see," Lord Rothlan explained gently, "kidnapping Clara is really his only chance of getting hold of the spells."

"I wouldn't worry about it too much, Janet," the MacArthur said, doing his best to comfort her. "Believe me, once he has all the spells, he'll release her."

"I don't know about that," John MacLean looked unconvinced. "She's been gone for a couple of days now and if what you say is true, well ... it wouldn't take her all that long to write them down, would it?"

There was a short silence as they digested the truth of this remark. "What really gets me," Neil remarked, "is why he tried to kidnap me as well? There were two of them, you know — real tough guys." He frowned as he thought of them. "I mean, *I* never had the talisman and *I* don't know any of the spells."

"Yes, but Lord Jezail wouldn't know that, would he?" Prince Kalman pointed out. "He would naturally assume that you'd read the book as well."

It was while they were all pondering the implications of this that the MacArthur's crystal started to glow and as all eyes turned to it, Lord Jezail's face appeared. He was frowning furiously, a bloodstained bandage was bound loosely round his head and it was obvious to everyone that he was spitting with rage.

Mrs MacLean gave a cry of fear and pressed both hands to her lips. This, then, was the terrible magician who was holding her daughter prisoner.

John MacLean clenched his fists and Arthur let out a fearsome roar of rage that echoed round the cavern. The witches froze in their chairs and watched as the MacArthur, accompanied by Prince Kalman and Lord Rothlan approached the crystal.

The MacArthur's face was stony as he met the magician's furious gaze. "Well?" he demanded abruptly.

Neil raised his eyebrows and glanced at his father. He'd never known the MacArthur to be rude before. Neither, for that matter, had anyone else. Even Jaikie and Hamish exchanged sidelong glances before concentrating once more on the glowing crystal.

Lord Jezail's eyes narrowed at the insult and, as they watched, his expression of utter fury was replaced by one of such evil that even the MacArthur recoiled.

At the sight of Lord Jezail's face, Prince Kalman gripped Lord Rothlan's arm. So Neil had been right all along, he thought. This, then, was the face of the real Lord Jezail; for despite Neil's assertion that it had been Lord Jezail who had hexed both him and his father to steal the Sultan's Crown, he had secretly had his doubts. Now he had none. The face in the crystal was a mask of venom. Gone was the memory of the austere but kindly old man whom he'd thought of as a friend. This was, without doubt, the true Lord Jezail.

"You are forgetting, MacArthur," Lord Jezail said softly, "that I have the girl in my power." He paused. "If you want to see her again, then I suggest you do as I say!"

Prince Kalman pressed the MacArthur's shoulder and, stepping forward, took his place in front of the crystal. Tall, fair-haired and handsome in his gorgeous robes, it took a few seconds before Lord Jezail recognized him and when he did, the shock on his face was apparent to each and every one of them.

"Prince Kalman," he stuttered, disbelief etched in every line of his face.

"Did you think I was dead, Lord Jezail?" the prince smiled in mock amusement. "How very disappointing for you! Your hex, as you see, didn't quite work as planned. I'm very much alive and once more a Lord of the North!"

"A Lord of the North?" Jezail's voice was thick with contempt. "Do you *really* think I'm impressed?"

"I think you should be, Lord Jezail," Lord Rothlan stepped forward, his face grim, "for, as you know, we are not without power. First of all, however, I suggest that we resolve this affair peaceably. Return Clara to us and we will take no action against you and allow you to return to Ashgar."

"My dear Alasdair, how very pleasant to see you again after all these years of ... er, exile," Lord Jezail returned smoothly, "and still," he sneered, "as honest and upright as ever."

"You haven't told me what you think of my suggestion," Lord Rothlan said evenly, ignoring the taunt.

Jezail shrugged his shoulders. "Oh, that," he said casually. "I will, indeed, return Clara to you, but," he leant forward, his face a mask of hatred, "only in exchange for the *Book of Spells*!"

Prince Kalman spoke again. "Clara knows all the spells by heart. You only have to ask her to write them down. We agree to that." He looked round swiftly as Lord Rothlan and the MacArthur nodded assent.

Jezail's hand reached for the bandage round his head and even as he pulled it off, blood ran from the deep lacerations that scored his head. "This," he snarled, holding out the bloodstained bandage, "is all Clara's doing."

Despite the seriousness of the situation, Neil grinned. Obviously, Lord Jezail wasn't having everything his own way! Clara was fighting back!

Prince Kalman and Lord Rothlan, however, eyed one another seriously. Clara was too brave for her own good and angering Lord Jezail hadn't been a wise move on her part.

"So," Jezail snarled, wiping the flow of blood from his forehead, "now, at least, you understand why I will ask Clara nothing! And," he continued, "let me make one thing quite clear — if you do not give me the book you will never see her alive again. It's the book or nothing!"

There was a horrified silence as they all looked at one another in disbelief.

"But ... that's quite impossible, Lord Jezail," the MacArthur interrupted, quickly. "There's no way the Lords of the North will give you the *Book of Spells*!"

"No?" he looked at them contemptuously. And, stretching out his hands, he lifted up the crystal that held Clara so that they could see her, curled in its centre. "Then perhaps you should all go to the circus this evening. I think you might change your mind when you see what I have in store for Clara!"

# 15. Cats and clowns

The circus tent was huge and the tiers of seats encircling the arena were packed with people; men, women and children, all thrilled and excited by the smell, colour and magic of the circus. The band, resplendent in bright red uniforms heavy with gold braid, played rousing numbers from a raised platform and, as the music blared, ponies, performing dogs, trapeze artists and acrobats all performed their acts.

Trumpets sounded as the ringmaster cracked his whip and brought on the clowns. John MacLean stiffened as soon as they appeared. "I think this is it," he whispered, taking his wife's hand. "Look, one of the clowns has a crystal ball. See him?"

Mrs MacLean swallowed hard and Lady Ellan looked at her apprehensively. Knowing the state she was in, everyone had tried to persuade her to stay at home but, predictably, Janet had insisted on coming. Clara was her daughter and she wanted to be there for her even if she couldn't do anything to set her free. Now she sat straight and stiff in her seat, her eyes round with worry.

Sitting beside her, Lady Ellan, too, was worried, but for a different reason; for the minute they'd arrived, her husband and Prince Kalman had headed for the back of the circus tent to suss things out as they'd really no idea what Lord Jezail intended to do. Where were they now, she wondered as she scanned the outlandish figures of the clowns with their painted faces, long shoes and ridiculous clothes. Had they, perhaps, merged with the clowns to try to get the crystal back? And Neil? What had happened to him? He was supposed to be sitting with her in the audience but, she thought, seething with irritation, he'd obviously had his own ideas and had managed to lose himself in the crowd. There wasn't a lot she could do about it, either. Apart from his firestone, he had no magic to speak of and if he were to cross Lord Jezail she didn't give much for his chances. Why couldn't he do as he was told!

Mrs MacLean gave a sudden moan and pressed her hands against her mouth as one of the clowns tossed the crystal ball through the air to another who pretended to miss it but caught it as it almost hit the ground. The clowns then threw the crystal ball to the jugglers who tossed it in the air with gay abandon.

It only took Lady Ellan a few minutes to work out that the crystal had been hexed. "It's all right, Janet," she whispered. "Lord Jezail must have put a spell on it. Whatever happens, it'll land in someone's hands."

"Are you sure?" John MacLean asked sharply.

"Trust me," Lady Ellan said, smiling grimly. "It's all an act!"

Janet MacLean heaved a huge sigh of relief

but despite the knowledge that it would never fall and break, her heart was in her mouth as, over and over again, she saw the crystal caught in the nick of time. In the end, she could hardly bear to watch. Where, she thought anxiously, were Prince Kalman and Lord Rothlan? They had told her that they would rescue Clara and as far as she could see, nobody was doing anything at all to save her.

It was then that the tigers entered the ring.

There was a horrified hiss of indrawn breath from the audience, the band faltered in mid-note and, as the music petered out in a discordant wail of sound, the ringmaster whirled round to see why — and then blanched visibly as three tigers padded softly forward and halted in front of him.

Tigers on the loose! His worst nightmare! And there was no audience protection either! His mind raced frantically as he glanced at the petrified clowns who were now backing slowly and carefully into the audience. His legs suddenly felt very shaky indeed. Running away was out of the question. The tigers would down him in seconds. He clutched his whip tightly. What on earth was he going to do?

The audience, quick to notice that the band seemed to have totally lost the plot, shifted fearfully. Was this part of the act or not?

Neil, however, didn't have time to take in the reaction of the audience. He was too busy trying to control his tiger who, to put it mildly, had a forceful character of its own and had quickly sensed that whoever was inside it could, at a push, be overruled.

It was all *such* a mess. Tigers were the last things they'd wanted to merge with and he knew that Lord Rothlan and Prince Kalman, too, must be absolutely livid. But they really hadn't had much choice in the matter for the yobs who had thought it great fun to let the tigers loose had got more than they'd bargained for when the tigers, with terrifying growls, had leapt from their cages with startling speed and headed straight for them.

It was then that Prince Kalman and Lord Rothlan had appeared from beside the circus tent and, seeing Neil, Lord Rothlan had snapped at him to merge with one of the tigers. As the alternative was allowing three tigers to run loose round the circus, he had seen his point but, nevertheless, it had taken every ounce of will-power he possessed to force his tiger to back off.

The broad entrance to the circus ring had emptied swiftly as Prince Kalman led the tigers into the blazing spotlights. His heart was heavy for he had hoped to merge with one of the clowns and knew that as tigers, they'd find it almost impossible to rescue Clara, wherever she was.

Sensing the waves of panic emanating from the audience, Prince Kalman sent a hex flying through the air and as the feeling of fear faded, he approached the white-faced ringmaster and sat down beside him. Taking their cue from the prince, the other two tigers did the same and looked at the petrified man through glowing amber eyes.

The ringmaster, to this day, can't explain the voice he heard in his head. "Don't worry about us," it said. "We won't harm anybody. Just keep calm and get the band to go on playing!"

Totally stunned, he looked into the tiger's eyes and, to his amazement, saw a lively intelligence there.

"Go on, man!" Prince Kalman urged. "You don't want the audience to panic, do you?"

The ringmaster gulped and, gathering his scattered wits, realized that the tiger was right. If there wasn't going to be blind panic in the audience, he had to play along.

"Don't worry," the tiger repeated, accompanying his words with a gentle hex, "no one's going to get hurt, I assure you."

Meeting the tiger's eyes, the ringmaster was suddenly reassured. He didn't know what was going on but he knew instinctively that he could trust the animals. Relief swept through him and still half wondering whether or not he was dreaming, he bowed low to the tigers and, with a magnificent flourish of his whip, gestured to the band to play on.

The bandmaster, looking understandably doubtful at this gesture of supreme confidence, gulped noticeably, but seeing that the tigers seemed quite peaceful and that the ringmaster was obviously determined to go on with the show, he lifted his baton. The petrified band then launched, albeit rather shakily, into the catchy tune of the circus march.

Lady Ellan, mind racing, sat up straight in her seat, guessing immediately what had happened. Tigers? she thought incredulously! Surely they could have chosen clowns or even circus hands to merge with! "I'll have to go," she whispered hurriedly and before Janet could reply, pressed her arm reassuringly before slipping quietly down the aisle towards the circus ring and the clowns. The tigers, she knew, were going to need her help.

The audience, now quite relaxed, watched with increasing fascination as the bandmaster, blessed with inspiration, started to play the opening bars of the tigers' routine. The tigers, tilting their heads to one side, listened to the familiar music and finding themselves on their home ground, so to speak, calmed down considerably.

Neil breathed a sigh of relief. He was finding it difficult to keep his tiger from running amok and it was only the presence of Lord Rothlan and Prince Kalman on either side of him that had kept his beast in check.

It was then that the principle clown, called Charlie, moved into the ring. Seemingly unafraid of the tigers, he carelessly tossed a crystal ball from one hand to the other. Clara! Neil thought, glancing apprehensively at the other two tigers. Like them, he knew she was there. He could just make out her tiny figure, curled in the middle of the ball.

For a moment, he was tempted to let his tiger attack the clown, for one look at Charlie's triumphant face was enough. Lord Jezail had merged with him. Prince Kalman and Lord Rothlan obviously thought so, too, for their tigers bared their teeth and a low growl rumbled in their throats.

Jezail, however, merely shrugged and, gesturing to the other clowns to come forward, started their act all over again. The petrified clowns, however, had other ideas. They knew exactly how fierce the tigers were and as they threw the crystal half-heartedly among themselves, a ripple of unease swept through the audience.

By this time, both Prince Kalman and Lord Rothlan had worked out that the crystal ball was hexed but apart from attacking Lord Jezail — and freaking out the audience in the process — there didn't really seem to be a lot they could do. And Jezail obviously knew it!

Aware that he had the upper hand, the magician smiled contemptuously and proceeded to make a fool of the tigers. Throwing the crystal confidently over their heads to one of the more daring of the clowns, he cavorted round them, pulling funny faces that set the audience roaring with laughter.

It was then that Prince Kalman noticed that the clown with the crystal hadn't thrown it back but was tossing it carelessly into the air as if deciding whom to throw it to next. Hope rose in his heart. Could it possibly be Lady Ellan?

He watched as Jezail's eyes sharpened. He was becoming suspicious at the delay and as the magician's arm rose to throw a hex, the prince decided it was definitely time to take a hand in matters. If Jezail could play the audience for laughs, why then, so could he! He gave a grim smile, threw a hex and waited ...

The huge square of shiny, yellow plastic that suddenly appeared beneath Jezail's feet took the magician by surprise. It appeared inoffensive enough but it was only when he took a step forward that he discovered it wasn't nearly as innocent as it looked. Indeed, it had the kind of surface a skater would have died for. He gave a howl of dismay as, despite frantic efforts to stay upright, his feet slid from under him and he landed flat on his back with a resounding thud that knocked the breath out of him.

The audience, thinking it all part of the act, cheered him on as he heaved himself furiously to his feet. He was hampered, however, by his long clown's shoes which now seemed to be doing their best to trip him up. Try as he might, he just couldn't keep his balance and, waving his arms wildly was left, once more, lying on his back.

His face, as he scrambled to his feet once more, was a picture of seething rage. Rage, Prince Kalman knew, at not being able to hex the clown who had so cleverly stolen the crystal from him. Lady Ellan, he thought, had stepped in just in time.

Then he fell again! The band could barely play for laughing, the clowns were helpless and the audience near hysterical.

Neil creased up. He couldn't help it.

The tiger, of course, felt Neil's laughter and looked somewhat bemused. Being a tiger, it wasn't a sensation that it had ever experienced before but as Neil went on laughing, the tiger opened its mind to the feeling and found itself joining in. Before long, it was totally helpless, rolling on its back in the sawdust, flapping its paws in the air and roaring with a strange gurgling sound that was obviously its version of laughter.

The other two tigers turned, eyebrows raised, to look at it disapprovingly — it was hardly standard tiger behaviour, after all — then *they* caught the feeling. Creasing up, they all roared, howled and cried with laughter as Charlie, still persevering in his attempt to stay upright, floundered furiously on.

It was only when the exhausted tigers could laugh no more that Prince Kalman noticed that the animal trainer had arrived. Some of the clowns, too, had gone to help Charlie off the slippery plastic square and, as if that weren't enough, a group of circus hands was hurriedly clipping together the barred segments of a shield round the ring to protect the audience from the tigers. They'd obviously done it many times before and were working fast. At the rate they were going, he reckoned, the cage would be completed in minutes.

He nudged Neil. It was definitely time to demerge from the tigers — and it had to be now, while escape was still possible. Yet they couldn't risk the tigers turning on them either. He eyed Lord Rothlan and receiving a nod of understanding, hexed all the lights.

The animal trainer strode up as the lights came on again and looked down at his exhausted tigers in surprise. The tigers, however, proved remarkably docile and, obviously pleased to return to their familiar routine, did their best for him. It was only towards the end of their act that they caught sight of a rather puzzled-looking Charlie who, peering at them through the bars, was still trying to work out what had actually happened to him that evening.

The audience, however, hadn't forgotten — and the tigers certainly hadn't. Neil's tiger gave a hysterical gurgle and, with a shake of its head, waved a helpless paw. That set the others off and as the audience roared with laughter, all of the tigers joined in. The animal trainer, looking at them in baffled wonder, hadn't a clue what everyone was on about but decided there and then that if Charlie was *that* funny, he'd definitely include him in the act from then on.

No one in Arthur's Seat that evening felt like laughing, however. One look at the crystal ball had told them all they needed to know. The curved shape that they'd thought was Clara was nothing more than a twisted scrap of cloth.

Clara wasn't in it. The crystal was empty. She was still Lord Jezail's prisoner.

# 16. The tournament

There was no question about it — Arthur's Seat had been totally transformed. Its grassy heights rose gently above the array of gleaming white tents and pavilions that formed the background for the tournament. It was, as Sir James had predicted, a wonderful spectacle. The grassy concourse was filled with people in mediaeval costume, visitors thronged the stalls and, mingling with the crowds, were jesters in multi-coloured clothes, their belled hats tinkling as they moved while pedlars, carrying trays of scarves, bangles and beads, shouted their wares. Even the usual vendors of popcorn, candy floss and ice cream had taken care to dress for the occasion.

The sun shone, flags fluttered in a gentle breeze and as crowds started to stream in from the High Street, the tiers of seating gradually started to fill up, while those unable to get tickets valiantly climbed the slopes, unfolding rugs, chairs and picnic hampers as they found a vantage point and settled to watch the spectacle from on high.

Neil looked at the scene with interest, glancing every now and again at Prince Kalman and Lord Rothlan who sat beside him. Dressed in their customary velvet robes and ruffled shirts, they were, in the circumstances, not at all out of place.

"Your mother didn't object to your coming?" Prince Kalman queried.

"No, she was fine about it," Neil answered. "I had to promise not to get up to mischief, though," he grinned.

Lord Rothlan heard the conversation and smiled slightly. Although Neil didn't know it, his parents had been hexed to cope with his sister's disappearance and even his mother, who normally would have been worried sick, felt both comforted and secure in the knowledge that the world of magic would come to Clara's rescue.

It was then that a very slight breath of magic filtered through the air. Although little more than a tremor it was enough to make Lord Rothlan stiffen slightly and look round curiously. Catching Prince Kalman's eyes, he knew that he, too, had picked up on it. They looked round a trifle warily; nothing to worry about unduly but certainly close enough to ruffle their senses.

Thank goodness, the prince thought, that they'd put a strong protective shield round Neil. At least the boy was safe. His eyes searched the crowds as he tried to home in on the source of the magic but when the opening parade started, the feeling diminished and was lost altogether as the pipe bands marched past, heading a long line of performers. Groups of Scottish country dancers waved as they passed by, followed by Highland dancers, a troop of precision marchers and many, many more. The applause, however, grew to a deafening roar as, standards fluttering bravely in the breeze, Peter and Simon, the Black Knight and the Red Knight, splendid in shining armour, rode by majestically on their beautifully caparisoned horses; undoubtedly the stars of the show.

A bubble of fear shivered through Arthur as, from the depths of Arthur's Seat, he watched the procession through the crystal, his eyes fixed on the Black Knight and his dreadful black flag. Sir Pendar's flag! The Black Knight was once more going to go into battle on the slopes of Arthur's Seat! The MacArthur had warned him what to expect and he knew that Prince Kalman and Lord Rothlan were in the audience to guard against trouble but seeing the flag filled him with dread. It was like living a nightmare all over again.

Seeing the terror in his eyes, Archie, Jaikie and Hamish exchanged glances and did their best to calm him down. It was all a pretence, they said. The swords were made of rubber, the lances were plastic and the knights' armour was little more than painted cardboard. Nothing, they said reassuringly, was going to happen to him.

Arthur, however, barely heard a word of what they were saying. He was a dragon, after all, and had powers that were not given to the faery folk or the magicians either, if it came to that. A sixth sense told him that things were not as they seemed and he knew, beyond a shadow of doubt, that someone, that very afternoon, was going to kill him.

The procession finished to rousing cheers from the audience and it was only when the speeches

began that the eye of the crystal veered away from
Colonel Jamieson who had risen to welcome the
audience to the tournament.

The stable tent was huge and a hive of activity.
The horses looked magnificent and after the
excitement of the procession, seemed to know that
today was going to be their day; the day they had
trained for.

The black horse stood calmly as one of the red
headed grooms adjusted its face armour carefully;
its breastplate had already been tightened and
it was now used to the feel of the long black
cloth that hung over its back to the ground.
Embroidered with golden swords, it was uncannily
like that worn by Sir Pendar's horse hundreds of
years before.

The grey, undergoing the same treatment,
stamped nervously. The loose folds of the scarlet
cloth draped over its back was bothering it and as
it whickered and pawed the ground restlessly, the
Red Knight whispered to it soothingly, calming its
nerves.

"He's a bit nervous, Simon," the groom said,
joining him. "Knows it's the big day, I reckon!"

Simon, the Red Knight, smiled. "I'm a bit
nervous myself, Mac," he admitted as the groom
nodded and made to move on. Simon caught his
arm. "Hang on a bit, Mac," he said, thrusting
the horse's reins into his hands, "could you take
over for a while? Thanks," he added as the groom
nodded, "I just want to go over something again
with Peter. Won't be a second!" He waved and
moved off.

"Nervous is he?" Kenzie wandered up and stroked the grey soothingly.

"They both are!" Mac grinned. "Horse and master!"

Kenzie shrugged. "They'll forget their nerves when they start," he said. "Simon's a pro. He'll be fine!"

The afternoon wore on, event following event, until it was the turn of the knights. This was what everyone had been waiting for! The Black Knight and the Red Knight mounted their horses and, lances held aloft, set forth to try their fortunes in the lists.

"Come on," Kenzie said to the rest of the grooms, "let's find a good place to watch."

They made their way to a small rise and watched as the Black Knight and the Red Knight took their positions at either end of the concourse and, at a signal from Colonel Jamieson, urged their horses forward. The jousting had begun.

Neil leant forward excitedly as the two knights, lances at the ready, galloped towards one another in a thunder of hooves. The Black Knight's lance hit the Red Knight's shield squarely in the middle and the impact threw the Red Knight off his horse.

There was a gasp of horror from the crowd but the Red Knight was unhurt. He sprang to his feet almost immediately and bowed low to the cheering crowd. Highland dancing followed the jousting, giving the knights time to prepare for their next event — fighting on horseback.

The Red Knight was ready first and, steadying his prancing horse, waited outside as the Black

Knight adjusted the visor on his helmet so that only his eyes could be seen. It was then that Kenzie, checking the girth, noticed the golden hilt of the sword in his scabbard. His face changed and he looked up in alarm. It wasn't one of the fancy rubber swords they'd been given; this was a real sword!

"Hey, Peter!" he grasped the Black Knight's arm and looked up at him questioningly, "that's a real sword you've got there! You can't fight with that! It's ... it's not ... allowed ..." His voice petered out as he met the knight's eyes ...met them and flinched.

Instinctively, he took a step backwards as fear gripped him, for Peter's brown eyes were grim, ferocious and, somehow, triumphant. Dark and fierce, they seemed the eyes of a stranger.

# 17. Dragonslayer

Kenzie fell back with a cry as the Black Knight snapped his visor shut and, pushing him roughly out of the way, spurred his horse forward and cantered out of the tent to join the Red Knight.

"What was all that about?" Mac asked, looking at Kenzie anxiously.

Kenzie ignored the question. He was too busy looking after the two knights who were now riding together towards the concourse. "Look at the Black Knight's scabbard, Mac," he whispered. "He's got a real sword there!"

"*You're joking!*" Mac looked flabbergasted.

"That's not all! When I tackled him about it just now ... well ..."

"Well ... what?"

"I don't think it was Peter on that horse. It was someone else. I saw his eyes through his visor. It wasn't Peter, I tell you!"

"You're out of your mind," Mac said, looking at him in disbelief. "Of course it was Peter! Who else could it be?" Then he frowned as he thought of the sword. "But," he stammered, "what on earth did he bring a real sword for?"

Remembering the look in the knight's eyes,

Kenzie hesitated. "To kill Simon?" he said, hazarding a guess.

The grooms looked at one another in horror.

"Come off it!" Mac objected. "They're good friends!"

"Well, I don't *know*, do I?" Kenzie muttered. "Hurry up! We might be able to do something!" And with that, they ran towards the crowds.

From the stands, Neil looked on in fascination as the two knights cantered briskly towards the dais. Their visors were closed and Neil wondered just how much they could see through the holes that decorated the front. Both knights and horses looked magnificent. The Black Knight, in trappings of black and gold, carried a black shield with a shining golden sword in its centre. His opponent, the Red Knight, sitting astride a beautiful silver-grey horse, was equally richly attired but his horse was draped in red and a red dragon rampant reared ferociously in the middle of his silver shield.

Lord Rothlan stiffened as they approached and looked at Prince Kalman with raised eyebrows; for the feeling of magic that swept from the knights wasn't the mere whisper they'd sensed before. It was strong and powerful and it emanated from the Black Knight!

Completely oblivious, Simon, the Red Knight, smiled behind his visor. He was tense with excitement and full of confidence. They'd practised the fight over and over again; every move had been carefully choreographed and they both knew exactly what they were going to do and when they were going to do it. It would, of course, look alarmingly real to the watching crowds but, if the truth be told, there was really nothing dangerous about the fight whatsoever.

The two knights reined in their horses in front of the dais and it was then that Neil choked and gripped Lord Rothlan's arm as, with a grand gesture, they drew their swords and saluted the assembled gathering.

As the Black Knight held the sword aloft, so that it shone and glinted in the sunlight, a tremor of fear and excitement gripped the crowd. Prince Kalman swore softly under his breath and Neil bit his lip. Dragonslayer, he thought, his heart sinking. It couldn't be anything else. Magic blazed from its blade! He knew that the MacArthurs would be watching and almost wished he was with them so that he could comfort Arthur.

Dragonslayer blinked in the sunlight. Then it saw the familiar slopes of Arthur's Seat and glowed with happiness as the years rolled swiftly back. The only thing that took the edge off its feeling of delight was the fact that it was not Sir Pendar who held it in his grasp; for Lord Jezail was a weakling by comparison. He could barely hold the sword, far less wield it with the strength needed to kill a dragon! Indeed, it was only when it had suggested that Count Vassili take his place that the furious magician had downed half a dozen dragon pills and, bursting with new-found energy, had managed to convince it that he had the skills, and the strength, to kill a dragon.

Inside the hill, the MacArthur drew an unsteady breath as he saw the Black Knight holding the sword aloft. It was as though Sir Pendar had returned to life. The Black Knight was once more on their doorstep and Arthur was once more at risk. He was under no illusions for he knew the strength of the magic the sword commanded.

Arthur gazed at the crystal, his eyes fixed on the sword. It was then that he realized that he'd secretly known all along that, one day, Dragonslayer would return to claim him and this — this, it would seem, was the day.

Archie, looking devastated, clung to the dragon in an agony of fear. The MacArthur reached out and grasping Jaikie's arm, nodded towards the magic mirror, bidding him to tell the Lords of the North what was going on. Minutes later, they arrived, stepping one by one in all their finery to stand by the MacArthur's crystal and watch the happenings on the slopes of Arthur's Seat.

"Who is the Black Knight?" queried Lord Alarid.

"I think it might be Lord Jezail," the MacArthur said shortly.

"And the Red Knight?"

The MacArthur shrugged.

"I *still* can't understand it," Lord Alarid frowned. "There's *now ay* that Dragonslayer could undo the hex I put on it!"

The MacArthur glanced at him, pursing his lips. "It's Dragonslayer all right," he said heavily. "I mean, just look at it!"

And as all eyes turned again to the crystal, they saw the magic that shone from the sword in a triumphant blaze of golden light.

It was as the knights turned from that crowds

and faced one another, ready for battle, that the Red Knight noticed the sword for the first time and looked at Dragonslayer blankly. What the devil was Peter up to, he thought, poncing around with a real sword! Even from where he was, he could see that it was razor sharp. It would cut his sword in half the minute they began their fight, for goodness sake!

The Black Knight approached him threateningly, sword at the ready. Simon, still not sure what was going on, edged his horse backwards, holding his shield fearfully in front of him. He sensed that this wasn't a game anymore. The Black Knight was deadly serious. But why on earth would Peter want to hurt him?

To Simon's surprise, however, the Black Knight made no move to attack. He merely urged his horse forward, pointed his sword at his shield, and said some strange words. They were, of course, the words of a hex, but they were enough to convince Simon that Peter had chosen the worst of all possible moments to go completely bonkers.

It was then that his shield became heavy on his arm; so heavy that he balanced it on the side of his saddle to keep it from falling to the ground. He didn't notice that the red dragon in its centre gleamed suddenly bright in the sunlight as Dragonslayer's power drew Arthur from the safety of the hill to the grassy slopes outside.

The Lords of the North gasped at the power of the hex but could do nothing to counteract it, they could only watch as the great dragon gave a dreadful cry as he shimmered and disappeared before their eyes. Turning in horror to the crystal, they then saw the painted dragon on the Red Knight's shield become ever larger as Arthur emerged from it in a sinewy, rippling tide of red.

Utterly petrified at the sight of the dragon, the Red Knight backed hastily away, his horse, rearing and whinnying shrilly. It took all of his skill to control the frightened animal and it was only when it was quiet that he hastily dismounted and led it quickly to one side. He not only needed to calm the trembling beast but also had to steady his own shattered nerves. A dragon! This hadn't been in the script!

What on earth was Peter up to? He looked fearfully at the Black Knight who now stood in front of the dragon, sword at the ready. He must be mad! For the dragon, he knew, was real. He'd seen and felt its body writhe out of his shield. What was Peter thinking? How could he stand there, face to face with a dragon? Even as he watched, the great beast sent a stream of sparkling fire curling across the grass and his heart sank. The dragon was huge and obviously meant business!

The crowd tensed with excitement at the sight of the huge beast. Its appearance was totally unexpected and many people started to flick through their programmes, wondering how on earth they'd missed reading about this utterly fantastic act.

Colonel Jamieson, however, almost had a heart attack. He stiffened and leapt to his feet. looking totally stunned. A dragon! Where on earth had it come from? More to the point, who had organized it without telling him? It looked frighteningly

real and the blasts of fire worried him. It had
certainly never been planned as part of the
tournament and his heart sank as he thought of
Health and Safety ...

Some people clapped at what they thought were
the most fantastic special effects they'd ever seen
but the applause faded and a ripple of unease
replaced the initial excitement as Arthur stood
before the Black Knight in all his splendour. He
was a magnificent dragon and, spreading his
wings, blinked in the bright sunlight. He had
lived in the hill for so long that he'd forgotten the
incredible blueness of the sky on a summer's day,
the all-pervading warmth of the sun and the sweet
smell of newly mown grass. How wonderful the
world was.

In front of him, the black horse reared and
bucked nervously, drawing Arthur's attention to
it and its rider. The Black Knight! He wondered
if the MacArthur was right in thinking that it
was Lord Jezail. Lord Jezail who had kidnapped
Clara! His eyes narrowed dangerously for the
very thought of Clara in the magician's clutches
made him forget his fears. He roared furiously,
a thing he hadn't done in years and, if the truth
be told, gave himself a bit of a fright! But noticing
that the Black Knight had backed away slightly,
he roared again and then, wings outstretched,
clawed his way over the grass towards him,
blowing great gusts of flame that licked round
the horse's legs, making it rear in panic. Gone
were the days when he had trembled before Sir
Pendar. He was now a fully grown dragon and

more than capable of looking after himself.

Now, angry dragons are not to be trifled with at the best of times and, despite the powerful hexes that surrounded him and his horse, Jezail trembled at the sight of the fearsome creature moving steadily towards him. The sword, feeling his fear and afraid that the magician might turn tail and run, sent a wave of power through him that did much to steady his nerves so that Jezail, regaining his confidence in an instant, relaxed and smiled nastily. Holding his horse with an iron hand, his eyes gleamed with triumph as the sword's magic gripped him. He knew exactly what he was going to do and where he was going to strike.

He raised Dragonslayer aloft as Arthur gave another dreadful roar and, wings beating the air furiously, flew at the knight in a blinding blaze of fire.

In the stands, Neil watched, his heart in his mouth, as the Black Knight spurred his terrified horse forward to meet the dragon. "Arthur," Neil whispered, his breath catching on a sob. "Arthur," he pleaded, grasping Lord Rothlan's sleeve, his eyes still on the dragon. "You must save him!"

"Wait," Lord Rothlan said curtly.

Ignoring the great gusts of flames that Arthur blasted round him, Jezail galloped straight towards him and, lifting Dragonslayer, gave a cry of triumph as he thrust the sword deep into the dragon's heart.

The whole crowd rose screaming to their feet as Arthur gave a great, shrieking cry, his body arching in pain as he writhed furiously in the air before collapsing in a heap on the grass.

# 18. Hoax hex

Peter dismounted from his horse and looked at the sword in his hand incredulously. It was a real sword! How on earth did he come to have it in his hand? And where had the dragon come from? It was enormous. He took a few steps towards it but it didn't move. It must be dead, he decided. But then, who had killed it? He looked again at the sword in his hand and turned white. Had *he* killed the dragon in some sort of dreadful dream? Was it possible?

He started in surprise as a gorgeously robed old man appeared at his elbow. A magician, Peter thought, without quite knowing why.

"Give me the sword!" the old man snapped and then, seeing that Peter was still in more than a bit of a daze, grasped it roughly from his hand. It was only as the sword flashed triumphantly in the sun that Peter dimly began to understand what had happened.

"Stay where you are," the old man snarled. Peter blinked in surprise for although he'd worked out that the sword had made him kill the dragon, it hadn't entered his head that anyone else might be involved, far less a magician.

Lord Jezail left him standing and ran quickly up

to the dead dragon. He knew it wouldn't be long before the magicians retaliated with a barrage of hexes but he was desperate to have some trophy of his great kill. Let him at least have the dragon's tongue! His heart thudded and his black eyes gleamed with triumph! He'd done it! He'd killed a dragon!

It was only as he approached the dragon's head that the suspicion dawned that something wasn't quite right. His eyes sharpened. The head looked ... well, it looked rather like rubber. Horrified, he bent down and touched it, his face incredulous. It *was* made of rubber! But it couldn't be! His brain worked furiously. It had been a real, live dragon he had killed. He was sure of it!

He became aware of a hissing noise and, looking at the vast bulk that was Arthur, saw that the dragon seemed to be shrinking by the second. Poking the red scales on the dragon's side with the blade of his sword, he stiffened angrily as the sudden burst of escaping air made the rudest of rude noises.

It was then that realization struck him.

The dragon was nothing more than a great big balloon!

"You didn't really think that we'd let you kill Arthur, did you?" Prince Kalman said conversationally.

Lord Jezail whirled round, an expression of fury on his face, to find Prince Kalman and Lord Rothlan standing behind him.

"You!" he mouthed venomously, realizing too late that he'd been outwitted. "You think you're so clever, don't you! But don't forget," he hissed, "don't forget that I still have the girl — and," he waved the sword threateningly, "I have Dragonslayer as well!"

And, before they could answer or make any move to stop him, he muttered the words of a hex and disappeared.

"Look out," Archie shrieked as Prince Kalman's hex returned Arthur to the hill in a roar of sound, fire and fury.

No one needed to be told. The MacArthurs took one look at the dragon and scattered — for Arthur, unaware that he was no longer confronting Lord Jezail, was a terrifying sight as, wings beating strongly, he roared his way furiously round the cavern. Great sheets of flame scorched the walls and several banners and wall hangings were reduced to ashes before he discovered that he was no longer in the open air but back in the safety of a strangely deserted hill.

Where, he thought, looking round in amazement as he swooped down to land, where had everyone gone? It was only when he saw scared faces peeping apprehensively from behind rocks round the cavern's edge that he realized the sensation he'd caused and, feeling more than slightly guilty, landed beside the MacArthur and the Lords of the North who had watched his sudden arrival with heartfelt relief.

"Well done, Arthur!" the MacArthur smiled broadly as he jumped to his feet, delighted to see him safely back.

Archie, Hamish and Jaikie rushed up together
with the rest of the MacArthurs who crowded
excitedly round the dais. They looked rather
shame-faced at having run away but really, as
Archie said later, you could hardly blame them;
for the fearsome dragon that had soared into
the cavern belching smoke and flames all over
the place was nothing like the Arthur they knew
and loved.

Conscious that he'd done well, Arthur's eyes
glowed with happiness as Archie flung his arms
round his neck. No longer fearful and timid, he'd
stood up to Lord Jezail *and* his magic sword.

It was then that Neil arrived with Prince
Kalman and Lord Rothlan.

"Arthur, you were wonderful!" Neil said, rushing
forward. "Absolutely brilliant!" he added, looking
at the dragon with real respect. He still couldn't
quite believe that Arthur could look so terrifying.

It was when the MacArthur cleared his throat
that they noticed the Lords of the North and
hastily moving towards them, bowed low.

The MacArthur, nodding approvingly, gestured
to Hamish and Jaikie, who immediately brought
chairs forward for their visitors. It was only when
Amgarad flew over to perch on Lord Rothlan's
shoulder and everyone had settled comfortably
that Arthur breathed a very gentle cloud of smoke
down his long nose and looked questioningly at
the magicians. "What happened?" he asked
simply.

Prince Kalman smiled. "Well, we'd no intention
of letting Lord Jezail kill you, Arthur. You know

that. I just waited for the right moment and hexed you back into the hill."

"So I disappeared?"

"Well, not quite," the prince confessed. "I, er ... I left your image behind ... in the shape of a huge balloon. The people watching didn't know the difference."

"Neither did Lord Jezail," added Lord Rothlan. "In fact, his face when he discovered that he'd just killed a balloon was really quite something!"

"I bet he was gutted!" Neil grinned.

"Something like that," the prince admitted, his eyes gleaming appreciatively.

Amgarad hissed as Lord Rothlan rose to his feet and approached the small table that held the MacArthur's crystal. With a muttered few words, he passed a hand over it but to no effect. The crystal remained dull and cloudy. "No joy there," he remarked. "He's still hiding himself from us."

"*And* Clara!" Lord Alarid said somberly.

Lord Rothlan nodded. "Actually, those were his final words," he said, looking dismayed as he remembered the triumph on Lord Jezail's face. "He has Clara and he has the sword ..."

"He won't hurt Clara, will he?" Neil asked hesitantly.

"No, but he'll force Clara to give him the spells," Prince Kalman's voice was grim, "and I wouldn't be surprised, either, if he has plans for Dragonslayer. Or, more likely, that Dragonslayer has plans for him."

Lord Rothlan looked startled. "You mean he'll attack the Valley of the Dragons?"

At his words, a murmur of unease ran round the circle of assembled lords and Amgarad gave a cry of distress.

Neil looked at the MacArthur. "You mentioned that before," he said, trying to visualize a valley full of dragons. "It's in Ashgar, isn't it?"

Lord Rothlan nodded. "Yes, and once Jezail returns to his citadel in Stara Zargana, I think the sword will most definitely take charge of him. Lord Jezail will become another Sir Pendar."

"Not necessarily, Alasdair," the MacArthur disagreed. "Sir Pendar wasn't a magician and once Jezail has the spells from Clara, he might well be able to control the sword."

"Oh, no," the prince leant forward to emphasize his words. "He won't want to! One of Jezail's main complaints, was the price he had to pay for his dragon pills. He was never a well man and he's very old, you know, even in our terms. He used to say that if it weren't so dangerous, he'd have a go at killing some of his own dragons to save himself the expense. Jokingly, you know ... but underneath it all, I think he was quite serious."

Lord Rothlan smiled sourly. "You're right, Kalman," he nodded in agreement. "*Once* a Dragon Seeker, *always* a Dragon Seeker!"

Arthur gazed at Lord Rothlan in horror. He'd heard stories about the Valley of the Dragons when he was very young; a fabulous place set among fantastically shaped cliffs that hid caves and deep gorges. No human ever went there for the dragons were fierce and could kill with one long breath of flame. Now, from what

Prince Kalman had said, the dragons were in real danger. Worry gripped him. He knew only too well the strength of Dragonslayer's magic. The dragons wouldn't stand a chance and even if they tried to hide, there would be no escape. Lord Jezail would use the sword to seek them out, pick them off one by one and kill them all! He had to go there and warn them. Now! At once!

He was just about to say so when Lord Alarid rose to his feet and looked at them all in turn. "Now that we know his true nature, I think we must make plans to stop Lord Jezail before he does any more damage," he said seriously.

There was a general murmur of agreement at his words.

"Quite right," Lord Dorian said grimly. "The man's a menace. He's always been full of crazy schemes and, if he gets the spells from Clara, he'll be a threat to the entire region!"

"Very true," Lord Alarid nodded, "but first of all, we have to rescue Clara from his clutches, and then," he continued, "do what we canto protect the Valley of the Dragons from Dragonslayer."

Prince Kalman and Lord Rothlan looked at one another. This was going to be no mere skirmish.

"You're talking about a massive undertaking, Alarid," Lord Alban said seriously.

"I am, indeed," Lord Alarid said. "I'm talking about war!"

"War?" Neil gasped as everyone sat up, looking more than slightly startled.

"War," Lord Alarid repeated sternly. "It's the

only way! We must end Jezail's rule in Ashgar forever!"

Hamish and Jaikie looked at one another in alarm but Arthur's eyes lit up at Lord Alarid's words and, with a roar of approval, he sent a long, curling stream of fire streaking across the cavern.

They were going to Ashgar!

# 19. An unexpected guest

They rose like a cloud to meet him.

Dragons! Dragons of all shapes and sizes! So many of them that they darkened the sky!

Arthur flinched at the sight of the oncoming horde and almost fell out of the sky in fright as they flew towards him. He'd expected a reception committee of some sort for he was quite sure that the Valley of the Dragons would be well guarded, but this was something else! There seemed to be hundreds of them and, he noted apprehensively, they didn't look particularly friendly either for the silver-grey soldier dragons in the front rank were breathing clouds of smoke and great bursts of fire.

His eyes dilated suddenly when, at a signal from a very old dragon who seemed to be their leader, the mass of dragons split in two and, swerving to both right and left, swept round him in a mass of horned heads, steadily beating wings and ripples of fire.

The ancient dragon, whose scales had quite definitely seen better days, spoke in a somewhat wheezy voice. "I am Gladrin the Great, Lord of the Valley of the Dragons," he announced. "Who are you and what is your name?"

"They call me Arthur, Milord," Arthur replied.

The old dragon searched his memory. "Arthur?" he repeated slowly. "If you are the Arthur I have heard of then you must have travelled far ..."

Arthur relaxed. He bowed his head respectfully. "Milord, I have come from Scotland," he replied, his voice friendly but steady. "I bring a message from the Lords of the North who send you their warmest greetings."

Gladrin's expression changed. He had heard of the Lords of the North and if this was the dragon he'd heard tell of in ancient tales then they were, indeed, honoured; for Gladrin, like all dragons, was well versed in history and knew Sir Pendar's story. He dipped his wings and bowed his head. "Welcome, Arthur," he said graciously. "Welcome to the Valley of the Dragons."

So it was that Arthur, escorted by Gladrin and a whole host of dragons, soared high over the dizzily towering peaks and pinnacles that guarded the fabled Valley of the Dragons and landed in quite the strangest place he'd ever seen.

Apart from the open stretch of ground where they'd landed, it was a place of light, cream-coloured rocks. Jagged hills and rocky ravines rose steeply towards the surrounding cliffs that stood, almost white, against a sky of the brightest blue. While the hills and high peaks blazed brightly in the sunshine, dark marks here and there indicated the presence of what Arthur thought might be doorways or entrances to tunnels.

And there were dragons everywhere.

Before the alarm had been raised, the Valley

of the Dragons had presented a peaceful scene that hadn't changed much over the centuries. Draped lazily over smooth shelves of rocks, the female dragons spent much of their day sprawling idly in the heat of the sun watching over their adventurous young in case they flew beyond the high peaks that protected them from the outside world. Now, however, they looked on, wide-eyed and anxious, as dragon after dragon soared in to land. They'd no idea what was happening. Visiting dragons were more or less unheard of, but of one thing they were quite sure — a stranger in their quiet valley meant that change was on its way.

Unaware of the consternation he was causing, Arthur was quite overwhelmed. The Valley of the Dragons was a fantastic place, he thought, looking round in amazement. Never in his wildest dreams had he imagined it being quite like this. And if the cliffs were the homes of the dragons, there must be hundreds of them for the valley seemed to stretch for miles.

Bowing to Arthur, Gladrin gestured to Nestor, captain of the grey soldier-dragons who, carrying slender, spiky spears in their claws, immediately formed a guard of honour. Then, at a sharp word of command, they all made their way towards the high, steep slopes that fringed the valley.

Arthur had been right in his assumption that the dragons lived in caves and marvelled as he saw a myriad of openings hidden deep in the craggy clefts of the rocks. Gladrin escorted Arthur into what was, obviously, his cave. The opening, although wider than the others, narrowed quickly and the passage that sloped steeply downwards had walls that had been brushed smooth by the wings of countless dragons over the ages.

Gladrin's halls, when they reached them, were not nearly as grand as those of the MacArthur but were stern and impressive in a dragon sort of way. Ancient hangings lined the walls but what took Arthur's attention was the enormous fireplace that dominated one side of the hall, the iron baskets by its side piled high with logs. He smiled slightly for the MacArthur had told him that in winter the snow in Ashgar lay deep in the mountains.

The floor around the fireplace was scattered with a variety of rugs and cushions and it was here that the dragons settled, looking expectant and excited — for word had swiftly spread that their unexpected visitor was none other than Arthur, the legendary dragon of Sir Pendar's famous story.

Once Arthur had been introduced to the notables of Gladrin's court he looked at them all and lowered his eyes sadly as they waited expectantly to hear the reason for his visit. They were all so polite, so interested, so excited to see him and yet he knew that within the space of the next five minutes he was going to give them news that would destroy their nice, comfortable little world. Nothing would ever be the same again.

Perhaps the dragons sensed this for, as the silence lengthened and Arthur said nothing, Gladrin spoke gently. "You come bearing bad news, Arthur?"

Arthur nodded his head. "I do," he said sadly. "It ... it concerns Lord Jezail."

The dragons stiffened where they sat and eyed one another apprehensively. Some of them hissed angrily, remembering how, in times past, the Dragon Seeker had hounded them from mountain to mountain until they had found safety in their precious valley. They blew clouds of angry smoke down their nostrils, but still no one spoke.

"We have the power to deal with Lord Jezail," Gladrin frowned, looking puzzled.

"It's a bit more serious than that," Arthur said, unhooking a bag that hung round his neck. He pulled at it with his claws until it opened wide enough for him to tip the crystal ball it held, onto the carpet. "Lord Alarid wishes to speak to you personally, Lord Gladrin," he said. "He wants to tell you himself why the Lords of the North have decided to declare war on Lord Jezail and why he is bringing an army to Ashgar."

"War?" Gladrin looked and sounded astounded, as well he might, and a hiss of unease rippled among the assembled dragons.

"The Lords of the North will explain everything," Arthur assured him. "It's a long story. In fact, it started when Sir Pendar tried to kill me with Dragonslayer all those years ago ..."

Dragonslayer! The very mention of the word sent a piercing stab of terror through the heart of each of the assembled dragons.

Before they could start asking him awkward questions, Arthur hastily placed the crystal on a cushion where it rested in full view of the dragons and, conscious that they were all watching him, passed a rather shaky claw over it. It was the

first time he'd used a magic crystal and his heart
beat faster than usual as he muttered the magic
words and wondered what would happen if it
didn't work. The crystal, however, as if sensing his
anxiety, behaved beautifully and glowed brightly.

The dragons gasped in awe and regarded Arthur
with great respect; for a dragon to use a magic
crystal — that was really impressive! Arthur,
quite weak with relief, hid his trembling claw so
that they wouldn't see how nervous he'd been and
smiled thankfully as Lord Alarid's face appeared
in the crystal.

Once the initial polite greetings had been gone
through, Lord Alarid, in a sombre voice, told the
dragons the story of the earthquake and how
Lord Jezail had hexed Sir Pendar's sword. He
also mentioned Clara's part in stealing the *Book
of Spells* from the witches but, Arthur thought,
it was doubtful if many of the dragons heard this
part of his story as the thought of Lord Jezail and
Dragonslayer had sent their minds into a complete
spin.

As the enormity of situation dawned on Lord
Gladrin, he looked at Lord Alarid with fearful eyes.
"You must know that we are defenceless against
the magic of Dragonslayer," he said apprehensively.

"That's why Arthur insisted on flying out to
warn you," Lord Alarid explained, "so that you
would be aware of your danger."

"We are more than grateful to him, Lord Alarid,"
Gladrin nodded, "and you can be quite sure that
we will welcome you and your army to Ashgar.
Dragonslayer is a threat to us all."

# 20. Stara Zargana

"There now," Maria said with a smile. "Don't you think you look pretty?"

Clara looked at her reflection in the long mirror and nodded. She did, indeed, look pretty in the new clothes that Maria had brought her. They were a big improvement on her jeans and T- shirt which now lay in a heap on her bedroom floor. She'd been wearing them ever since they'd arrived back in Ashgar and they looked indescribably tatty.

Looking round the bedroom she found it hard to believe that she was in a foreign country and wondered how they'd travelled. Probably by magic, she thought. Not that she remembered anything after Lord Jezail's hex had hit her, but she assumed that she'd been put back in the crystal again for she was still quite stiff.

"All the young girls in Stara Zargana dress like this," Maria chattered on. Smoothing the print skirt with its colourful braid trim, she adjusted the gathered neck of her white blouse, and stood back to admire her. "Now try this on," she instructed, holding up a little black jacket. "The weather's not nearly as warm as it was yesterday and we can't have you catching a cold now, can we!"

"Thank you, Maria," Clara said gratefully, looking at the pile of new clothes that lay scattered across her bed. "You've been very good to me and ... well, you didn't need to buy me so much."

"I got you a few winter things as well," Maria confessed. "The summer's almost over and the wind's really quite chilly this morning." Her eyes, however, were troubled and more than a little afraid. She liked Clara and would do what she could to protect her, but using a hex to attack Lord Jezail hadn't been at all wise and her master had by no means forgiven her. "Come downstairs and have some breakfast," she urged, banishing her worries from her mind.

Clara sighed. Really, she couldn't have had nicer jailers than Maria and Count Vassili. They were both very kind to her but although they did everything they could to please her, she was still conscious of being a prisoner, for they were careful never to leave her alone.

"Doesn't she look lovely, Count Vassili?" Maria said as they stepped from the narrow, stone, spiral staircase into one of the lower rooms of the tower. Compared with some of the other rooms in the citadel, it was quite simply furnished, for which Clara was grateful. Ornate crystal chandeliers, tapestries and Persian carpets weren't really her thing at all and she liked her little sitting room with its homely, carved furniture and deep, comfy armchairs.

Vassili looked up and nodded approvingly. "What have we here?" he queried, smiling. "An Ashgari princess?"

Clara gave a mock curtsey as he gestured towards the table where breakfast was laid. She was hungry and, pulling out her chair, missed the look that passed between Maria and the count. It was one of extreme unease for earlier that morning Lord Jezail had informed them that he wished to speak to Clara later on in the day. His tone had been grim and uncompromising and the count knew that he wasn't going to take any nonsense from Clara. This time, she would have to copy out the spells and if she wouldn't, he would use force. The thought made him wince as both he and Maria knew the pressures that could be brought to bear on her.

They chatted quite cheerfully throughout breakfast. Maria had mentioned a walk through the town and Clara was quite anxious to see it. The quaint, red-roofed houses of Stara Zargana had fascinated her and she longed to explore the narrow, twisting little streets that she could see from the slit window of her bedroom.

"Are you going to come with us this morning, Count Vassili?" she enquired.

The count, looking startled, glanced at Maria. "Where were you planning to go?" he asked.

Clara smiled as she buttered a piece of toast. "Maria promised me yesterday that she'd take me on a walk through the town this morning ..."

Her voice petered out as she saw his expression change.

"I ... er, I don't think Maria meant today," he said, avoiding her gaze.

Clara looked at him fixedly, her heart sinking.

"Lord Jezail wants to speak to me, doesn't he?" she said, her voice little more than a whisper. "He wants me to write down the spells!"

Maria gave a sudden cry of distress and, pressing her napkin to her mouth, rushed from the room.

"Clara," the count reached forward and grasped her wrist. "Clara," he repeated, looking into her eyes, "this time you *must* write the spells down for him. *All of them.* If you don't, he'll *make* you — and, believe me, that won't be very nice."

Fear flickered in her eyes but, as the count sat back satisfied that she'd taken his warning to heart, she spoke again, her voice thoughtful. "Can I ask you something, Count Vassili?"

He looked at her in surprise. "You can ask me anything you like," he said.

"Would you promise not to tell Lord Jezail what I asked?"

"He is my master," he reminded her dryly.

"I know, but ... sometimes you don't approve of him, do you? Like just now, when you told me he might hurt me to get me to write down the spells."

The count pressed his lips together and, pushing back his chair sharply, walked over to the window. Staring unseeingly at the mountains he suddenly longed for home. He'd had more than enough of Lord Jezail and his schemes. If it weren't for the book he was searching for, he'd have left his service long ago.

"You see," Clara said, rising to her feet and catching him by the arm, "there are some spells that I don't think Lord Jezail ought to know."

"I can't advise you, Clara," he said, holding her by the shoulders and looking at her straightly. "You must do as you think fit."

"Do you think he would know if I didn't tell him them all?" she whispered anxiously.

He paused and released her. "There's no way that Lord Jezail knows what's in the *Book of Spells*, Clara. Does that make things easier for you?"

She nodded and her face cleared as she smiled in relief. "It does," she said. And then she added in a strange voice. "You have been very kind to me, Count Vassili. I won't forget it."

Maria came back into the room and, seeing from Clara's face that she knew what was in store for her, ran forward and hugged her hard. "Don't you worry," she said in a voice tinged with tears. "You just tell him what he wants to know and everything will be all right!"

# 21. Spellbinding

Lord Jezail glowered at Clara as she entered the sitting room at the side of the count. She swallowed hard at the sight of him for he looked just as scary and horrible as ever. There were no words of greeting. Lord Jezail ignored her completely.

"Well?" he asked, glaring at the count. "Have you told her what she has to do?"

"Clara has agreed to write down the spells for you," the count replied.

"Excellent," Lord Jezail leant back, smiling nastily. "Sit her at that table over there," he nodded sharply towards the window. "She can start at once."

Clara went over to the round mahogany table where a stack of paper and a pen had been laid out in readiness. She hesitated and looked at him anxiously. "I need to touch the talisman," she said, her voice rising nervously. "You *do* know that, don't you? The spells won't come unless I'm touching it."

The count hastily drew another chair towards the little table and gestured to his master. "If you rest your arm here, Milord. As you did before ..." he said, his voice trailing off.

"Yes, but no tricks this time," Jezail growled. Rising grudgingly to his feet, he sat beside the little table and pulled his sleeve up to reveal the talisman. It shone, a bright band of silver, round his thin wrist as he rested his arm on the edge of the table.

Clara pulled her chair as far away from him as she could so that when she stretched her arm, it was only the tips of her fingers that touched the talisman. It was enough. Its magic flowed through her like a river and again she felt its happiness at being close to her.

"Write!" Lord Jezail snapped impatiently. "The faster the better. This is going to take all day as it is, without you wasting time!"

Count Vassili moved the pile of paper further along the table so that Clara could start.

"Are the words there?" he asked.

Clara nodded as she saw the spells in her mind and hastily started to write as Jezail twisted round in his chair to watch her, his eyes black and sharp.

Time passed and it all got a bit boring. Sun slanted in through the slit window as she wrote down page after page of the *Book of Spells*. Jezail sat beside her, slumped in his chair dozing fitfully while the count lay back in an armchair on the other side of the room, tapping his fingers worriedly as he wondered when the Lords of the North would arrive. He was pretty sure that they'd come in force to rescue Clara. So was his master, for that matter; which was why, after they'd laid their plans and organized the garrison of the citadel, he'd insisted that Clara write the spells down immediately.

It hadn't proved quite as easy as that, however. Clara had been inside the crystal for a considerable length of time and had slept for the best part of two days before she woke up to the world. Maria had sat by her bedside the whole time, worried out of her mind, and Vassili, too, had been afraid; for he'd no idea if Clara might suffer any after-effects from her imprisonment. Watching her, however, eased his mind and he smiled as, now totally absorbed in her work, she finished a page, laid it on top of the growing pile in front of her and automatically reached for the next one.

As Clara continued writing, the silence deepened. Once or twice she stopped to stretch her arms, watching to see if Jezail would notice or if Count Vassili would raise his head enquiringly from across the room. Neither moved. She was pretty sure that Jezail was asleep as his rasping breath had become a slight snore but Vassili ... she looked at him closely. His head had fallen back against the cushion and he was completely relaxed. He *must* be asleep.

Trembling slightly, she laid her pen carefully on the table and, looking at the last spell she had written, quietly folded the sheet of paper until it was small enough to go into the pocket of the little black jacket Maria had given her. In the course of the next half hour, she repeated this three times and then, with a sense of relief, continued writing. Lord Jezail would surely never know the difference.

It was Maria's knock on the door that woke the two men. Jezail snorted and sat up with a start while Vassili opened his eyes, looking casually towards the door as Maria entered.

"I thought you might like lunch now," she said, looking at Clara to see if she was alright.

Jezail muttered and, taking his arm off the table, rubbed it hard. It had become stiff and cramped and he wasn't amused.

"Have you nearly finished, Clara?" the count asked.

Clara shook her head and stretched her fingers. "It's a long book," she said tiredly. "I'm only about half way through."

"Maybe, we should leave the other half for tomorrow," the count suggested, looking at his master.

Lord Jezail shook his head. "We'll have lunch," he said determinedly, "and then she can go on writing until dinner if needs be. Maria can take your place if you like, but I want the whole book finished today!"

It was dark and Maria had long since lit the lamps before Clara finally reached the last spell. With a sigh of relief, she put down her pen and slumped back in her chair. Her eyes closed. She was dead tired and all she wanted to do was sleep for a week.

"You've finished?" Maria queried, rising from her chair. "Thank goodness!"

Lord Jezail stirred.

"Master," Maria shook his arm. "Master, Clara has finished writing."

Lord Jezail looked from the neatly stacked pile of papers on the table to Clara. His eyes were suspicious. "Did you write down *all* of the spells?" he asked. "You didn't leave any of them out, did you?"

Clara looked him in the eye. "I wrote them all down," she said firmly, "and I didn't leave any of them out."

Her gaze was direct and honest and Jezail knew instinctively that she was telling the truth. He turned to the table and fingered the sheets of paper, his black eyes gleaming in triumph. The *Book of Spells!* It was his at last! Hands trembling, he picked up the top sheet of paper and scanning the spell greedily, started to read.

Seeing her master so totally absorbed, Maria took Clara's arm and led her gently to the door. "Come on, Clara," she whispered. "You'll feel better once you've had some supper."

Clara nodded, feeling the gentle crackle of paper in her pocket as she followed Maria down the spiral staircase. She hadn't actually lied to Lord Jezail, she thought guiltily, for she had, indeed, written down every spell in the book — what she hadn't mentioned was that four of them nestled safely in her pocket.

# 22. The road north

Count Vassili rose to his feet as they entered and pulled out a chair for her. She sat down, surprised to see that he had changed out of his velvet robes and was now dressed in a high-necked black jacket, breeches and riding boots. Not only that, a heavy fur-lined cloak lay over one of the chairs. Where, she wondered, was he going at this time of night?

She knew better, however, than to ask and, completely forgetting to tell him of the spells in her pocket, reached for her napkin, while looking in astonishment at the many steaming dishes on the table — quite different from their usual simple supper. "What's this?" she asked, feeling somewhat light-headed, now that her ordeal was over. "A feast?"

The count lowered his eyes. "Not so much a feast as a farewell dinner, I'm afraid," he answered a trifle grimly.

Alarm sparked in her eyes. "A farewell dinner?" she questioned, catching her breath.

"Yes," he replied. "We leave the citadel tonight."

"We?" she queried, meeting his eyes in startled surprise. "Me, too?"

He nodded. "Maria's coming with us as well. She'll be down in a second. She's just gone upstairs to organize the packing."

"So that's why she bought me so much ..."

"No," he said, shaking his head. "She didn't know we'd be leaving the citadel any more than I did." He rose to his feet and spooned a generous helping of beef stew onto her plate. "Please don't worry about it, Clara," he added, seeing her anxious face. "You know that you're safe with us. Now," he smiled reassuringly, moving the potatoes and vegetables to within her reach, "eat well. We have a long journey ahead of us."

A long journey! Hope sprang suddenly in her heart and she sat up straight, her eyes shining. "Count Vassili! Are ... are you taking me home?"

His eyes dropped and he fingered his fork idly. Of course she would think that. She'd done what his master had asked, after all. His lips set in a straight line and he had to force himself to meet her eyes calmly. "No, Clara, actually, we're going to ... to Dragonsgard, one of Lord Jezail's castles near the northern border."

Angrily, Clara pushed her plate to one side. "But I did what he asked," she protested, blinking back tears. "I wrote down all of the spells! *Why* can't I go home?"

The count shrugged uncomfortably. "I don't know Clara. He obviously wants you to stay in Ashgar — and it's his decision, you know. I only obey orders. We leave for Dragonsgard within the hour!"

"Dragonsgard," she whispered. The word sent a chill tingling through her. It sounded every bit as grim as the citadel. "I ... will I like it there?" she asked dubiously.

The count was saved from answering by the entry of a black-uniformed officer who bowed low and clicked his heels together smartly. "We'll be ready to leave by midnight, Count Vassili," he announced.

"Midnight?" the count queried, looking up as Maria entered and slipped into the chair beside Clara. "Surely you can be ready sooner than that?"

"Lord Jezail has instructed me to provide you with an escort. I've detailed six men to accompany you."

Maria and the count exchanged brief glances but the count's voice remained calm. "That was extremely thoughtful of Lord Jezail," he remarked. "There might well be brigands on the road."

"With your permission, Sir, we'll be loading extra stores on the coach."

Coach? Clara picked up on the word. They were going to be travelling by bus?

"Of course," the count agreed. "Oh, and Colonel Braganz ..." the count added, before the man could turn away.

"Sir?"

"See that there are plenty of thick blankets in the coach for the ladies. The night air is cold and we've a long journey in front of us."

"Yes, Sir," the colonel saluted briskly and left.

It was well after midnight, however, before Clara and Maria, clutching warm, hooded cloaks round them, walked down a shallow flight of steps into the deep courtyard of the citadel.

Torches flared on the high walls sending fantastic
shadows across the cobbles where a coach drawn by
six black horses waited in the moonlight. Behind
the coach, a troop of cloaked horsemen with an
officer at their head, waited in twos, ready to
move off, their horses moving restlessly, harnesses
jingling as they tossed their heads, snorting softly.

Clara stopped dead, her eyes widening in
amazement. A coach, she thought, a proper old-
fashioned coach! How could she have been stupid
enough to think Lord Jezail would have anything
as ordinary as a bus! Anyway, the thought crossed
her mind fleetingly, where would he get petrol
from? Dismissing the bus from her mind, she
gazed in awe at the coach: its wheels were huge
and brass fittings gleamed fitfully in the light of
the flares as the horses stamped impatiently. The
coachman, perched at the front, was well wrapped
up against the chill breeze and holding the reins at
the ready, watched them approach.

A sudden clatter of hooves interrupted her
thoughts and she swung round to see Count Vassili
riding across the courtyard towards them. He
pulled up beside the coach, returning the salute
of the officer in charge of the escort, and looked
enquiringly at Maria. "Do you have everything you
need for the journey?" he asked briefly.

Maria nodded as a soldier stepped forward and,
opening the carriage door, pulled down a step so
that she could enter easily. "I think so," she said,
nodding to the cases and boxes strapped at the
back of the coach.

"Good! Then we're ready to set off! In you get,

Clara," he gestured as she hesitated at the door of the coach. "There are lots of blankets inside, so you can stretch out and get some sleep."

"Sleep?" Clara looked at him, her eyes sparkling. She was so excited at the thought of travelling in a coach that her tiredness seemed to have left her.

The count smiled ruefully, knowing that within the hour she'd most likely be bored stiff and probably quite uncomfortable; for the road to Dragonsgard was unpaved and, in some places, little more than a pot-holed track. "I'll be riding beside you," he said, pulling his cloak round him, "so you only have to call if you need anything."

Clara gave a final glance round the high walls that enclosed the courtyard and climbed into the roomy interior of the coach. Settling herself comfortably, she grinned across at Maria. The coach could, she thought, hold six people comfortably, not just two. Then she turned and peered through the little side window as an order was given.

The soldiers who'd been holding the horses' bridles, promptly stepped back from their heads and, as the coachman shook the reins, the six black horses pulled on their harnesses. With a jerk and a rumble of wheels, the coach started forward. They were off, Clara thought excitedly, peering out as they passed slowly under a dark archway into the night.

As the great doors of the citadel closed slowly behind them, the horses picked up speed, sending the coach rattling across the curved, stone bridge that divided the citadel from the narrow streets of the town. Clara craned her neck and could just see the frothing, white water of the rushing mountain stream that passed below.

Despite the lateness of the hour, a few people in Stara Zargana were still awake and curtains parted fearfully in the windows of several houses as the coach, with its escort of dark-clad riders, clattered swiftly through the winding streets, heading towards the great road that led north.

# 23. Magic carpets

As the first fingers of daylight slipped across the morning sky, a fleet of magic carpets soared across the tree-clad mountains that marked the western border of the tiny state of Ashgar. It had been a long journey and the carpets, cold and tired, sighed with relief at the thought that there wasn't much further to go. Not that anyone had seen them, of course, as the MacArthur's mighty army had travelled across Europe quite invisible to human eyes.

Neil woke up as the sun rose and, blinking tiredly, felt a moment of panic as he felt the wind on his face. Then he remembered. He wasn't cosily tucked up in bed at home; he was cold, stiff and shivering on his magic carpet! Sitting up carefully, he drew his cloak closer.

Although he couldn't see any of the carpets around him, he knew that they were there, flying in tight formation. Prince Kalman's carpet was to his left and Lord Rothlan with Amgarad, his great eagle, flew to his right. Ahead, however, lay the invisible host of magic carpets that carried the MacArthur and his troops, into battle. Interestedly, he peered over the edge of his carpet and saw thick forest stretching almost to the horizon.

"Good morning," he called tentatively, wondering if the others were awake.

It was Prince Kalman who answered. "Good morning, Neil," he replied. "I was wondering when you were going to wake up!"

Lord Rothlan then chipped in. "Are you all right, Neil?" he asked, amusement colouring his voice. "I was just about to send Amgarad across to peck you awake!"

"Morning, Lord Rothlan," Neil replied. "I slept like a log, I'm afraid. I must have been really tired! Are we nearly there?"

"Not far to go now," Rothlan replied. "We've just crossed the border into Ashgar. That road, down there on your right, beside the river, runs to Plevitz, the capital. It's more of a big town than a city."

"The rest of the country hasn't changed in centuries," Prince Kalman added. "Just small farms and the like — and forests, of course. Most people still travel round on horseback."

"Just as well that we have magic carpets," Lord Rothlan observed thankfully. "It'd take us the best part of a week to get to Stara Zargana otherwise."

Although they chatted now and then, the time passed slowly. Neil felt a lot better when the sun climbed higher in the sky and warmed him through. Everyone had brought sandwiches and bottled water for the journey and he didn't take long to finish his. The cold mountain air had given him an appetite.

When his carpet started to lose height Neil felt a thrill of excitement. "Are we nearly there?" he queried.

"Yes, that village ahead's called Hilderstein," Prince Kalman said. "The old hunting lodge I told you about is just a few miles further on."

The hunting lodge, Neil knew, was to be the base of their operations. In years gone by, when they'd regarded Lord Jezail as a friend, the prince and his father had lived in it while hunting wild boar in the forest. Indeed, it was a map the prince had drawn showing the lie of the surrounding countryside that had done much to convince the MacArthur that its position, although isolated, was ideal. It was so remote that, with any luck, none of Jezail's spies would ever guess that they were there.

The only problem, Neil thought, was that he was going to have to stay at the lodge, kicking his heels, while the others enjoyed all the excitement of going to war. The MacArthur had been quite definite about it. There was no way he would allow him to take part in the battle for the citadel.

No one expected the hex that hit the MacArthur's army.

Not that they knew anything about it, since Lord Jezail was a wily soul as well as being a powerful magician. Leafing through Clara's spells, he had chosen the hexes carefully. The first was a quiet, subtle hex that immediately sent all of the MacArthur's troops into a deep, deep sleep. He followed this up with another which, if anything, was the more dangerous of the two, for it knocked all of the magic carpets completely off course.

Looking out idly from the window of his study, Jezail smiled nastily. Wherever the MacArthur and his army ended up, it certainly wasn't going to be *anywhere* near Stara Zargana!

His black eyes glowed with satisfaction as he turned to his desk where the sword lay, glowing gently. Dragonslayer! He could still hardly believe that it was his! Lifting it up, he held it in the palms of both hands and told it of the spells he had just cast. "They were from the *Book of Spells*," he said proudly. "I made the girl write them all down."

The sword glowed red with anger. "You didn't tell *me* she had written them all down!" it said furiously. "I would like to have questioned her about them. Some of them might have been useful to me! Didn't you think of that?"

Lord Jezail had, indeed, thought of just such a possibility; which was why he'd had Clara write the spells out in his sitting room rather than in his study. He'd seen enough of the sword's magic to know its power and, as far as he was concerned, giving it access to the *Book of Spells* was quite out of the question.

"Bring her here!" the sword said commandingly. "At once!"

"Oh, she's not here anymore," Lord Jezail answered, shaking his head. "Once she'd finished writing the spells, I sent her away."

The sword fizzled with rage.

"I thought it best," Lord Jezail explained, stiffly. "So far, I've dealt a deadly blow to the Lords of the North *and* their army but they might well recover. Anyway," he continued, "if there *is* going to be any fighting here, I certainly wouldn't want a child in the citadel. I've sent her to Dragonsgard."

"Dragonsgard?" asked the sword.

"A castle of mine, on the northern border."

"Why?" queried the sword, sharply. "Surely the girl would be more useful here? If things go against you, you could use her as a bargaining chip!"

"Actually, sending her to Dragonsgard was mostly an excuse for getting rid of Count Vassili," Jezail admitted, scowling suddenly. "I've been suspicious of him for a while. Not that he's been plotting against me or anything like that but he's become tiresome; always finding fault and objecting to my plans." He paused and then added. "For instance, he would have done everything he could to stop me from taking you to the Valley of the Dragons."

A wave of approval burned through the sword.

"He's in for a surprise when he arrives at the castle, too," Lord Jezail added, smiling nastily. "You see, Vassili is a magician of sorts and I can't have him interfering in our plans. I gave the officer in charge a letter for the Governor of Dragonsgard instructing him to imprison them all, the minute they arrive."

Dragonslayer glowed. The magician had, indeed, done well and although he didn't approve of the girl being sent away, she could still be useful if things didn't work out as planned. All in all, everything was working out nicely, for now that the magician had hexed the MacArthur's army, the threat of battle had been nipped in the bud leaving the magician free to march to the Valley of the Dragons.

As the strength of the sword's desire swept through him, Lord Jezail fell under its spell and immediately started to make plans. The Valley of the Dragons lay in a remote corner of Ashgar. There was work to be done!

While Lord Jezail busied himself, making arrangements for his forthcoming journey, the MacArthur's army on their magic carpets continued to sail majestically through the sky, totally unaware that they were completely off course *or* that their riders were fast asleep.

All except Neil, that is. He sat up abruptly as the carpets changed direction. What was going on? He heard Amgarad give a loud squawk of alarm and fear gripped him.

"Lord Rothlan!" Neil shouted. He waited, but there was no answer. "Prince Kalman!" he called. Again there was silence.

"Amgarad!" Neil shouted. "Amgarad! What's going on?"

Neil gave a sigh of relief as Amgarad became visible as he left Lord Rothlan's carpet in a flap of wings, then promptly disappeared again as he landed on Neil's shoulder. "Ouch!" Neil winced as he felt the bird's claws penetrate the thick stuff of his cloak.

Amgarad was too angry to apologize. "It was a hex, Neil," he said grimly. "We should have known Jezail wouldn't let us fly in unchallenged. Everyone's asleep on their carpets and I've no idea where we're heading. The carpets have changed direction completely!"

"Do you think they're heading for Stara Zargana?" Neil hazarded a guess.

"I don't think so," Amgarad said. "We seem to be heading south ..."

"Can't you wake Lord Rothlan up?" Neil asked.

"I tried," Amgarad said, "but it was no good. He's in a magic sleep. He'll only wake up when the spell is lifted ..."

"... and by then he might be Lord Jezail's prisoner!" Neil finished the sentence.

The great eagle nodded its head worriedly.

"And me as well," Neil added grimly. "What can we do, Amgarad? If I could get off the carpet, I might be able to help in some way."

Amgarad looked at him in surprise. "Of course you can get off," he said. "Anytime you like! All you have to do is merge with me!"

Neil's eyes gleamed. He'd forgotten about merging. Nevertheless, he hesitated. It wasn't an ideal option for he'd no idea if he'd see his magic carpet again but at least if they were both free they might be able to rescue the prince and Lord Rothlan. Looking back, he searched for Hilderstein and saw it nestling among farmland at the edge of the forest. "Let's go to that village, Amgarad," he said. "Then we can ask someone where the hunting lodge is. If the spell's lifted then that's where the prince will come looking for us."

Amgarad looked unsure but with every second that passed, the village was drawing further away. Neil didn't hesitate. He put his arms round the eagle and immediately merged with him.

It was really quite fantastic, he thought, for in an instant, he saw the world from a different perspective. Now he knew the meaning of "eagle-

eyed" for as Amgarad flapped his great wings
and swooped downwards, he could see the earth
beneath in the most fantastic detail down to the
smallest blade of grass. The flight, however, was
all too short and stepping out of the bird onto a
footpath, he looked round in a bit of a daze. He
couldn't believe he'd merged with an eagle. It was
amazing!

Amgarad had landed at the edge of a wood
and, perching on an old fence, barely waited until
Neil demerged before flapping his wings to soar
skywards again.

"Amgarad?" Neil was startled. "Where are you
going?"

"I've just realized that I can't leave the carpets,
Neil. I have to stay with them, at least until I know
where they're heading. I'll come back for you as
soon as I can. I must go. I've got to catch up with
the carpets!"

The carpets, however, had travelled for quite
a few miles before he managed to catch up with
them and by that time he was regretting having
left Neil alone on the ground. They hadn't thought
it through properly and now Neil was on his own
in a strange land. He had an uneasy feeling that
the prince and Lord Rothlan weren't going to be at
all pleased with him.

As for Neil, he waited and worried beside the
fence for hours — but Amgarad didn't return.

# 24. Night watch

Arthur went to bed early that night, completely worn out by his long stint of sentry duty, for he had insisted on doing his bit in protecting the Valley of the Dragons. Within seconds of rolling himself into a comfortable position among the rocks that formed his bed he was fast asleep. Indeed, so deep was his sleep that he didn't hear the red dragons as they closed the entrance to his cave. This was the first task of the night watch and the dragons took their duties seriously, moving round all the caves in the valley, closing the openings with huge boulders that fitted snugly into the entrances of the tunnels.

It was exhausting work, for the boulders were heavy, but the dragons were strong and as their leader flew round to make sure that no cave had been left open to the night air, they flew to their perches atop high pinnacles of rock, their eyes sharp and alert for they knew that *she* would be hungry. It was many months since she'd managed to kill and eat a baby dragon — and every night since had been a battle of wits as she crept cunningly between outcrops of rock, trying to reach the caves on the hillside where the dragons slept. Tonight was a dangerous night, for the full moon shone brightly on the creamy rocks of the valley, leaving deep areas of shadow where ... she ... could move unseen.

She was there. And she was hungry. Very hungry. Slithering upwards, the great serpent rose from the depths of the deep crevasse she called home and, stealing through the shadows, slipped silently across the smooth rocks to feast, hopefully, on dragon flesh. Preferably baby dragon flesh, she thought, hissing softly to herself; so much more tender and appetizing than the tough, ancient, hundreds-of-years-old variety and *so* much easier to swallow!

Her tongue flickered several times as she smiled in cold amusement, for her chances this time were more than good. The dragons had been careless that morning. So excited were they at the arrival of this new dragon that they hadn't noticed her watching. But she had been close. So close that she had heard them talking of Arthur in hushed tones. Arthur, she thought contemptuously. What kind of a name for a dragon was that, for goodness sake! And, putting Arthur out of her mind, she cast the red dragons a calculating glance as she slithered slowly and carefully upwards towards the cave entrance she'd marked out as her target for the evening. It had, she'd discovered, housed a rather nasty baby dragon who was so badly behaved that it drove its mother to distraction. It really deserved to be her supper. In fact, she reckoned she'd be doing the mother a favour, getting rid of such an awful brat! She certainly wouldn't miss him and as he was on the plump side, her mouth watered in anticipation.

Reaching the entrance to the cave, she reared her thick length behind her in undulating curves and pushed against the side of the boulder. It was moving, she thought excitedly. She only needed a small opening to get through and once in the dragon's lair, a quick bite would be enough to put the dragons to sleep. Getting out again with a young dragon filling her stomach, however, was definitely something else and gently, ever so gently, she widened the hole. Slithering softly down the tunnel, she arrived in the cave where the dragons lay on their rocky beds, snoring loudly, blissfully unaware of their danger.

It was all the fault of the wretched child, she thought afterwards, nursing her burns and bruises. Who else, after all, would have left sharp stones lying around in the dark! Her hiss of alarm as they'd pierced her scales had been more than enough to wake the dragons and the father had got in a good few searing blasts of fire before she'd managed to turn round and streak back up the tunnel again.

Then, of course, the red dragons, alerted by the noise, were already diving towards her, flames belching from their mouths. It had been a tricky journey home. The thought of it made her shudder as, slithering in a mad panic from rock to rock, shadow to shadow, she'd done all she could to avoid them. Lashing out with her tail when they got too close, she knew she'd caused them some damage but there were so many of them that her

efforts had been of little use as they swooped on
her unprotected body, raking it with their claws.
The flame of their breath lit the valley and sent
the shadows fleeing so that her last, few, painful
yards, in full view of her attackers, had been a
nightmare of pain and horror.

Arthur rose bright and early the next morning
and stretched lazily on the heap of rocks and
stones that served as his bed. It wasn't quite what
he was used to, of course, and for an instant he
thought longingly of Arthur's Seat and the ever-so
comfortable heap of wonderful treasure that he
snuggled down into each evening. He sighed
inwardly, missing the gleam of gold, the sparkle of
precious jewels and the slippery slide of sovereigns
under his claws. But then, he supposed, this was
an adventure and you couldn't really expect home
comforts.

It was then that he discovered that it was dark.
He frowned, knowing that by this time light should
have been streaming into his cave. Something was
most definitely wrong! Feeling his way over to the
tunnel, he scrambled upwards and, on reaching
the top, found the way barred by the huge boulder
that fitted across the opening. Not a chink of light
shone through and he was just about to put a
shoulder to it when the rock rolled away from the
entrance, leaving him blinking in the dawn light.

The red dragon was very apologetic and more
than slightly ashamed. "I'm very sorry, Arthur,
Sir," he gabbled distractedly. "I'm a bit late today.
*She* was on the prowl last night, you see, and she

made it into one of the caves. Fortunately the dragons woke up and ... it was quite a battle, I can tell you!"

Arthur noticed that one of the dragon's wings was badly torn.

"Did you manage to kill her?"

The red dragon shook his head. "No, she escaped into her den but she was badly injured.

You must excuse me, Arthur, Sir," he said pleadingly. "I'm late as it is this morning and I've loads more rocks to remove."

"Go ahead," Arthur answered, looking across the valley to where a veritable army of red dragons was hurriedly removing the great round boulders that blocked the tunnels that led down into the dragons' caves.

"Thank you, thank you," gabbled the little red dragon as he flew, rather precariously given his damaged wing, over to the next pinnacle of rock where he proceeded to shoulder a round boulder from the entrance to a tunnel.

Arthur looked on as the red dragons went about their duties. What, he wondered, had gone on in the night? He wished that he, himself, had been on guard duty so that he could have seen the great serpent that had obviously petrified the wits out of the red dragon.

Gladrin told him the story later on that morning and Arthur looked thoughtful. The Valley of the Dragons, so peaceful on the surface, wasn't quite the paradise he'd thought when he first arrived. He kept his thoughts to himself as he didn't want to raise false hopes for, although there was no way that the dragons could get into the deep clefts where the serpent lived, he was fairly sure that, between them, Prince Kalman and Lord Rothlan might well be able to rid them of the ugly monster that ate their young.

# 25. Morven helps out

"What on earth is Amgarad trying to do?" A puzzled frown crossed Lord Dorian's face as he gazed into the crystal ball.

The other lords rose to their feet and wandered over.

"It looks as though he's trying to wake Lord Rothlan up," Lord Alarid's voice was tinged with anxiety.

"Something's going on," Lord Alban said in alarm. "Widen the image, Dorian, and let's see the rest of the magic carpets."

"Dear goodness," Lord Alarid whispered as he viewed the sleeping army, "they're ... they're all asleep!"

"It looks as though Jezail was waiting for them and got his hex in first," Lord Dorian said sourly as the eye of the crystal passed over the fleet of carpets.

"Oh! Come on, Dorian!" Lord Alban protested. "The MacArthur's not a fool! He had a strong protective shield round his army."

Lord Alarid raised a hand to silence him. "Shhh! Amgarad knows we're watching," he interrupted as the eagle raised its head eagerly.

"Amgarad," he spoke to the bird, "tell us what happened."

"It was a hex," the bird replied. "It sent everyone into a deep sleep and not only that, it's altered the direction of the carpets. I've no idea where we are!"

Lord Alban, still pondering the strength of a hex that could break the MacArthur's protective shield, looked towards the *Book of Spells* that lay open on a carved bookrest. If Clara had written out the spells for Lord Jezail, he thought grimly, then it was more than likely that he'd find the hex within its pages.

Leaving the little group that clustered round the crystal, he strode hurriedly over and, leafing carefully through the pages of thick parchment, stopped abruptly, his eyes gleaming in sudden triumph. "This *must* be it!" he muttered, hastily lifting the heavy book off its stand. Carrying it over to the table where the crystal still shone brightly, he laid it down reverently. "What do you think, Alarid?" he gestured towards the page. "Do you think he's used this one?"

Lord Alarid read through the hex and then nodded. "It's more than likely," he agreed. "Stand back, Amgarad," he instructed, gazing deep into the crystal. "We think we can reverse the hex!" He then took a deep breath and read the spell backwards, word by word.

There was an anxious few seconds when nothing happened and then a sigh of relief rippled through them as they saw Lord Rothlan stretch lazily and sit up. Amgarad flapped onto his master's arm and when he'd finished telling him what had happened, Lord Rothlan looked up, knowing that the lords could see and hear him.

"It looks as though everyone's awake," he said grimly, as raised, angry voices echoed round him. "There's a real hullabaloo going on."

"I'm not surprised," Lord Alarid remarked dryly. "Your carpets seem to be heading south instead of east!" He looked up as Lord Alban, leafing hastily through the book, nodded his head and pointed to another spell.

"Let me try this one," Lord Alban said, his fingers moving backwards over the words of the spell as he read it aloud.

The fleet of magic carpets fluttered uneasily as the hex was lifted. What had happened to them? They felt sick, ill and incredibly tired. All they wanted to do was land, curl up and rest.

Lord Alban bent over the crystal. "Your carpets should be alright, now," he said grimly. "Just be careful, Alasdair! With the *Book of Spells* in his hands, Jezail can get up to a lot of mischief!"

Rothlan nodded. "Thank you, Lord Alban," he answered gratefully as the carpets began to lose height. "We'll be careful!"

It was later on that evening when they had organized their camp and eaten dinner that Amgarad returned with bad news. Neil was nowhere to be found. He was quite sure that he'd returned to the same place and had searched for him until darkness fell.

At much the same time, the MacArthur arrived

back from his inspection and, with a brief word to
the sentry, pulled the flap of the tent to one side
and looking round the lamp-lit interior, sat down
heavily on a pile of cushions. One look at his face
was enough. More trouble, Lord Rothlan thought,
his heart sinking.

Seeing the MacArthur, Amgarad repeated his
story, his head bowed in shame. He knew he'd
made a bad mistake in leaving Neil but just
couldn't work out where the boy had got to.

The MacArthur didn't say anything but looked
grim. Losing Neil was a problem they could well
have done without.

Prince Kalman looked at him shrewdly.
Something other than Neil's disappearance had
upset him and he raised an eyebrow enquiringly.

"It's the carpets," the MacArthur said briefly,
catching his glance and coming straight to the
point. "They say they're sick and can't fly."

"Can't fly?" Prince Kalman interrupted. "What
do mean, they can't fly? We need them!"

The MacArthur accepted a cup of tea gratefully
and took a sip before answering. "I don't know
what's wrong with them," he admitted, eyeing
them all in turn, "but I believe what they're telling
me! And if they say they can't go any further then
they can't," he added stubbornly.

Prince Kalman and Lords Rothlan exchanged
glances. This was serious.

"It's been a long journey and when they say
they really *are* exhausted, I believe them," the
MacArthur said apologetically, "but as for feeling
sick and ill! Well, if you ask me, that's another

of Lord Jezail's hexes! Sick and ill, I ask you! Just tell me! Since when have magic carpets ever complained of feeling sick and ill?"

Amgarad squawked and flapped his wings but Archie, Hamish and Jaikie said nothing and even Lord Rothlan and Prince Kalman didn't argue. The MacArthur, Lord Rothlan thought, was probably right.

Prince Kalman looked round, tight-lipped and angry with himself for underrating Jezail's power. He should have known from the start that he'd have some powerful hexes up his sleeve. Too late, he remembered the citadel's massive library of books on magic lore. Now, to cap it all, Jezail had Clara's version of the *Book of Spells* to add to his collection!

"In that case, I think we'd better camp here for the next few days," he said, looking at the MacArthur for approval. "Amgarad can start looking for Neil first thing tomorrow morning while we do what we can to make the carpets comfortable. I'll ask Lord Alban if he can help."

The MacArthur nodded. He'd been just about to suggest it.

The prince, looking ruefully at Lord Rothlan, took a small crystal ball from the pocket of his cloak and set it on a nearby cushion." Time to tell the Lords of the North the mess I've made of things, Alasdair," he said bluntly." But first of all, we'll have to find out if Lord Jezail used a hex from the *Book of Spells* to make the magic carpets sick — for we can't reverse it until we know which one it was!"

"Don't blame yourself too much, Kalman," Lord Rothlan said, leaning forward and putting an arm round his shoulders. "It's not your fault that the carpets are ill."

"You *do* realize that if they don't recover soon, we'll have to *march* to Stara Zargana," the prince said grimly as Lord Alarid's face appeared in the crystal.

Hamish and Jaikie, who had a fair idea of the distance involved, looked at one another in dismay. It would be a long walk!

"I'm not looking forward to it either," the prince said seriously, seeing their faces, "but we've no choice. Getting Clara back *must* be our first priority!" Then, turning to the crystal, he told Lord Alarid what had happened.

"And Neil?" queried Lord Alarid when he'd heard the story. "What about him?"

"Apparently, Jezail's hex didn't affect him," Lord Rothlan interrupted. "Amgarad took him off his carpet to safety before flying back to try and help me."

"So he's on his own?" Lord Alarid sounded shocked.

Archie, Hamish and Jaikie looked at one another apprehensively for although Neil wore a firestone, he had no magic to speak of.

"He's in a dangerous position," Lord Alarid said sharply. "Jezail will have spies everywhere."

"He's a sensible lad," Lord Rothlan frowned. "I'm sure we'll find him."

Lord Alarid turned from the crystal as though someone were talking to him. "Excuse me, Alasdair,

I won't keep you any longer. Lord Alban is working his way through the *Book of Spells* at the moment. I'll let you know the minute he finds the hexes you're looking for."

As his face faded, Lord Rothlan looked at Prince Kalman regretfully. They both knew that Lord Alarid wasn't at all amused at the turn events were taking.

"Neil must be worried sick," Lord Rothlan said, "and he'll be hungry, too," he added.

"He's wearing a thick cloak so he ought to get a reasonable night's sleep," Prince Kalman said slowly, seeing his distress. "You're right, Alasdair, he *will* be hungry but he'll last out until morning."

Lord Rothlan nodded. "I'll send Amgarad out to look for him as soon as the sun comes up."

# 26. In the forest

I hope nothing's happened to him, Neil thought, shading his eyes against the sun as he scanned the skies for the hundredth time. Where, he wondered, had Amgarad got to? He knew he wouldn't have let him down without a reason, which made things even more worrying. Glancing anxiously at his watch, he decided to give him another hour. If he hadn't turned up by then, well ... he'd have to work out what to do next.

Spreading his cloak over the grass, he settled himself against the trunk of a huge oak tree that stood at the edge of the wood. Although the sun was warm, summer was fading. The great tree was already losing its leaves and acorns lay scattered among the grass. Birds twittered and chattered among its branches and an old crow regarded him with beady eyes from its perch on the rickety old fence that bordered the path. It watched him for a while and then, stretching its wings, flew off. Apart from the distant roofs of the village, there was little else to see, for the forest around him seemed to stretch for miles; a green blanket of trees that covered the countryside.

The hour passed incredibly slowly with no sign

whatsoever of the great eagle although he kept
his eyes fixed on the sky all the time. He felt
worried and depressed. They'd set off for Ashgar
in such high spirits and now all this had happened!
Everything had gone wrong.

Time passed and he half-dozed in the sun.
Stretching lazily, he checked his watch yet again
and looked expectantly at the sky but there was
still no sign of Amgarad. His spirits fell as worry
set in and the dangers of his situation started to
dawn. If Amgarad didn't come back, he was on his
own — on his own in a strange country. What was
he going to do now?

He looked at the roofs of the houses that showed
through distant trees. He could, he supposed, work
his way over towards them and ask someone for
directions to the hunting lodge and perhaps, too,
someone might give him something to eat. It was
a long time since he'd had breakfast ...

He looked doubtfully at the sky, willing the eagle
to appear for he knew that if he moved on, Amgarad
would never be able to find him. "I think I should
stay put, at least until morning," he said aloud, "and
if he hasn't turned up by then ...well, then I'll know
something really *has* happened to him!"

It was a grim thought. He leant back against the
trunk of the tree and sighed, his eyes scanning the
horizon yet again. The only thing in the sky was
a flock of crows. He watched idly as they swooped
through the sky towards him. Flock, he thought,
was the wrong word. A flock of sheep, a herd of
cattle ... he searched his mind and then it came to
him ... a *murder* of crows.

It was as the crows drew closer, however, that he sat up and scrambled to his feet in alarm, gripped by a sudden feeling that the crows were heading straight for him! Grabbing his cloak, he ran into the shelter of the forest; but the trees didn't stop the crows. They dived in underneath the branches and cawing loudly, swooped after him. It was as he floundered through a scatter of bushes that he thought of his ring! He looked at it in some surprise, amazed that he could have forgotten it. "Stupid idiot!" he muttered to himself as he changed the ring over to his other hand and promptly became invisible.

The crows almost fell out of the air with surprise at his sudden disappearance and fluttered round, unsure of what was going on. There were so many of them that they flew into one another; wings got tangled and, as tempers flared, several of them pecked out angrily.

Neil stayed very still, knowing that they would sense the least movement and the slightest rustle of leaves. Half an hour passed but they were a determined lot, flapping here and there, chattering and cawing loudly. By then, Neil was so stiff that he worried about getting cramp. It was ages before the crows decided that enough was enough and, at a squawked command from their leader, flapped heavily into the air. Neil watched in relief as they rose into the sky, thinking that they had given up the search for him. The crows, however, had other ideas and although they didn't enter the forest again, they didn't leave it either but flew around above the tree tops, cawing loudly.

A murder of crows, Neil thought grimly as he relaxed and stretched his weary limbs. "If they *had* got hold of me, they *would* have murdered me," he muttered, thinking of the size of their beaks. But how had they known he was there, why had they hung around for so long and who had sent them? Maybe, he thought, they were Lord Jezail's spies; and it was then that he remembered the old crow that had been sitting on the fence.

Scared to go back to the place where Amgarad had left him, he made his way quietly through the trees until he stumbled on a track. It was by no means straight, but meandered gently among the thick growth of trees. It must go somewhere, Neil reasoned and, as he followed it deeper into the forest, the squawking of the crows gradually faded. It was only when he couldn't hear them anymore, however, that he changed his ring back over to his other hand and strode along, hoping to find a hut of some sort where he could shelter for the night.

It was as darkness began to fall that the trees gradually thinned out. The path rose steeply over outcrops of rocks, leading him to a sparkling stream that bubbled cheerfully downhill. Cupping the water into his hands he drank his fill and then sat back, wrapping his cloak around him for warmth. The path seemed to have petered out and he was seriously worried about going any further. It was with a heavy heart that he finally lay down and soon, worn out by tiredness and worry, his eyes closed. But before he fell asleep, he'd decided that first thing next morning he would follow the path back through the forest and wait once more for Amgarad to return.

The night darkened, stars glittered and the light of a full moon bathed the hillside in its gentle glow. It wasn't the moonlight that woke Neil, however. He opened his eyes in alarm and sat up, suddenly very wide awake indeed. Something, some noise, had penetrated his dreams. What was it? In the moonlight he could see the outline of the forest against the night sky and the bare hillside around him. Everything seemed very still and quiet; the only sound being the chuckling gurgle of the little stream as it tumbled over its rocky bed. He listened hard and had just decided that maybe an owl or some creature of the night had disturbed him when the sound came again.

This time, he knew exactly what it was. Turning white, he straightened abruptly as the howl of a wolf echoed eerily through the still night air. Wolves, he thought. Wolves! It was more than possible. This was Central Europe, after all, and he knew that wild animals still roamed the forests. Hadn't Prince Kalman talked of hunting wild boar?

Another wolf howled. And this one, he thought, sounded a lot closer.

He saw them as they emerged from the forest — dark, slinking shapes, darting here and there, noses to the ground as if they were following a scent. Which they were, he thought. His scent! They were closer now. He could hear their snuffling breaths and the scrabble of their claws on the rocks as they bounded upwards in great leaps.

Neil thought of changing his ring over again but dismissed the idea as soon as he thought of it. The wolves weren't like the crows. They'd follow his scent and track him down wherever he went. He swallowed hard. He could see them quite clearly now; at least seven or eight of them. There was nothing nearby that he could use as a weapon, either. Not even a stick or a loose stone. In minutes, he was surrounded by the creatures.

# 27. Dragonsgard

This was all she needed, Clara thought as the coach pulled up yet again. Never had she been so totally and utterly fed up. What with being bored to tears, worried at what awaited her at the end of the journey and feeling sorry for the horses as they laboured up the side of the mountain, she'd had a trying time. Maria had done her best to lighten the atmosphere but it had really all been a bit nerve-racking — for it had been a slow, difficult climb over the pass. The road, for a start, hadn't been intended for coaches and they'd had to stop several times so that rocks and boulders could be cleared to one side. As it drew up at the side of the track for the umpteenth time, she consoled herself with the thought that at least the exhausted animals, breathing heavily through their nostrils, would be glad of the rest.

"Are we nearly there?" she asked, looking up enquiringly at Count Vassili who had reined in his horse beside the door of the coach. He opened it for her and as she jumped down onto the stony verge, the blustery wind that scoured the high slopes of the mountain blew cold around her.

"Careful, Clara!" Count Vassili warned.

It was just as well that he did so, for she found herself standing unexpectedly close to the edge of a high cliff. Wrapping her cloak around her, she looked nervously over the wide valley that lay before her and drew in a sudden breath. This couldn't be it, she thought in disbelief. It just couldn't! For the scene that met her eyes was the stuff of nightmares. Even Maria, peering through the window of the coach, looked shocked.

Clara paled. There wasn't a blade of grass in the valley below, nor room for one to grow. The entire landscape was one monstrous jumble of rocky slabs, thrown here and there as if by a giant hand. And, dominating this terrible valley, rearing high on a jagged spur of rock, loomed the massive, towering bulk of a huge, grey castle, its tall towers outlined against the blue sky. It just *had* to be Dragonsgard!

"Is ... that ... Dragonsgard?" Clara whispered, looking up at the count.

"Yes, I'm afraid it is," he said shortly. He, too, was appalled at the sight of it, for he'd forgotten what a truly dreadful place it was. Meeting Maria's warning glance, he dismounted hastily and walked over to Clara. She was standing stiff and still and, he thought grimly, was probably fighting back tears. As if she knew it was going to be her prison ...

"We'll make you as comfortable as we can," he said awkwardly, knowing that the horsemen were within earshot and would most definitely be listening to anything that was said.

A strong gust of wind blew the hood of her cloak from her fingers and set her hair blowing wildly. Good, she thought, it would hide her face from the watching soldiers. They wouldn't see the tears that were streaming silently down her cheeks. Smothering a sob, she ignored the count and climbed blindly back into the coach. Maria leant forward to comfort her but she shrugged her hands away and threw herself miserably along the bench seat. She'd been Jezail's prisoner for ages, she thought helplessly. Why, why, why had no one tried to rescue her?

Maria looked despairingly at the count and even more despairingly at the jagged grey towers of the huge castle that brooded threateningly over the valley. She shivered as a cloud of unease dampened her spirits still further. Dragonsgard! She knew, without being told, that it was a dreadful, evil place.

The coachman cracked his whip and the coach once again jerked forward, rumbling carefully down the rough track that clung to the side of the mountain. Maria didn't look out of the window. She had no head for heights at the best of times and the drop to the valley floor was staggering.

By the time they reached Dragonsgard, Clara had mopped up her tears and was sitting upright, red-eyed and silent. The horses, now bone-tired, hauled the coach up the last steep slope to the castle. A drawbridge had been lowered across what appeared to be a deep moat and the sound of the coach's wheels changed as it rattled across. Clara looked down as they crossed. The moat was certainly deep but there was no water in it. Only rocks. There seemed to be nothing else in the valley. Just rocks and more rocks ...

They entered a wide courtyard surrounded by the high, grey walls of the castle. Grooms appeared from an arched tunnel and, hurrying forward, bowed low to the count before taking charge of the horses, leading them wearily away towards what must, Clara thought vaguely, be the stables.

Their arrival had obviously been expected, for a tall man dressed in uniform stood at the top of a shallow flight of steps and saluted them briefly as they approached. "Major Strelitz," he announced. There were no words of welcome, Clara noted, as he stood back stiffly and gestured to them to enter.

They glanced at one another grimly as they looked round the large hall. Clara wasn't impressed. Paved in huge stone slabs, it was bitterly cold and looked unutterably shabby and depressing. A table and chairs sat in the centre and although some threadbare armchairs were grouped round a huge fireplace, no fire burned; nor, she noticed, was there any sign of logs in the iron baskets that stood dusty and untended at its side.

Maria looked at the count apprehensively. This was worse than either of them had thought and she was glad that she'd packed lots of warm clothes in the suitcases. They were obviously going to need them!

As they were standing looking around in dismay the officer in charge of the guard marched forward and, saluting smartly, handed Major Strelitz a letter. Count Vassili looked at him sharply and felt a stab of anxiety. Any letter from Lord Jezail should surely have been entrusted to him.

Major Strelitz took a long time to read the letter although it was obvious that it only covered part of a page. Clara felt the tension in the atmosphere. What was happening now? Nothing good, she thought, from the look of fear on Maria's face.

Displaying no emotion whatsoever as he passed the letter to Count Vassili, the major's face was unreadable. The officer, however, shot the count a triumphant glance. From what Lord Jezail had said to him before they left, he had a good idea of its contents.

The count's lips twisted in an angry smile as he read the letter through. There was, as the saying goes, good news and bad news. The good news was that Lord Jezail had dispensed with his services. The bad news was that he was to be held prisoner in Dragonsgard.

He looked at the major shrewdly and then, lowering his eyes to the page, pretended to read it again. All the time, however, his mind was working with lightning swiftness. As a prisoner, he'd be of little use to Clara. It was best that he escaped now, while the great door was open and the drawbridge down.

"I'm afraid that you are to be my prisoner, Count Vassili," Major Strelitz said smoothly.

"So it would seem," the count admitted, handing the letter back and adding the words of a powerful spell to the sentence in a very ordinary voice that gave no one cause for alarm. Indeed, Clara was still trying to work out what he'd actually said when the count, in a shimmer of light, changed into a wolf.

There were a few moments of complete astonishment. Maria cried out, Clara took a hasty step backwards and the officer's mouth dropped open in amazement. Count Vassili had been with Lord Jezail for so long that he'd tended to forget that he was of the Onegin, the wolf people of the north.

Vassili, taking advantage of the stunned silence, was through the great door and heading for the drawbridge before anyone had recovered their senses. The soldiers in the courtyard looked at him in some surprise as he streaked past but made no move to stop him and by the time the major rushed out, shouting for the drawbridge to be raised, the count was over and away.

Maria started to cry, but Clara comforted her. "He did the right thing," she whispered, putting her arms round her. "It's better that he's free. He'll find a way to help us."

The hall was now a scene of complete confusion. Soldiers rushed in and rushed out again, voices shouted orders that no one seemed to pay any attention to and the drawbridge, half-raised, had to be lowered again to let the troops across.

As the horsemen galloped across the bridge, the major frowned. He should have known that something like this was going to happen! Ever since Lord Jezail had spoken to him through the crystal he'd been uneasy. Guarding the northern border of Lord Jezail's domain was one thing and part of his job, but looking after prisoners in a place like Dragonsgard was quite another! And now one of them had escaped! Lord Jezail wasn't going to be pleased, he knew that for sure. The girl, too, looked very young — yet he had instructions to put her in the highest tower in the castle.

In the course of his duties, Major Strelitz had, on occasion, carried out some unpleasant orders. This one, however, stuck in his throat. He was a decent man and as far as he was concerned, he wouldn't have kept a dog in the highest tower of the castle for any length of time, far less a child. It was open to the winds and freezing cold even on the warmest of days and now that winter was setting in ...

He kept his opinions to himself, however, and found himself feeling rather glad that Count Vassili had escaped. Lord Onegin's lands were not far distant and the count should reach Trollsberg within the day if he travelled fast. Perhaps his father might negotiate the girl's release. Nevertheless, he looked frowningly at Clara — for Lord Jezail's face when he'd spoken of her through the crystal, had been a vicious mask. Why did he hate the girl? Hate her enough to imprison her in Dragonsgard!

# 28. Wolf pack

Seeing the fear on Neil's face, the wolf materialized immediately. The boy wasn't all that old and it seemed a shame to scare him, but he really had to find out who he was and, more importantly, what he was up to. Lord Jezail's spies, after all, didn't waste their time attacking nobodies and the crows had been very persistent.

The shimmer of light that had miraculously transformed one of the grey wolves into a soldier left Neil gaping open-mouthed at the tall, dark-haired man who now stood before him. Resplendent in a grey tunic trimmed with gold braid, breeches and jack boots, Major Sallis was as impressive as he was unexpected.

The Onegin, the wolf people, Neil thought excitedly as he leapt to his feet, his eyes full of hope. He then took a couple of steps backwards as the wolves, fur bristling menacingly, showed their teeth and growled warningly. Two of them even darted forward and snapped at the edge of his cloak.

"Get off, will you," Neil said, pulling it round him.

There were a few moments of utter silence as the wolves looked at one another, their pale blue eyes mirroring their astonishment. Major Sallis stiffened, just as dumbfounded. An *English* child!

"I know who you are," Neil said. "You're wolf people, aren't you? They call you the Onegin." He bowed low, saying his name as he did so.

A slight smile twisted the major's lips as he inclined his head in acknowledgement. "I am Major Sallis of the Onegin Guard," he said. His tone was pleasant but even as he spoke his mind was working furiously as he wondered what on earth was going on! He hadn't heard of any English people roaming the countryside, far less children! Indeed, had it not been for the crows, he might never have picked up on this one. He'd obviously missed something vital along the line which was unusual to say the least. He prided himself on knowing everything that was going on in Ashgar and wasn't accustomed to surprises. Certainly not surprises like this, for his sharp eyes had noted the T-shirt, jeans and trainers under Neil's cloak. "Tell me," he queried, "how does an English boy know of the Onegin?"

His voice wasn't unfriendly and Neil took heart. "Actually, I'm Scottish," he said, meeting the major's pale blue eyes honestly, "and I know Count Vassili."

There was another silence.

"And ... where exactly did you meet Count Vassili?"

"I met him in Scotland. Last year."

This was true. All of the wolves knew it.

"And how did you come to Ashgar?" queried the major.

"I came on a magic carpet," Neil answered. He didn't see any point in telling lies. If the Onegin worked for Lord Jezail, then they'd very soon hear about the magic carpets.

"On a magic carpet!" Major Sallis took a deep breath. "Well, well ..."

"Honestly, I did," he added, seeing the look of disbelief on the major's face. One or two of the wolves shifted restlessly but the major quietened them with a wave of his hand.

"And why would you come to Ashgar on ... a magic carpet?"

Neil saw the amusement on the major's face. He thinks I'm lying, he thought angrily, feeling his temper rise. "Can I ask *you* a question first," he said abruptly.

"Go ahead," the major said.

"Do you work for Lord Jezail?"

Again there was a silence. The wolves looked at one another. By sheer accident they seemed to have stumbled on something that could be important.

At the mention of Lord Jezail's name, the major's face changed abruptly. Gone was the easygoing friendliness. His expression turned as hard as stone and his blue eyes were icy as he raised an eyebrow. "What do you know of Lord Jezail?" he asked coldly.

"You haven't answered my question," Neil pointed out, standing up to him bravely.

"I've no intention of answering it," the major said. "You will come with us to Trollsberg to be interrogated properly."

"And if I don't want to go?" Neil queried, his voice wary.

The major smiled but there was no amusement in his eyes. "The choice is not yours," he said, holding out both his hands towards him. "Take my hands," he instructed.

As the circle of wolves growled threateningly, Neil realized the folly of making himself invisible. If he tried to run, he wouldn't get far. They'd smell him out! Grudgingly, he moved forward and placing his hands in those of the major, felt a shimmer of warmth.

It was when the comforting warmth was replaced by a decidedly chill breeze that Neil opened his eyes. The dark hillside had disappeared to be replaced by the battlements of a stone castle. This, he thought, must be Trollsberg, wherever it was. He'd never heard Prince Kalman mention it and yet the castle was rich and very grand. The soldiers, smart and well-dressed, all wore heavy woollen cloaks to protect them from the cold and the steel helmets that hugged their heads were emblazoned with the head of a snarling, grey wolf.

Armed sentries led them from the battlements to the interior of the castle. It was quite a long journey and made him realize just how large it was. Several flights of stairs and miles of stone corridors later, they arrived at a busier part of the castle, eventually reaching a tall, arched door. Pushing it open, the sentries stood by and saluted.

With a gasp of amazement he looked down the length of what was obviously the castle's Great Hall. A multitude of banners fluttered from the ceiling, tapestries hung between the rows of pillars set into the walls and the entire hall was filled with grey-clad, jack-booted soldiers.

Major Sallis stopped dead at the entrance, catching his breath in surprise at the sight that met his eyes. Looking at him sharply, Neil felt that this was not what he had expected to see.

The soldiers, seeing the newcomers, fell silent and stood aside to let them through; looking somewhat curiously at Neil as he walked beside the major down the long red carpet that ran length of the hall towards a raised dais where a tall, grey-haired man dressed in heavy velvet robes sat on a grey stone throne. His nobles turned as they approached and the sudden murmur of excited conversation died as Major Sallis halted and bowed low. Neil followed suit and waited to see what would happen.

"Lord Onegin," the major began, "Please forgive me for interrupting your discussions, but I bring you a Scottish boy that I found in the hills near Hilderstein. He has a strange story to tell and ... er ..." he raised his eyebrows doubtfully, "he claims to know Count Vassili."

"Does he indeed?" Lord Onegin said, a smile curving his lips. "Well, that is a matter that is easily solved. What is your name, boy?"

Neil bowed but before he could open his mouth an amused voice spoke. "His name," it said, "is Neil MacLean."

Major Sallis's head jerked and he drew his breath in sharply. Count Vassili! Here! In Trollsberg! He was falling down on the job! What else had happened in Ashgar that he didn't know about?

Neil, for his part, almost fell over, such was his surprise. He hadn't recognized the count among all the splendidly dressed nobles of Lord Onegin's court.

"Count Vassili!" his voice mirrored his relief. "Thank goodness you're here. I need your help ... really badly."

"Now, why am I not surprised?" Count Vassili said, hiding a smile as he stepped forward to grasp Neil's hand.

Neil grinned. He knew his German teacher of old and, despite his association with Lord Jezail, trusted him. "Just wait," he said, looking him straight in the eye, "until you hear what I have to tell you!"

Count Vassili shot a glance at his father and receiving a nod of assent looked at the major. "We will talk to Neil in the Blue Room, Sallis," he commanded. "At once!"

# 29. Dragon quest

Colonel Braganz, entering Lord Jezail's study, saluted smartly. "The troops are ready to depart, Milord," he announced.

His voice was even enough, but inwardly the colonel was a very worried man. He'd discussed the matter with his master the previous day and still couldn't believe that Lord Jezail had ignored his advice. The magician, he decided, must have gone mad for, as far as he was concerned, it was the height of folly to make the journey to the Valley of the Dragons while an enemy army lay virtually on their doorstep. And to leave the citadel so lightly guarded ... it was just asking for trouble!

He was not to know, of course, that it was the sword that had filled Jezail's mind with the urgency of making a journey to the Valley of the Dragons. It only cared about killing dragons and the fate of the citadel meant nothing to it. Indeed, such was its power that it didn't enter Lord Jezail's head for a second that he was actually being controlled. That being the case, he'd shrugged off Colonel Braganz's arguments quite casually; for even the troubling thought of the MacArthur's army had somehow become quite unimportant.

Now, crouched over his magic crystal, Lord Jezail looked up at this announcement with an expression on his face that made the colonel stiffen. What, he wondered, had happened to put his master into such a fearful temper?

Gathering his robes round him in a swirl of velvet, Lord Jezail rose to his feet and started to pace up and down the room, muttering to himself furiously. He was beside himself with rage for Major Strelitz had just told him of Count Vassili's escape from Dragonsgard. It was the last thing he'd wanted to hear — and on today of all days, when he was about to set out with Dragonslayer on their Great Quest!

It was all arranged! They would leave the Citadel in grand style, flags flying and weapons gleaming; just like the knights of old! Now this had to happen! His frown deepened. Setting off with his men for the Valley of the Dragons should have been a glorious moment of triumph for him and now it was *totally* ruined! It was utterly *typical* of Vassili to have spoiled it! He wished now that he'd hexed him instead of sending him to Dragonsgard!

"I'll be ready in a few minutes, Braganz," he snarled furiously. "Keep the men waiting!"

Colonel Braganz saluted again and left the room without a word. The honour of stepping into the count's shoes as aide to Lord Jezail had, at first, filled him with a pleasing sense of importance. Now, however, he was beginning to appreciate the difficulties of serving such an eccentric and demanding master. No wonder the count had spent his spare moments in the relative peace and quiet of the library: his master's temper was enough to fray anyone's nerves!

The minute the door shut, Lord Jezail started to pace the room once more. So Vassili had escaped from Dragonsgard, had he! And probably gone straight to his father at Trollsberg! He relaxed slightly as, mind working swiftly, he realized that there was little that Lord Onegin could do. He had his own problems to attend to and he didn't see him launching an attack on Dragonsgard any time soon. The castle, anyway, was virtually impregnable and, despite what Colonel Braganz said, the MacArthur certainly wasn't going to prove a problem! He and his army were stuck miles away and, given the hex he'd thrown, his precious magic carpets ought to be as sick as parrots by this time. He smiled at the thought. They wouldn't be taking anyone anywhere in a hurry. His mind skated swiftly over the strangely clad boy that his crows had found. Probably just a poor village child, he decided, certainly not worth bothering about.

He walked over to the glass cabinet by the window where Dragonslayer hung by its hilt. The sword had wanted to see the sky, the sunlight and the forests and he had quite happily agreed to its request. Now, he unlocked the cabinet carefully and reverently removing the sword from its hook, reached for its scabbard. "It's time for us to leave," he told it briefly. "The troops are ready and waiting to start. It'll only take a few days to reach the Valley of the Dragons and then ... then you will be able to kill as many dragons as you like!"

The sword glowed with delight and breathed a delicious sigh. It was just like old times, it thought happily, when it had bumped along contentedly at Sir Pendar's side as he travelled throughout the country seeking their next dragon.

There was a great stir in the little town of Stara Zargana when the sound of trumpets suddenly blared out from the battlements of the citadel and the great doors opened slowly to reveal armed horsemen carrying tall spears. Flags and colourful pennants fluttered in the morning breeze as the horses stamped and shifted impatiently.

At a given signal, the black-clad riders urged their horses forward and, walking at a steady, majestic pace, crossed the high, curved bridge that separated the citadel from the town. Word spread quickly. The townspeople left their work and tumbled hastily into the street to watch this latest spectacle, gasping in amazement at the seemingly never-ending stream of horsemen that poured from the arched gateway.

Lord Jezail rode, straight as a ramrod, on a jet-black horse and looked neither to right nor left as the cavalcade made its way through the winding streets. Everyone knew who he was, although few people had actually seen him. They knew, too, that he was ancient, but the sight of his proud, triumphant face caused unease and a creeping sensation of trouble to come.

The initial, excited muttering of the crowd when the first soldiers had ridden over the bridge now died away and the people watched in fearful silence as they moved in a black snake-like procession

through the town towards the road that led to the
northern border. A few in the crowd remembered
the coach and horses that had galloped through
the streets the previous week but this ... this was
something else! Where on earth was he going with
so many men and what were the strange flat carts
that some of the horses pulled? They were huge
affairs and so broad that many of the townspeople
had to press themselves against the sides of the
houses to let them through.

The soldiers swore silently under their breaths
for the carts were long, unwieldy and seemed to
have minds of their own. They hadn't a clue as to
how they were going to get them over the steep
mountain passes, but knew it wasn't going to be
easy! None of the soldiers were supposed to know
where they were going nor what the flat carts were
for, but the citadel held few secrets and word had
quickly got round that their master had a magic
sword and was going to the Valley of the Dragons
to kill a great dragon; more than one if he could.

It was also whispered that the flat carts were
going to be used to bring back the bodies of dead
dragons.

# 30. Neil tells all

The Blue Room was warm and comfortable. Neil headed immediately for the log fire that burned in a huge white marble fireplace and warmed his hands gratefully while Count Vassili and Major Sallis settled themselves in armchairs as footmen, carrying trays laden with food, proceeded to lay the table.

On the way there, Neil had, rather nervously, asked the count about Clara.

The count, however, had been brief. "I saw her yesterday morning," he'd said quietly. "She's still a prisoner but she's well. No one has harmed her."

Neil felt an enormous weight lift from his shoulders. Clara was okay. He'd known all along that she'd be alright but sometimes, he thought ruefully, things didn't always work out as planned. He loved Clara dearly, but there was no getting away from it; she had a mind of her own and it often got her into trouble.

It was only after they'd eaten that Neil told the count what had happened to him. He felt relaxed and relieved for, during the course of the meal, the count had mentioned that he no longer worked for Lord Jezail, and Neil believed him.

"Well, Sallis," the count said thoughtfully when they had finished listening to Neil's tale, "it seems we have more than one problem to attend to!"

The major nodded as Neil looked enquiringly from one to the other.

"We must, of course, help the McArthur and his men," the count said.

"But we don't know where he is," Neil interrupted, "the carpets could be hundreds of miles away for all we know."

The major smiled. "We have eyes and ears everywhere and it won't be long before my spies find them."

Just as they picked up on me, Neil thought, eyeing him shrewdly.

"Then there's Lord Jezail," the count continued. "We heard this morning that he's left Stara Zargana — with Dragonslayer, of course! He and his men took the road north so they are obviously heading for the Valley of the Dragons!"

"Arthur's there already," Neil said, "at least I hope he is! He went to warn them that Lord Jezail had Dragonslayer."

"Did he, indeed!" the count sounded surprised.

Neil then told them the story of the tournament and when they'd finished laughing, the count's face again became serious. "Nevertheless, Dragonslayer is still a threat to the dragons. They'll need help from us if they're going to survive Jezail's attack."

"If Jezail and his men have left the citadel," Neil interrupted, "then we could quite easily rescue Clara." He stretched out his hand so that the count could see the magic ring on his finger. "If

I became invisible, I could walk in, free her and more or less walk out with her. She has a magic ring, too, you know!"

"I *do* know," the count said with a wry smile, "but Lord Jezail has it now. It was the first thing he took from her when she was captured. Besides which,' he paused, "Clara isn't in the citadel any longer."

"Not in the citadel!" Neil exclaimed, looking alarmed. "Then where is she?" he demanded, sitting forward in his chair.

The count then told them everything that had happened from the time that Clara had been hexed into the crystal ball at the circus to their arrival at Dragonsgard.

"Dragonsgard," Neil repeated. "It sounds ... *exciting*," he said.

The count's face hardened. "As far as I'm concerned," he said with a frown, "Dragonsgard is among the most terrible places in the world. Lord Jezail's own soldiers dread being posted there. It's high in the mountains and even in summer the temperature is close to freezing. Now, with winter on the way, the castle will be like an icebox."

There was a silence as Major Sallis looked at the count apprehensively.

"What's more," the count added heavily, remembering the fateful letter, "Lord Jezail has instructed that she's to be kept in the topmost tower of the castle."

He stopped abruptly, not wanting to worry the boy more than necessary and shot a warning glance at the major, who had stiffened at his words.

Like everyone else, Major Sallis had heard tell of the dreadful room in the topmost tower of the castle and cringed inwardly at the thought of the circle of deep slit windows that gave no protection whatsoever from the biting, icy winds that swirled round the mountain tops. It was no place to keep a grown man far less a child.

"Would it be difficult to rescue her?" Neil asked, doubtfully.

A mental picture of the grim, grey fortress flashed through the major's mind. "Virtually impossible," he said quietly, "but we'll have to try."

# 31. The topmost tower

"It's time to go upstairs," Major Strelitz said.

Maria looked at him but his face showed no expression whatsoever. "Can't she sleep a little longer," she asked.

The major's eyes flickered over to the couch by the fire where Clara lay, fast asleep.

"I'm afraid not," he answered. "I only brought you in here so that you could rest while my men got your ... your room ready for you." He hesitated, "You, yourself, are not a prisoner, you understand," he added. "Lord Jezail made that quite plain. You can come and go as you please but given the circumstances, I think it's better that you spend most of your time with the girl. If you need anything, you only have to ask. I'll have a sentry outside your door all the time."

His voice woke Clara, who sat up sleepily and glanced round the unfamiliar room. Then she remembered where she was and smiled at the major. Really, she thought, he had been very kind. Rather than have them wait in the cold hall of the castle, he'd taken them to his own quarters and given them an excellent lunch.

"What's happening?" she asked.

The major didn't answer and Maria broke in hurriedly. "Our room is finished now, Clara," she said, hurrying over to help the girl to her feet. "The major's men have been getting it ready for us. They're ... they're not used to having ladies, you see."

"I've had your cases taken up," the major said briefly, "and I've added a few things that you might be able to make use of. Furs and the like ..."

"Furs?" Maria shot him a shrewd glance.

"I've done the best I could for you," he said abruptly, "and you mustn't worry about meals. I'll make sure you're well fed."

It was then that Maria realized that the major, for all he tried not to show it, was extremely upset. Her heart sank. What on earth was their new prison going to be like?

He took them up to the tower room himself. It was years since he'd ventured to the top but he wanted to make sure that the beds and bedding were sufficient. His soldiers had been toiling up and down the spiral staircase for the best part of the day and the language that had floated down to him when the thin single beds had stuck in the steep curves of the stairwell had been colourful to say the least.

Clara was exhausted by the time she was only half way to the top. "I've got a stitch in my side," she complained as she leant against the wall, panting for breath. "Is it far to go?"

"Not much further, I hope," the major muttered. He, too, was breathing heavily. Glancing casually out of one of the slit windows, he blenched at the

sheer drop to the valley below and, for the first
time that day, appreciated the effort his men had
made to lug all of the cases and bits of furniture
up the stairs. He only hoped it had been enough to
make the tower room habitable.

With effort they continued up the winding stone
spiral. It seemed to go on and on forever and, when
they reached the shabby wooden door at the top, it
actually came as a surprise that they had, at last,
arrived.

The major turned the huge key in the ancient
lock and pushed the door open. The wind, however,
almost slammed it in his face again. Once more he
pushed it open and standing with his back against
it, ushered them inside.

The wind whirled round them, blowing their
cloaks and tangling Clara's long hair.

White with shock, Maria rounded on the major,
who, himself, seemed horrified. "You can't keep
us here," she pleaded desperately, "you can't!
It's not a room ... why, we may as well be out
on the battlements!" Her eyes darted round the
deep slit windows that curved all the way round
the room. "There's no shelter," she whispered, "no
shelter at all! And what if it rains?"

"We'll get soaked!" Clara said, answering her
question. Her brown eyes turned to the major.
"How can you leave us in a place like this?" she
demanded scornfully.

A shadow of shame crossed the major's face.
"These were my master's orders," he answered in
a flat voice. "You ... you must understand that I
daren't disobey them. He will use his crystal to

see that I have done as he commanded."

Tears sprang to Clara's eyes as she realized what her days were going to be like in this awful room.

Maria, however, noted the thick carpet on the floor, the fur covers on the bed and two screens that lay folded on the floor. They would give them a little shelter. And he had promised them food. The major, she reckoned, had, indeed, done his best for them.

She put her arms round Clara, whose face was wet with tears, and hugged her close. "I appreciate all the extra things you've put in the room," she said, looking at Major Strelitz gratefully. "You've done your best for us and we ... well, we'll just have to do the best we can."

The major saluted and eased himself out of the room so that the door didn't slam in the wind. They heard the key turn in the lock and, seconds later, the sound of his footsteps clattering down the stairs.

They were alone. It was then that they turned and looked at one another. How were they going to survive in this nightmare of a room?

"Just you help me with these screens, Clara," Maria said in a business-like tone of voice as the wind blew her hair in all directions. "If we open them up," she said, shoving one against a couple of windows, "then at least we'll have a bit of shelter." The screen, however, only remained standing for the space of a couple of seconds before the wind sent it crashing to the floor.

"If we prop the beds against the screens then maybe the wind won't be able to knock them over," Clara said, hauling a bed over the carpet.

It took some time to adjust the beds and the screens but by the time they'd finished, there was a small area of the room where the wind didn't blow with such force. Maria unpacked the winter clothes she'd bought in Stara Zargana. Rough, country clothes made from heavy wool; much warmer than the cotton jeans and tops that Clara had insisted on wearing for the journey.

"They're not fashionable," she apologized, holding up a knitted hat, a pair of black woollen tights and a bright scarlet dress that was so thick and heavy that it almost stood up on its own. "The winters here are really cold."

Clara grabbed at the clothes and shivering in the cold air, swopped her jeans for the black tights and hurriedly pulled the red dress over her head. It had long sleeves and reached well past her knees. She probably looked an absolute fright, she thought, but she didn't care. She was deliciously warm and that was all that mattered.

"The hat," Maria said, handing it to her. "You must keep it on all the time, even when you're sleeping. Yes, I know it sounds crazy," she added, seeing Clara's face, "but body heat escapes through the head, surely you know that?"

"I do, actually," Clara nodded. "It's why people in olden days wore nightcaps. There was no central heating to keep the bedrooms warm."

"Anyway," Maria said comfortingly as she sorted out some of the clothes for herself, "there's only me to see you!"

Clara nodded and, propping up the pillows, turned back the furs that covered the bed and slipped between the sheets. Looking round the curve of slit windows she could see dark billowing clouds. She'd been worried about rain but these clouds looked as though they might hold snow.

She sighed. What were they going to do all day? They were alone in this dreadful tower with only the wind and the weather for company.

# 32. Eagle eyes

Amgarad flew high, his sharp eyes scanning the countryside. Where, he wondered for the hundredth time, had Neil got to? There was no sign of him and as the morning progressed he became increasingly anxious. The forest was so thick that he could be flying over him without realizing that he was there!

He swooped over the trees, quartering the forest carefully, his screeching cry echoing over the treetops. Apart from sending the small animals of the forest diving for the nearest hole, however, there was no answering call or sign of movement. He flew far and wide until his wings were tired and had just decided to return to the MacArthur's camp when he noticed the wolves.

Now Amgarad knew little about the behaviour of wolves but he was fairly sure that dancing wasn't a feature of their everyday lives. Neither was his presence a threat to them. They were big enough to take care of themselves and, indeed, it was a brave eagle who would dare take one on. Why, then, were they running round in circles, leaping into the air and howling their heads off?

A sudden suspicion crossed his mind as he

swooped down to investigate and, as he passed over them, it was confirmed; for one of the wolves changed into a man; a man who was looking up at him and waving his arms frantically.

He landed amongst them in a flap of great wings. By doing so, his back was to many of the wolves and, had they attacked him, he would have been severely mauled. Appreciating his trust, the wolves moved to stand beside their leader and sat themselves down at his side. A soldier, Amgarad noted; a soldier of the Onegin!

The soldier snapped to attention and saluted the great bird. He had never seen such a huge eagle in his life and stared in fascination at its black shining eyes and fearsome beak.

"You are Amgarad? Lord Rothlan's eagle?" he questioned eagerly.

Amgarad nodded. "You are of the ... Onegin, the wolf people?"

"On – yeg – in," the soldier corrected him with a smile. "Yes, we are. I have a message for you from my master, Lord Onegin."

"About a boy?" Amgarad asked hopefully.

The soldier looked a trifle taken aback. "A boy?" he repeated. "Oh, yes, the boy is quite safe. He is in my master's castle at Trollsberg."

Amgarad sighed with relief. The wolves must have come across Neil and rescued him.

"You needn't worry about him," the soldier assured him with a smile. "Count Vassili is looking after him."

"Count Vassili?" Amgarad's face darkened in alarm and he spread his wings, ready to take off in an instant should things turn nasty, for he knew that the count had been Lord Jezail's right-hand man for many years.

"Count Vassili is not in Lord Jezail's service any longer," the soldier assured him hurriedly. "The boy told him how he'd come to Ashgar with the MacArthur's army and the count gave me a message for you."

"A message?" Amgarad repeated.

"He asked me to tell you that Lord Jezail has left the citadel at Stara Zargana and is heading for the Valley of the Dragons with his men. It'll take him many days to reach it and, of course, we'll put obstacles in his way to delay him, but now that the citadel is only lightly guarded, the count thinks that the MacArthur could take it quite easily if he were to attack. He's also anxious to speak to Prince Kalman and Lord Rothlan."

Amgarad looked more than doubtful. Why on earth would Jezail leave the citadel when he knew that the MacArthur's army was in Ashgar?

"You *will* deliver the message to Prince Kalman and Lord Rothlan, won't you?" the soldier said urgently, sensing his doubt. "It's most important. So important," he added with a slight smile, "that Count Vassili ordered every wolf in Ashgar to be on the look-out for you today!"

Amgarad bent his great head and met the captain's blue eyes seriously. "Please thank Count Vassili for the message," he said formally, "and tell him that I am returning to my master immediately to give him the news. It is, indeed, important information and I'm sure he will be very grateful for it."

The soldier saluted and, as Amgarad spread his wings and took to the air, he followed the bird's flight with his eyes for many minutes before reverting, once more, to being a wolf.

"So Neil's at Trollsberg!" Prince Kalman repeated thoughtfully as Amgarad, once more back in the MacArthur's camp, perched on the trunk of a fallen tree and told of his encounter with the wolves.

"That's what the soldier told me," Amgarad said tiredly, settling his feathers. "I think the wolves must have found him wandering around and taken him there."

"Where is it?" the MacArthur asked interestedly.

"Trollsberg?" repeated the prince. "It lies to the north of us. Lord Onegin has a castle there."

"It's a relief to know that Neil's safe!" Lord Rothlan said thankfully. "And *if* what you told us about Lord Jezail travelling to the Valley of the Dragons is true," he continued thoughtfully, "then perhaps Clara is still in the citadel. I can't see Lord Jezail taking her on such an expedition! Maybe he's left her behind?"

"Perhaps that's what Count Vassili wants us to think," the MacArthur interrupted. "How do we know we can trust him? It might be a ploy on Jezail's part to catch us out ..."

"No, no, I'm quite sure it isn't," Prince Kalman said decisively. "He and Clara between them more or less saved my life when we were in the snow witches' palace last year. I'm *sure* we can trust him and to tell you the truth, I'm not surprised that he's left Jezail's service. In fact, I've never really understood why he stayed with him for so long. He's a bit of a riddle is our Vassili!"

"I've been wondering about him, too," Lord Rothlan said pensively, "and I rather think it's because Lord Onegin wanted his son to keep tabs on Lord Jezail."

Prince Kalman's eyes sharpened. "What do you mean, Alasdair?"

"Well," he pointed out, "there's the hex that Jezail put on your father, for a start."

There was a brief silence. At the time, no one had known that it was Lord Jezail's hex that had made Prince Casimir steal the Turkish Sultan's magic crown and, when caught, his punishment had been severe. The furious Sultan had turned him into a djinn and he'd spent many years imprisoned in a deep well out in the desert.

Lord Rothlan continued. "You know as well as I do, that Jezail's hex must have been a fairly complicated affair," he pointed out, "and it wouldn't surprise me if some of the staff got wind of it. You can't keep anything secret in a place like the citadel. It's more than likely that whispers about that little episode got out and reached Lord Onegin's ears."

"You mean he sent Vassili to keep an eye on what Lord Jezail was up to?" Prince Kalman finished.

"It's more than possible," Lord Rothlan answered.

"You know, I think you're right," the prince nodded, as realization dawned, "for if Jezail *had* got his hands on the Sultan's crown, he would have been a serious threat to his neighbours. Just think of the power it would have given him! In fact," he added, meeting Lord Rothlan's eyes, "he'd probably have started a war! And with the crown in his possession, he'd have won!"

There was a short silence as they digested this. If their suspicions were correct then Vassili had certainly served his father well.

"So," the MacArthur said as the conversation drifted to an uneasy halt. "What do we do now? Head for Stara Zargana?"

Prince Kalman looked at the darkening sky. "We'll start early tomorrow morning," he decided. "What do you say, Alasdair? I know that the carpets are fine now but it's a long way to Stara Zargana and a good night's sleep will set them up for the journey."

Amgarad shifted on his perch. He, too, had had a tiring day and a good night's sleep was just what he had in mind. Tomorrow was, indeed, another day and it looked as though it were going to be an exciting one at that!

# 33. Trollsberg

Lord Onegin, elderly and grey-haired, smoothed the velvet of his long robes and rose to greet his visitors as they marched down the length of the red carpet. Lord Rothlan he picked out immediately; who else, after all, would have a great eagle perched on his shoulder! The other, tall and fair, must, he decided, be Prince Kalman.

The two magicians bowed low before Lord Onegin and it was only once the initial introductions were over that he indicated the ornate chairs that had been set beside the throne. It was then that Count Vassili stepped forward and, eyeing Prince Kalman rather hesitantly, smiled a welcome. "I hope that witch looked after you," he said diffidently, referring to their last meeting at the snow witches' palace. "I threatened her with hell and damnation if she let you die!"

Prince Kalman smiled and, grasping both of his hands, clasped them firmly. "You saved my life, Vassili," he said quietly. "I won't forget that in a hurry."

The conversation was general for a while and then turned to more serious things for Lord

Rothlan and Prince Kalman had come straight from Stara Zargana.

"You say that the MacArthur now has control of the citadel?" Lord Onegin queried.

Lord Rothlan nodded. "It was very much a surprise attack," he said. "Jezail's men didn't put up much of a fight. They knew they were totally outnumbered."

Lord Onegin sat back in his throne with a sigh of relief. "Over the years Lord Jezail has been a great source of worry to me," he admitted, "as my son well knows." Looking over at Count Vassili, he smiled gratefully. "Vassili sacrificed a great deal by becoming his aide but it was only by placing him in the citadel that I could find out what schemes that ... that madman ... was hatching."

"We thought as much," Prince Kalman smiled.

"Also ... but I'll tell you about that later," Lord Onegin hesitated. "First of all I think we must discuss how we are going to rescue Clara ... and Maria, of course." He glanced at Vassili. "My son is very worried about them."

"I suggest we move to the Blue Room," Count Vassili suggested swiftly, rising to his feet. "We can talk in private there," he smiled cheerfully, "and Neil, of course, is more than anxious to see you both!"

Amgarad flapped his wings. Now they only needed to rescue Clara and they would all be together again!

Major Sallis rose to his feet as Lord Onegin was ushered into the room with his guests. Neil, too, sprang up and bowed low as they entered and then beamed happily at the sight of Lord Rothlan, Prince Kalman and Amgarad.

Prince Kalman eyed him shrewdly as they settled into the deep sofas and armchairs that clustered cosily round the fireplace. He was bright-eyed and happy, certainly none the worse for his adventures.

"I'm really sorry I wasn't where you left me, Amgarad,' Neil apologized, turning to the eagle, perched comfortably on his master's shoulder. "You see, some crows attacked me. I reckon they must have been Lord Jezail's spies, and, well, I had to run into the forest to escape ...and then I was afraid to go back to where you left me, in case the crows found me again. I followed a path until it got dark and ... well, that's when the wolves found me," he finished, looking at Major Sallis with a smile.

"It was the crows that alerted us to you," the major admitted. "The fact that they were attacking you meant that you were Jezail's enemy ... and *our* friend. That's why we came looking for you!"

"Thank goodness you did!" Neil said, appreciatively. "But what happened to you, Amgarad? You didn't come back for me! I was out of my mind with worry!"

Prince Kalman then recounted everything that had happened, even down to the carpets feeling sick and ill. It was fortunate, he said, that the Lords of the North had been quick to find the spell that Jezail had used to hex them for, once they'd reversed it, the carpets had soon recovered. That was when they'd got ready for battle and flown to Stara Zargana.

"You could hardly call it a battle," Lord Rothlan said with a smile. "We were invisible when we flew in on the carpets and when we materialized ... well, Jezail's men saw that we outnumbered them so completely that ... well, they just laid down their arms. We took the citadel without a single casualty."

"I still can't believe that he left the citadel with so little protection," Count Vassili said in disbelief. "Jezail isn't a fool! Nobody knows that better than I do! He *must* have known you weren't all that far away ... what was he thinking about?"

"Dragons, I should imagine," Lord Rothlan said. "Don't underestimate the sword's magic, Vassili. It's tremendously powerful. I'm not at all surprised that he left for the Valley of the Dragons. The sword would be urging him on!"

"That's more than probable," Lord Onegin nodded. "If Jezail had been in his right mind, he'd never have left the citadel open to attack."

Vassili nodded. "I was always suspicious of its intentions," he said slowly, "especially as Jezail was once a Dragon Seeker. The sword played along with his ambitions as long as they matched its own. I think it probably controls him now."

"Shouldn't we warn Arthur and tell him that Lord Jezail is on his way?" Neil asked, looking apprehensively round the circle of worried faces.

"Yes," the count looked at Lord Rothlan, "Neil told me that Arthur is already in the Valley of the Dragons! Is that correct?"

Lord Rothlan nodded. "He insisted on flying out to warn them. Actually, I was in touch with him this morning ... to tell him that we'd taken the

citadel and that Jezail is on his way to the valley.
Knowing Arthur, he'll have sentries on every
pinnacle of rock, believe me! Arthur knows the
power of Dragonslayer only too well."

"We'll attend to Lord Jezail in good time," Lord
Onegin interrupted briskly, "but we mustn't forget
Clara. Before we go any further, I think Vassili
should tell you *his* story."

Vassili looked round the circle of faces bathed in
the comfortable red glow of the fire and his face
darkened as he thought of Clara and Maria in the
high tower room at Dragonsgard.

"Clara," he began, "is being held in one of
Jezail's border castles." He held up his hand for
silence as an alarmed murmur ran round the little
group. "Once she had written down all of the spells
he had no more use for her. I think he thought she
might be useful as a bargaining chip if his plans
went wrong but," and here his face darkened, "he
was also determined to punish her for the hex she
cast when we were in Scotland."

Lord Rothlan looked at Prince Kalman,
remembering Jezail's scarred, bloodstained face
when he'd spoken to them through the crystal.

"He used magic to heal the scars," the count
continued, "but he didn't forgive Clara. That's the
*real* reason he sent her to Dragonsgard."

"Dragonsgard!" Prince Kalman sat up looking
thunderstruck.

"When he detailed an armed guard to accompany
us, I had a suspicion that I might become a
prisoner there as well," Vassili continued candidly,
"and as it happened, I'd guessed right! Anyway, I

managed to escape and came straight here to my father for help."

"Dragonsgard!" Kalman repeated. "I remember Lord Jezail talking about it. Doesn't it have a tower room where ... where ..." he stopped and with a glance at Neil, said no more.

"Exactly," Vassili said, "which is why we must rescue her at once."

Neil looked from one face to another. "What is it about this tower room that you don't want to tell me?" he asked.

Vassili pressed his lips together. "The tower room at the top of the castle has slit windows all the way round. There is no shelter from the wind and the rain. And being so high, it is always cold and windy ..."

"We can use magic to bring her in," Prince Kalman said confidently. "She *is* wearing her firestone, isn't she?"

Count Vassili looked at his father. "I don't know," he admitted. "We've already tried to bring her in by magic. It was the first thing we did."

"It didn't work," Lord Onegin added. "Of course, there could be a protective shield round the castle, you never know."

"We have our magic carpets," Lord Rothlan said confidently, "and," he added, looking at Neil, "I can borrow Neil's firestone for her to wear."

Lord Onegin shook his head as Neil reached up to unfasten the chain that held his firestone. "There's another problem," he added. "The slit windows round the tower are set deep into the walls and they're very narrow. I doubt if even a child could squeeze through one."

"*I* merged with Amgarad to get off the magic carpet," Neil said, looking round doubtfully. "If she's still wearing her firestone she ought to be able to merge with him if he flies up close!"

"As far as I know, Jezail didn't take her firestone," Count Vassili said slowly.

"Then I think Amgarad should go at once," Lord Rothlan said. "Even if he can't rescue her, he can at least tell her that help is at hand."

Everyone turned to look at Amgarad who, spreading his vast wings, flapped them eagerly. The very thought of Clara imprisoned in such a dreadful place was beyond bearing.

Major Sallis drew his breath in sharply, appreciating for the first time the strength, power and ferociousness of the great bird. Looking decidedly impressed, he hurried to open one of the windows as Lord Rothlan, with Amgarad on his arm, rose to his feet.

"Fly east, Amgarad," Major Sallis said, pushing the window wide open and pointing to some mountain peaks that reared in the distance. "Dragonsgard is on the other side of those mountains. You can't miss it," he added dryly.

There was a great flap of wings as Amgarad took off over the battlements of the castle. Watchful sentries looked up in awe as the huge bird soared overhead. They all knew who he was for details of the new arrivals had filtered swiftly round the castle. They noted, too, where he was heading and after a few minutes were quite sure.

The great eagle was heading for Dragonsgard!

# 34. A welcome visitor

Clara, peeping at her watch for the hundredth time that day, hurriedly stuck her hand back underneath the blankets and, with a shiver, drew them up under her chin once more. How, she thought, could five minutes last so long? A feeling of despair enveloped her. If she was going to have to stay in this dreadful place for any length of time, she was going to die of boredom. Tears filled her eyes. Only five minutes! They seemed to have taken five hours to pass! Huddling miserably in the little cocoon of warmth under the furs piled on the bed, she gazed unseeingly at the curve of slit windows that circled the room. Where, she thought, was Lord Rothlan? And what about Prince Kalman? She was quite sure they hadn't forgotten her but she couldn't understand what was keeping them. She'd been a prisoner for such a long time and yet no one had tried to rescue her! She looked across at Maria, bundled under a similar pile of blankets. She hadn't left her for a second even although she wasn't a prisoner. Then there was Count Vassili! He had escaped days ago. How many days ago was it? She couldn't be sure. Time meant nothing in this cold, grim room where the wind whistled and roared all day.

Maria heard it first and lifted her head slightly at the sound; the distant cry of an eagle. She thought nothing of it but when it sounded again, closer this time, Clara, too, heard it and stiffened, hope rising in her heart. Amgarad! Could it be Amgarad, she wondered? About to throw back the furs, she hesitated, for getting out of bed and rushing to look through one of the slit windows would make her a thousand times colder than if she stayed in bed and did nothing. And the cold was terrible. Should she risk it? But then, knowing her luck, she thought despairingly, it might well turn out to be just another eagle.

A frantic scrabbling at one of the slits, however, sent her dashing across the room, tears streaming down her eager face. It *was* Amgarad! He had come to rescue her!

Maria followed her, dragging some furs off the bed as she passed. "Here, Clara," she muttered, draping them over her shoulders, "put some of these round you, for goodness sake!"

"Amgarad," Clara cried, peering excitedly through the long, narrow slit of the window, "I thought you were never coming! What's going on? What's been happening?" she asked as the bird scrabbled to get a foothold on the lip of the windowsill. It was impossible, however, and as his claws slid off, he flapped his wings frantically to stay in the air.

"I'll tell you later," he answered. "First of all, tell me ... are you wearing your firestone?"

"Yes," she answered. "Lord Jezail took my magic ring but he didn't take the firestone. I don't think he knew I was wearing one."

"Right! That's fine. Now, listen! I want you to try and merge with me, Clara." Amgarad sounded a lot more confident than he felt for the windows were much deeper than he'd thought. "Stretch your arm through and try to touch me!"

Clara tried and it was as he'd feared. Quite impossible! She just couldn't stretch her arm far enough. His heart sank. She couldn't reach him.

"I can't reach you, Amgarad!" she cried hopelessly. "I can't reach you. The opening's too deep!"

"Wait a minute," Maria said, "I'll lift you up." She cupped her hands so that Clara could put her foot in them and heaved her up. Again Clara reached through the gap, her cheek pressed hard against the wall as her arm stretched as far as it could go.

Still she couldn't touch him! Tears welled in her eyes.

Reluctantly, she withdrew her arm and, peering through the opening, could see Amgarad's eyes looking at her in sheer frustration. She bit her lip. "It's no good, Amgarad," she said hopelessly. "My arm's not long enough! You'll have to think of something else."

"Don't worry, Clara," the eagle said, hiding his doubts and trying to sound reassuring. "Lord Rothlan and Prince Kalman are both here. We won't let you down!"

"I know you won't," Clara said. "But, Amgarad,

tell me what's been going on. I thought you were never coming! How did you get to Ashgar?"

"We came on magic carpets," Amgarad replied. "Lord Rothlan and Prince Kalman are at Trollsberg with Count Vassili. Neil's there as well. And the MacArthur's army has taken the citadel."

"Really?" Clara said excitedly. "That's great news! I hope they captured Lord Jezail!"

"No such luck," Amgarad admitted. "He's on his way to the Valley of the Dragons!"

Clara's face suddenly became serious as she thought of Arthur facing up to Dragonslayer again. "Amgarad," she said urgently, "you've really got to get me out of here. Please, tell Lord Rothlan it's most important!"

"Don't worry, Clara," Amgarad said. "We know just how important it is. We'll make new plans and I'll be back soon."

"Please tell Count Vassili that the major is looking after us," Maria called. "Tell him we're being well fed!"

Amgarad nodded his head and with a screeching cry, dropped away from the tower and flew off.

They watched him go, moving from one slit window to another to keep him in sight.

"He's going to Trollsberg," Maria said positively, watching as he faded to little more than a speck over the mountains.

Clara drew the furs more closely round her. Not that the cold really mattered any more. She didn't mind putting up with it now that she knew help was at hand. Amgarad's visit had raised her spirits and she felt like dancing with joy. She hugged

Maria, her eyes alight with excitement, quite sure that Lord Rothlan and Prince Kalman would think up another plan and come to rescue them soon. Indeed, such was her relief that the minute she curled up in bed, she fell into a deep and dreamless asleep.

Maria, however, lay awake and worried. Count Vassili, she knew, would do his best to rescue them but if Clara couldn't merge with the eagle then he'd have to take the castle by force. And that wouldn't be easy. Not easy at all ...

"Where's Clara, Amgarad?" Neil asked, his face falling in disappointment when it became obvious that Clara hadn't merged with the eagle. "What happened? Didn't you find her?"

He'd been so looking forward to seeing Clara again, jumping to his feet when Amgarad had flown in through the open window and rushing forward to hug her the minute she'd emerged.

"Didn't she merge with you?" he persisted. "She's alright, isn't she?"

Lord Rothlan raised a hand for silence. "Now, Amgarad," he said calmly. "Tell us what happened."

Amgarad shifted restlessly and settled his feathers before replying. He wasn't at all happy at what he'd seen. The size of the castle and its rock-strewn valley had taken his breath away. He looked at his master through bright, black eyes and sighed heavily. "The slit windows round the tower," he explained, "are a lot deeper and narrower than they look from the outside."

"And?" queried Prince Kalman.

"Clara was able to get her arm through the slit but," and here he paused worriedly, "she couldn't reach me. Her arm just wasn't long enough." He saw Neil's face fall and continued hurriedly. "I told her you were here and that we'd think of something. It gave her hope. She knows we'll rescue her, but ... well, merging is out of the question."

Neil bit his lip and Count Vassili, turning to rest his arm along the mantelpiece, stared into the fire, his mind working swiftly. This, he thought worriedly, was bad news, indeed, for their whole plan had rested on Clara being able to merge with the eagle. He straightened abruptly and, turning his back to the fire, looked across the room at Major Sallis. They both knew that without a sizeable army it would be virtually impossible to rescue Clara from Dragonsgard.

It was then that Lord Onegin rose to his feet. "I told you when we first met," he said quietly, "that my reason for sending Vassili to the citadel was to keep an eye on Lord Jezail and do what he could to ... er ... curb his visions of grandeur. It wasn't, however, the only reason."

Everyone looked at him in surprise.

"You see, over the years we, the Onegin, have been ... 'regressing', I suppose, is the word I should use. We are gradually finding it more and more difficult to keep our human form. Slowly but surely, we are becoming wolves again. Many of my people," and here he gestured to the forests that covered the surrounding hills, "many are now reduced to living in the forests as animals.

We've tried to keep it a secret, for if Lord Jezail ever finds out how weak we are ... well, he'd march on Trollsberg immediately. That's why I sent Vassili ..."

Seeing the distress on his father's face, Count Vassili interrupted. "Lord Jezail has a massive library full of books on magic. A fantastic collection," he admitted.

"Go on," Prince Kalman urged, puzzled to see where the conversation was leading. Years ago, he'd been in Jezail's library and knew that Vassili was telling the truth.

The count shrugged his shoulders. "Father sent me there to look for a book; an old book about wolf magic. We couldn't ask Lord Jezail for it, you understand. He would have been suspicious and asked questions ..."

*"Wolf Lore and Legends,"* Prince Kalman interrupted. "That's the one you mean, isn't it?"

Vassili looked at him in amazement. "How ... how do you know that?" he asked, his voice almost a whisper.

"I saw it there," Prince Kalman said simply. "Lord Jezail had it in his study. He showed it to my father and me. He told us it was valuable ..." his voice drifted to a halt, "and I remember now. I wondered what he meant at the time. He said that he kept it hidden, for it was more valuable to others than it was to him ..."

At his words, Lord Onegin bent his head, shielding his eyes with a thin hand. Vassili's face, however, darkened furiously. *"So he knew all along!"* he said bitterly, striding up and down in front of the fire. *"He knew that I was looking for it!* And all the time he had it in his study and was laughing at me!" He almost ground his teeth in rage.

Prince Kalman looked upset. "But ... do you think he *knew* that you were changing back into wolves?"

"I'm sure he did," Vassili almost spat the words out. "Time was on his side. All he had to do was wait — wait until we were too few to defend our lands!"

There was a dreadful silence.

Lord Onegin stood up. He looked frail and upset. "I hope you understand why we can't help you," he said with a sad smile. "We have very few troops ... barely enough to defend Trollsberg, far less take Dragonsgard ..."

Count Vassili and Major Sallis moved forward to grasp Lord Onegin's arm as he turned towards the door and together they helped him from the room.

"Well," Lord Rothlan said grimly as the door closed behind them, "I'm not a vindictive man but I rather think Lord Jezail deserves everything that's coming to him!"

There was a murmur of agreement. No one had any sympathy for him. Not after what they'd just heard.

"I know it's a tragic state of affairs," Prince Kalman said slowly, "but it's going to make it very difficult to rescue Clara. I was relying on Lord Onegin's help. I know we can use the MacArthur's troops but that will take time to arrange."

It was then that Neil cleared his throat nervously. "Er ... about rescuing Clara," he said hesitantly. "I think I've got an idea. I mean, I don't know if you can do it but ..." he looked round with anxious eyes.

"Any ideas are welcome, Neil," Lord Rothlan said with an encouraging smile.

"You see, I was thinking of *Alice in Wonderland*," Neil announced. And, with growing confidence, he told them his idea.

# 35. Drink me

"What does it say?" Maria asked, trying to peer over Clara's shoulder.

"I don't believe it!" Clara said thrusting the sheet of paper into Maria's hands. "I've never heard such rubbish!"

Maria scanned the letter and then looked at Clara doubtfully. "It might work," she offered. "They *are* magicians, after all. They wouldn't ask you to drink anything that would harm you ..."

"Well, whatever it is, I'm not going to drink it," she snapped. "A magic potion!" she snapped scornfully. "I bet it would taste foul!" With that, she stomped over to the bed and, pulling a blanket over her head, started to cry.

Maria looked at the paper, looked at Clara and heaved a sigh as she turned once more to the window where Amgarad did his balancing act against the window sill.

"She's not happy about it, Amgarad," she said, pressing her face to the opening.

Clara then threw the blanket to one side, rushed over and, ignoring the icy wind, pushed Maria to one side. "I just don't like the idea, Amgarad," she shouted. "It's ... it's like something out of *Alice in*

*Wonderland!* I don't want to be a couple of inches high! Whose idea was it?"

"Clara! It's the only way," Amgarad said firmly. "Once you become small, Maria will lift you up to the window so that you'll be able to merge with me." His claws scraped and scrabbled on the sill. "Prince Kalman and Lord Rothlan are working on it now."

"I'm scared," she admitted tearfully.

"Clara, please do as the letter says," Amgarad pleaded. "It's the only way to get you out of this dreadful place."

Clara didn't reply.

"I'll come with the bottle tomorrow morning," he added, his black eyes looking at her sharply. Her face looked thin and strained. Being shut up in the tower was telling on her, he thought grimly.

Clara shook her head despairingly and turned away from the window.

"I'll try to persuade her," Maria said, taking her place. "Please come tomorrow, Amgarad. The cold in here is terrible. We can't stand it for much longer."

The wind blew the little bottle through the slit and Amgarad, watching it anxiously, sighed with relief as Maria stretched out her hand and picked it up.

She stepped back, turning it over in her hand. The bottle was dark green, made from funny, swirly glass and had a little cork stopper. The white label had writing on it.

"What does the label say?" Clara asked sulkily. "I bet it says 'Drink Me!'"

Maria looked at her nervously. Now that she held the magic potion, she felt quite nervous. "Actually, it says, 'Clara, please drink this.' and it's signed 'Lord Rothlan.'"

Clara sniffed and held her hand out for the bottle.

Maria gave it to her nervously. "Be careful," she warned. "Don't drop it, for goodness sake!"

"I'm not going to drop it!" Clara answered stiffly.

"Please drink it, Clara," Maria urged. "Just think, in a few minutes you'll have left this place behind and Amgarad will take you to your friends."

Tears clouded Clara's eyes. "I'm scared," she whispered. "Scared of being ... just a few inches high."

"Don't think about it!" Maria advised. "Just be sensible. The magicians are your friends. They wouldn't harm you ... you know that!"

Clara nodded.

"I'll be very careful when I ... when I pick you up," Maria promised.

Clara shuddered at the thought.

"Why don't you smell the stuff inside," Maria suggested. "It mightn't taste all that bad."

Clara pressed her lips together and took a deep breath. She knew Amgarad was waiting outside. Well, she thought, here goes! With trembling fingers she carefully prised the little cork from the neck of the bottle and sniffed the magic potion. It smelt of oranges.

"Here," she held out the bottle to Maria. "Smell it! Orange flavour," her voice trembled as she tried to make a feeble joke. "Whoever heard of magic potions smelling of oranges!"

"It smells okay," Maria smiled in relief. "Not bad at all!"

Clara hesitated. "Where are the clothes I was wearing when we first arrived, Maria?" she asked. "I want to put them on."

Maria frowned. "It doesn't matter what you're wearing, surely," she protested.

"Yes, it does," Clara said stubbornly, thinking of the four spells that still nestled in the pocket of her black jacket. So much had happened that she'd almost forgotten them! She took a deep breath and, stoppering the bottle, laid it carefully on the bed, knowing she was going to *have* to drink the magic brew — for if Arthur was going to face Lord Jezail, then she *had* to be there to help him. She only hoped that she'd get a chance to use the spells; otherwise Arthur might well die. And that, she thought, didn't bear thinking about.

Maria sighed and walking swiftly over to one of the cases, drew out Clara's jeans and top.

"And the black jacket you bought me," Clara added, struggling out of the red dress and reaching for her top.

"There, now," Maria said when she'd finished dressing. "Just fasten the buttons of the jacket and you'll be ready to go."

Clara picked the little bottle up and looked at it again, her heart sinking. She had to drink it, she supposed. There was no other way. It was the sound of Amgarad's claws on the windowsill that made her decide and before she could think of changing her mind, she took the cork out, threw her head back and tipped the entire contents of the bottle down her throat.

Maria gasped and watched in amazement as Clara started to shrink ... and shrink ... and shrink. A terrible fear gripped her as she wondered what would happen if Clara just shrank away to nothing ...

Clara shut her eyes as she felt herself growing smaller. It was a strange sensation but not unpleasant. Thankfully, it didn't last long. The frightening bit was when she opened her eyes and saw Maria's shoes looming large on her horizon! Very large! She gulped. How tall was she? Two inches high? Three?

Maria looked down and saw the tiny figure at her feet. Very carefully, she knelt down and held out her hand so that Clara could jump on it. She didn't dare pick her up with her fingers in case she pressed too hard and squashed her!

Reaching the windowsill, she stopped in horror. Why hadn't she thought of it before? The wind, whistling through the narrow opening had been of no account when Clara was her normal size but to a child of three inches and a bit, it was a veritable hurricane! She wouldn't be able to keep her feet.

Amgarad, however, saw the problem and, jamming his body against the slit window, blocked the wind. Maria stretched her hand through the opening as far as it would go and watched as Clara's tiny figure ran towards the eagle. Then she stopped abruptly, spreading her arms out as though a pane of glass was stopping her from going any further.

Amgarad's heart sank. He knew immediately what had happened. Lord Jezail hadn't taken any chances. He'd put a protective shield round the tower! She still couldn't reach him.

Clara sank to her knees, sobbing bitterly in disappointment. She, too, realized what had happened and barely felt Maria's fingers as they lifted her gently back into the tower room. What was she going to do now?

Maria, however, had her own ideas. She stuck her head into the slit window and spoke rapidly to Amgarad. "Don't go away," she said briefly. "I'll see if I can take her outside." And with that, she put Clara carefully into one of the pockets of her cloak and moving towards the door, rapped on it sharply.

The sentry opened it immediately. "I'd like to talk to Major Strelitz," she said.

He stepped aside at once and let her through. The girl, he thought, must be asleep under the pile of blankets heaped on the bed. He shut and locked the door again as Maria set off down the winding spiral stair to the great hall of the castle.

Clara, crouched in the warm pocket of her cloak, heard what Maria had said and hoped frantically that her plan would work. She was also more than a bit nervous that she might grow back to her normal size. How long, she wondered, would the magic potion last?

The hall was more or less empty when Maria reached it. The few soldiers there paid little attention to her. They all knew that she wasn't a prisoner and many of them had wondered how

long she would stay in the tower with the girl
before giving herself a break.

Maria nodded to them and strolled as casually as
she could, out of the main door, feeling the warmth
of the thin morning sunlight on her face. After
a few minutes, she crossed the courtyard to the
drawbridge and waved smilingly to the guard who
nodded and waved back.

"I'm crossing the moat now," she said aloud
so that Clara could hear. "There's no one near
me and ... and Clara, there doesn't seem to be a
protective shield here at all."

Looking round, as though undecided which
direction to take, she sauntered round to the right
and stopping every now and then to admire the
view, was soon out of sight of the guard.

It was then that Amgarad flew down. Maria
gathered Clara out of her pocket and watched as,
arms outstretched, Clara reached into Amgarad's
feathers and merged into the bird.

Amgarad's bright eyes thanked Maria. He
bowed his head very low and then, with a flap of
his wings, rose into the air and headed straight
for Trollsberg, his heart as light as the sparkling
morning air.

# 36. Surprise attack

It hadn't, Colonel Braganz thought, been what you might call an easy journey. The track over the mountain would have been fine had it not been for the flat-bed trailers that Lord Jezail had insisted on bringing. They were long, heavy and awkward, sticking in every pothole and jamming round tight bends on roads that were precipitous, to say the least. They'd already lost one down a ravine and although he hadn't said anything, he was pretty sure that his exhausted soldiers had quite deliberately allowed another to fall off the side of a cliff.

Falls of rock had frequently barred their way and he had more than a shrewd suspicion that *they* were no accident either. Once or twice his sharp eyes had picked out grey shapes slinking through the boulder-strewn valleys. Wolves! At the thought of wolves, his mind turned immediately to Count Vassili. Idly, he wondered what had happened when he'd reached Dragonsgard. He knew perfectly well that there had been no real need for an armed escort to accompany the coach and reckoned that maybe the count had been taken prisoner along with Maria and the girl. If that were the case, he thought, it would certainly account for the wolves; for it wouldn't take long for word of Vassili's capture to reach Trollsberg. Like Lord Jezail, Lord Onegin had his spies everywhere.

Urging his horse to a canter, the major rode to the head of his troop of dispirited horsemen where he found Lord Jezail slouched wearily in his saddle. The initial thrill of the journey had long since died away and despite Dragonslayer's best efforts to keep him cheerful and focused, he was tired, fretful and in a thoroughly bad temper.

The major's face lightened, however, as two of his scouts appeared round a bend in the road and galloped up.

"What news?" he asked, praying that for once it would be good. His hopes, however, were swiftly dashed. The horseman saluted briefly. "There's been a landslide," he said quickly, avoiding Lord Jezail's eyes. "The horses might be able to pick their way over it but there's no way the trailers can get through. No way at all," he added.

There was a silence. Colonel Braganz looked enquiringly at Lord Jezail. "Milord?" he queried. "What do you want to do? We can go back and find another road," he suggested, "or perhaps we could go on ahead with the horses ... and leave some troops to find another route for the trailers?"

"Do as you like," Lord Jezail said sourly, waving a tired hand.

Colonel Braganz breathed a sigh of relief, and seizing the opportunity of getting rid of the remainder of the unwieldy trailers, issued brief instructions. "We'll camp here for the night," he ordered before his master could even think of changing his mind, "and tackle the landslide tomorrow."

The wolves attacked as dawn lightened the morning sky. It came as a complete surprise and was certainly the last thing that either Colonel Braganz or his men had expected. They were in their own country, after all, and even the posting of sentries round the camp had been little more than routine. Indeed, when dawn broke, the sentries' minds, far from dwelling on the possibility of a dawn raid, were firmly fixed on the rattle of cups from the mess tent where their morning tea was being brewed! It had been a cold night and the hot tea would be more than welcome.

Nevertheless, had the sentries been even slightly alert, they would have paid more attention to the horses. Tethered in long lines at the edge of the camp with heavy blankets draped over their backs against the icy wind, they'd spent a restless night — and it wasn't the cold that had disturbed them, either.

It was the wolves. Their nostrils flared as they caught the scent of them on the wind for although they couldn't see them, they could sense that they were near, hiding among the rocks on the hillside. Stamping nervously as the wolf-smell crept strongly round them, the horses whinnied anxiously and shifted on their hooves as the animals crept steadily closer as darkness faded.

It was only as daylight streaked the sky that the sentries looked in alarm at the horses who had started to rear violently, neighing with fear. By then, however, it was too late, much too late and for a few seconds they could only stare, open-mouthed, as a horde of grey wolves swept down the hillside towards them in a growling tide.

Not unsurprisingly, this totally freaked out the horses. Nervous to begin with, they reared in panic and, hooves flashing wildly, screamed shrilly. Breaking free of their tethers, they galloped, panic-stricken, round the camp, blundering into tents, knocking soldiers flat and one way or another succeeded in causing more havoc than the wolves themselves. Lord Jezail's tent collapsed round him as he sat up to see what all the fuss was about and by the time he managed to struggle free from the tangled folds of canvas, the wolves had long gone.

So, too, as it happened, had most of the horses.

Colonel Braganz strode furiously round the camp as his men made futile attempts to round up the few remaining animals while Lord Jezail clutching Dragonslayer to his chest, crouched quietly amid the debris.

"I didn't mean it to be like this," he muttered, looking down at the sword with tears of frustration in his eyes. "I wanted our journey to be ... magnificent. As befits a Dragon Slayer of old and a great sword such as yourself. We started off so well! And now look at us!" He gestured round the wreckage of the camp. "The whole journey's been nothing short of a disaster!"

The sword, red with anger, frowned and took a firm hold of its temper for it knew that with Jezail in this mood, it was never going to get anywhere *near* the Valley of the Dragons! "You forget, Lord Jezail," it said encouragingly, "that the journey isn't yet over. Don't forget that the knights of old encountered many setbacks on their quests. You did, too, as a Dragon Seeker, didn't you?"

Lord Jezail eyes dropped, his mind winging back to days long gone. "I was young then," he said, looking at the withered old hand that clutched the sword.

Sensing his sadness, the sword sent a gentle surge of hope through the magician's frail body. "Come, Lord Jezail, we haven't far to go now and with me in your hand, you will, indeed, kill a great dragon. That I promise you!"

As his spirits rose, Lord Jezail looked round the camp and rose to his feet. Soldiers were leading in some of the horses that had strayed, tents were being dismantled and there was a general bustle as Colonel Braganz restored order to the chaos.

The sword was right, he thought. There was no question of turning back. They would go on! On to the Valley of the Dragons!

# 37. Clara's return

"I can see him," Neil shouted. "Look, there he is!"

They crowded round the windows as Amgarad soared in over the roofs of the little town and headed straight for them.

Lord Rothlan breathed a sigh of relief as he saw the bird's triumphant flight. "He's got her," he said. "I'm sure he has!"

Major Sallis opened the window wide as Amgarad, claws outstretched, swept in over the battlements and sailed into the room to land, in a flutter of wings, on the arm of one of the settees.

There was a heart-stopping moment as everyone crowded round the bird and waited to see if Clara would emerge.

As it happened, they almost missed her, she was so tiny.

Neil gave a horrified gasp as he glimpsed her but Lord Rothlan threw a hex and, in an instant, Clara was her normal size again. She looked round, blinking in surprise at her sudden change in height.

"Clara!" Neil hugged her and to her surprise, she felt a sob shiver through him.

"Idiot!" she grinned, holding him tightly,

nevertheless. It was great to be back among friends. There was a babble of conversation as, smiling broadly, she hugged Prince Kalman and Lord Rothlan. Count Vassili introduced her to his father, Lord Onegin, and to Major Sallis who hovered uncertainly in the background.

Servants brought in trays, laden with a variety of dishes and it wasn't long before they were seated round the table enjoying a hearty lunch.

It was only when they had finished eating and were sitting grouped round the fire that they heard Clara's story of how she had been trapped in the crystal and kept prisoner in one of the old Border keeps.

"I was really glad you were there, Count Vassili," she said, smiling at the count, "but I knew you couldn't set me free while Lord Jezail was around. That's why I tried to escape by myself; and I almost made it!" she added thoughtfully. "I don't really remember what happened. I think Lord Jezail must have hexed me when I was running away. He did, didn't he?"

"You were lucky to get off as lightly as you did," Vassili said, his face grim as he remembered the incident. "I've never seen him so angry before!"

Prince Kalman raised his eyebrows and shot a troubled glance at Lord Rothlan.

"Yes, but I knew he wouldn't harm me, not with you and Maria around," Clara answered blithely.

The count said nothing but Neil thought that somehow he didn't look as though he believed her. "Er ... who's Maria?" he asked curiously, thinking it a good moment to change the subject.

"Maria used to be one of the maids at the citadel," the count answered. "Lord Jezail brought her along to look after Clara. You see," he confessed, colouring at the memory, "I'm afraid I let the cat out of the bag as far as the *Book of Spells* was concerned. I know I should never have mentioned it but ... well, I did. Of course, the minute he heard that Clara knew the hexes off by heart, he started making plans to kidnap her. He had it all worked out before we left for Scotland."

"I hope she's alright ... Maria I mean," Clara said, sitting up suddenly. "She smuggled me out of Dragonsgard in her pocket." She saw their glances of surprise. "There was a protective shield round the tower," she explained, "so when I couldn't reach Amgarad, Maria carried me outside so that I could merge with him. She wasn't a prisoner, you see. She could go anywhere she liked. So nobody stopped her."

"We obviously owe Maria a great deal," Prince Kalman said. "And you, too, Vassili," he smiled at the count as there was a general murmur of agreement.

"Just a minute," Clara's eyes gleamed suddenly. "I've got something for you, Count Vassili,' she muttered, fishing in the pocket of her jacket. To her relief, she heard the crackle of paper and pulled out some folded sheets. "This one," she said, separating it from the others, "is for you. I didn't have a chance to give it to you when we were at the citadel. Everything happened so quickly that night."

Vassili reached forward, smiling easily as he

took the paper from Clara's hands. He couldn't think what it was and gave it a brief glance. Then his expression changed abruptly and he leapt to his feet, his face white and his hands trembling.

Lord Rothlan rose to his feet, looking startled, and Prince Kalman put an anxious arm round the count's shoulders. "Are you alright, Vassili?" he asked.

Vassili ignored the prince and looked at Clara in sudden understanding. *"The Book of Spells?"* he said. "It was there?"

Clara nodded and blushed. "I thought it was quite an important spell," she said, "so I kept it for you."

"Look at this, Kalman," Vassili said, turning the paper so that the prince could read it. Prince Kalman took it in his hands and looked at it in growing amazement as a delighted Vassili stepped forward, gripped Clara round the waist and swung her, legs flying, round and round in a circle.

Lord Onegin blinked in surprise. His son had always been a bit too serious for his liking and yet, here he was, behaving like a teenager.

"I'm sorry, Father," Vassili apologized, putting Clara down and more or less grabbing the paper from the prince. He thrust it into his father's hands. "Forgive me! I should have shown you this first! Read it!"

"What is it?" Neil asked Clara as she recovered from her surprise and straightened her jacket somewhat dizzily.

"It's a wolf spell," Clara said, amazed at the excitement it had caused.

Prince Kalman, watching an expression of
wonder cross Lord Onegin's face as he read the
paper, shot her a strange glance. "Well done,
Clara," he said approvingly. "From the look on
Lord Onegin's face, I think you've just saved the
wolf people. Vassili's been looking for that spell for
years."

"We must call the wolves," Lord Onegin said
in a strong voice that nevertheless trembled with
emotion. "We must call them all."

No longer frail, he was filled with a new energy
that straightened his back, lit his eyes and
commanded complete respect. Major Sallis ran to
open the door for him. This was the Lord Onegin
of the past! And if the spell was what he thought it
was, then there was hope for them all!

They followed him out of the room; along
corridors, up flights of stairs and through doorways
until they came to the upper battlements of
the castle. By then, the entire castle knew that
something important was happening and a whole
host of people watched as Lord Onegin looked out
over his lands.

With trembling fingers, he unfastened a horn
from his belt and, raising it to his lips, blew a
series of long and short blasts.

The sound of the horn died away, and there was
an excited murmuring and a muttering among the
people of the castle. What had happened for Lord
Onegin to give such a signal? He was calling in all
the wolves from far and near.

As the sound of the horn echoed throughout
Ashgar there was a sudden silence. In the forests

and fields, by rivers and streams, wolf packs came to a halt and turned their heads towards Trollsberg. Blue eyes met blue eyes as the wolves took in the meaning of the summons. The signal to return. Frail wolves, thin wolves, sleek wolves, starving wolves, old wolves, young wolves ... all the wolves of Ashgar set their faces to the north and moved steadily towards Trollsberg. Whatever was in store for them, the call could not be disobeyed.

Count Vassili looked on, smiling tremulously. "They will come," he said.

"And we will make them whole again," his father replied. "With this spell, we will make them men!"

# 38. Dragon plans

Arthur looked up lazily as the crystal ball glowed with light, casting shadows over the walls of his cave. He stretched a clawed foot idly and wondered who it was this time. Probably Archie, he thought. The MacArthur, Lord Rothlan and the Prince kept in touch from time to time — principally to give him news of where they were and what was going on — but Archie talked to him every day. Although he hadn't said anything, he knew that Arthur had felt a bit left out of the whole adventure and was doing his best to make up for it.

Arthur knew this and was grateful for, although life in the Valley of the Dragons hadn't been dull, the fact remained that the fuss and excitement of his arrival had long since died away and even the sentries posted at intervals round the valley, seemed to have lost their initial drive and enthusiasm.

Archie and everyone else, on the other hand, seemed to be having a really exciting time. The MacArthur had taken the citadel and was now firmly installed in Stara Zargana while Lord Rothlan and Amgarad had somehow managed to rescue Clara. Arthur smiled as he thought of

Clara's excitement when she'd spoken to him. Maybe it would be her face he'd see in the crystal! Perhaps she wanted to talk to him again!

So it was with a comfortable feeling of happiness and relief that he got to his feet and, ambling over to the crystal, looked casually into its glowing depths expecting to see Clara's face or Archie's or even that of the MacArthur. Instead, he recoiled in horror, for the evil face staring triumphantly at him through the glass was none other than that of Lord Jezail himself.

Jezail saw shock and fear cloud Arthur's wonderful eyes and smiled scornfully. He wasn't going to have much trouble with this lily-livered excuse for a dragon, he was sure of that. He unsheathed Dragonslayer and held the sword in front of him so that Arthur could see it.

"Be afraid, Arthur," he hissed, "be very afraid! I am coming for you and this time there will be no mistake. I will kill you! Dragonslayer is hungry for your blood!"

And, before Arthur could make any reply, his face faded and the crystal misted over.

It was then that the alarm sounded; a screaming, dragon roar of warning that echoed among the jagged peaks. Arthur left his cave and, running up the tunnel that gave onto the valley, gasped in amazement as his eyes took in a scene of total confusion. There were dragons everywhere. Some circled the peaks while others, having hurriedly tumbled out of their caves, now huddled fearfully at the entrances, shielding baby dragons with their wings. All of them looked around in wonder and fright as the silver-grey soldier dragons criss-crossed the sky, screaming their warning to the heavens.

Arthur took the situation in at a glance but before he joined in, knew he had to pass the message on to the MacArthur and Lord Rothlan. This was totally unexpected ...

Hurrying back down the tunnel to his cave, he hastily passed his hand over the crystal and breathlessly spoke the magic words. The crystal glowed and it was Prince Kalman's face that looked at him.

Seeing the fear and worry on Arthur's face, the prince knew that this was going to be no casual conversation. "What is it, Arthur?" he asked sharply. "What's happened?"

Arthur took a deep breath and steadied his nerves. "Lord Jezail spoke to me a few minutes ago," he answered. "He threatened me with Dragonslayer. He ... he must be close to the Valley of the Dragons for the sentries have just called a warning."

Prince Kalman moved out of the way as Lord Rothlan appeared. "Don't worry, Arthur," he said reassuringly. "We're expecting the MacArthur's army any minute and the Onegin are almost ready to march. We'll be with you soon!"

Arthur breathed a sigh of relief. Help was at hand! He rushed up the tunnel once more, his heart beating hopefully. He had to tell Gladrin at once!

Gladrin was down in the valley, calling the grey dragons to him. As they swooped out of the sky to cluster round him, Arthur flew down to see what they had to say; although he could already guess.

They must have spotted Lord Jezail and his men.

The grey dragons were all talking at once but grew quiet as Arthur landed among them. Gladrin looked grave and his words weren't at all what Arthur had expected. "Lord Jezail has come," he said. "He is already in the valley and very close ..."

The grey dragons hissed and glanced round fearfully as though expecting him to appear there and then.

Arthur blinked his wonderful eyes and regarded the sentries accusingly. "Why didn't you raise the alarm when you saw him approach?" he asked. "How could you miss an army that size!"

Nestor, the commander of the grey dragons, stepped forward and bowed low. "Milord," he said respectfully, "there is no army; only the magician and a few soldiers."

Arthur felt a pang of anxiety at this, for the MacArthur had quite definitely told him that Jezail had left Stara Zargana with most of the soldiers in the citadel.

"They must have slipped in under cover of darkness," one dragon snarled angrily.

"Either that or they made themselves invisible so that we wouldn't see them," Nestor added grimly, "for we patrolled the outer ring of the mountains all night."

Gladrin looked enquiringly at Arthur, as did all the others and his heart sank as he realized that they were relying on him to defend the valley. Well, he thought, at least he had *some* good news to give them. "Help is at hand," he said reassuringly, looking round their anxious faces. "Even now, Lord Onegin is sending an army from Trollsberg and the MacArthur will soon be here, too. *His* army is travelling by magic carpet. Lord Rothlan and Prince Kalman are powerful magicians. They will protect us all."

A sigh of relief shivered through the assembled dragons as their eyes rose automatically to search the surrounding skies.

"I don't know exactly when they'll arrive," Arthur admitted, "but it will be soon."

"In the meantime," Gladrin took command once more, "we must defend ourselves as best we can. You, Nestor, will lead a ..."

"No!" Arthur interrupted. "No," he repeated in a softer tone. "That's not a good idea, Lord Gladrin. Lord Jezail will hex them out of the sky as soon as he sees them. He has come to the valley to kill dragons but it is Dragonslayer who rules his thoughts. You see, I have, in the past, felt Dragonslayer's magic and I know its power. Lord Jezail was once a great Dragon Seeker and although he wants to kill dragons, his sword has but one idea in its mind," he said gravely, looking round the circle of fierce horned faces. "Yes, I know it wants to kill you all — but before all else, it wants to kill *me*. Twice it has failed and this time — well, this time it *has* to succeed. It *must* kill me!"

The dragons eyed one another sideways and said nothing.

"Nevertheless," Gladrin said, speaking for them all, "you are our friend and we will be by your side in this venture. Don't forget that Lord Jezail is our enemy as well as yours."

There was a hiss of agreement as the silver-grey dragons flapped their wings and blew streams of fire from their nostrils. It was time to go into battle.

Arthur smiled sadly. He appreciated their support but he knew he had to face Lord Jezail and Dragonslayer alone.

# 39. Valley of the Dragons

Clara clung to Lord Rothlan's cloak as the magic carpets flew at breakneck speed towards the Valley of the Dragons. Hurry, hurry, she thought frantically as she saw the dragons circling the jagged peaks. They just *had* to be in time! Glad that Prince Kalman had taken the invisibility spell off the magic carpets, she glanced across at Neil, who was crouched beside the prince.

They had all been worried but it was Clara who had insisted that they set off for the Valley of the Dragons without waiting for the MacArthur and his army to arrive. Lord Onegin had listened to her arguments and in the end they'd all agreed with her on the need for speed. Lord Onegin and his army of wolf-men had left Trollsberg at much the same time as they'd taken to their magic carpets. They would travel swiftly, she knew, but not as quickly as the magic carpets.

Her fingers strayed anxiously to the pocket of her black jacket where the remaining spells nestled. Lord Jezail, she reasoned, must be really close to the valley to show himself through the crystal. Close and confident! Her heart sank as she thought of the problems that loomed ahead. She shuddered, knowing that she'd have to get pretty close to Lord Jezail to carry out her plan. Prince Kalman hadn't liked the idea but, as Clara pointed out, she didn't have much choice.

Neil's eyes scanned the peaks of the Valley of the Dragons as the carpets drew closer. White and creamy in colour, their sharp fangs rose straight from the plain. Clouds of black smoke, however, drifted among the jagged peaks where huge silver-grey dragons circled, emitting great bursts of fire.

It was as they neared the first peaks that Lord Rothlan saw a straggle of horsemen galloping towards the mountains. He looked across at Count Vassili, jabbing a finger downwards at the soldiers. Vassili peered over the edge of his carpet and seeing the black uniforms, cupped his hands against the wind and shouted across. "They're Jezail's men," he called, "but he's not leading them!"

The magic carpets were now very near the mountains and, as they soared between the first of the outlying peaks, Neil became aware of the noise of battle drifting towards him on the breeze. Peering ahead anxiously, he hoped that Clara's plan was going to work. He trusted Prince Kalman and Lord Rothlan to look after her, but knew perfectly well that if she made a mistake, Lord Jezail wouldn't spare her.

Lord Rothlan headed for the centre of the action, his eyes scanning the ground for the rest of Jezail's troops. He could see no sign of them and frowned anxiously.

Then Clara gripped his arm and pointed to where the silver dragons circled. "There's Arthur,"

she almost screamed. "Look! Down there! On that
flat bit of ground!"

Prince Kalman looked down and frowned. That
"flat bit of ground" as Clara had put it, ended in
a sheer drop into one of the valleys. What Arthur
was doing prancing around on the edge of a cliff,
he'd no idea.

Then he saw Lord Jezail and understood.

As Arthur had expected, it wasn't long before he
felt the magic of the sword calling him and as he felt
its strength, his mind winged its way back to that
dreadful day when, young, alone and friendless,
he'd faced Sir Pendar. Now, he reminded himself,
things were different but the call of the sword was,
nevertheless, just as powerful as it had been those
many years ago and he had no choice but to obey
its dreadful command.

The grey dragons looked at one another in alarm
as, without warning, his great body stiffened
suddenly, his wings flapped, his head reared and
his eyes glazed as the magic of the sword filled
his mind. He had already forgotten that the grey
dragons existed. All that mattered was the sound
of that sweet, enticing voice ... calling him ...

As Arthur rose into the air, Nestor, too, flapped
his wings and with one accord, all the grey
dragons soared skywards. Whatever happened,
they couldn't leave Arthur to his fate.

So it was that Arthur, followed by a host of grey
dragons, obeyed the siren call of the sword. Wings
beating strongly, he flew between the cream-
coloured peaks and dropped sharply towards a flat

ledge of ground that protruded from the side of the mountain.

Lord Jezail, Nestor thought in horror, had chosen the spot well for while there was room enough for him to fight the dragon, there was little space for unwelcome onlookers. The grey dragons circled wildly but couldn't land — for the broad ledge of rock ended in a sheer drop to the valley below.

Lord Jezail smiled triumphantly as, holding Dragonslayer aloft, he watched Arthur fly towards him, wings flapping strongly as he landed on the ledge. This time, he thought, things were going to turn out very differently and his face darkened with rage as he thought of the trick Prince Kalman had played on him at the tournament! Well, he thought nastily, *this time* there was no prince; *this time* there would be no dragon balloon; *this time Arthur would die!*

Arthur's brain was working swiftly as he saw the anger on the magician's face. Strangely enough, he felt quite calm and collected. He wasn't the least bit afraid and although he hoped the MacArthur's army would arrive soon, he was quite determined to do his best. Prince Kalman had put a protective shield round him before he'd left Arthur's Seat and hopefully the magic spells he'd taught him would stop the sword from doing him any real harm.

Lord Jezail smiled evilly as he moved towards the dragon, his heart swelling with pride with every step he took. The sword's magic had given him the strength and power of a young man. He was, once more, a Dragon Seeker! He could feel the sword's excitement and knew exactly what he had to do. He brandished the sword and, eyes narrowed, prepared for battle.

Eyeing him shrewdly, Arthur knew that the magician would have a protective shield round him and wouldn't be hurt by fire but, nevertheless, he put all his strength into throwing the biggest burst of flames that he'd ever given.

The result was quite spectacular. Enveloped in a cloud of fire and smoke, Lord Jezail staggered backwards, knocked off his feet by the force of the blast. The sword, with a scream of rage, fell from his hand as Arthur lunged forward, using his body weight to trample the magician.

It nearly worked.

Lord Jezail saw the dragon heading for him and, grabbing the sword, rolled over sideways. Springing to his feet, he rushed at the dragon. Arthur kicked out at him and once more the magician rolled in the dust. His face as he scrambled to his feet was a mixture of hatred and sheer frustration.

The sword, however, was absolutely livid and using its magic, forced the magician to attack again. "Get in close," it screamed, "and then thrust! Straight for the heart!"

Arthur threw one of the hexes that Prince Kalman had taught him and once more the magician stopped, doubled up in sudden agony. Again Arthur took advantage of his helplessness and with a flap of his wings, tried to herd the magician to the edge of the cliff.

It didn't work. Gathering his dust-covered robes round him, Jezail got to his feet, evaded the dragon and held Dragonslayer at the ready. This time there was going to be no mistake!

It was then that Arthur, who had been just about to breathe an enormous burst of fire at Lord Jezail, saw the magic carpets flying in behind the magician's back. Coughing and spluttering, he managed to choke it back, but his spirits rose. They had come! And just in time, too.

Taking advantage of Arthur's sudden fit of coughing, and totally unaware of the carpets landing behind him, Lord Jezail's lips twisted in a triumphant smile. Swinging Dragonslayer wildly, he darted forward to plunge the sword deep into Arthur's heart.

Dragonslayer almost burst with pleasure. This ... *this* was the moment it had been waiting for all these years. *This* time there was going to be no mistake. The magician knew his stuff! He was going to strike! Now! Now! Now!

Clara leapt off her carpet. It was the ideal moment. Lord Jezail's sleeve had fallen back over his arm as he held the sword up, ready to strike. The talisman was there! She could see it clasped round his wrist. Running forward, she spoke in the language of old magic and called the talisman to her. It obeyed immediately and as Lord Jezail felt it leave his wrist he stopped in mid-thrust and swung round.

The sword screamed its disappointment! What was the fool of a magician doing? It was the dragon that mattered, not some stupid talisman!

Lord Jezail paled, his face a picture of baffled fury as he saw the magicians. Then his eyes fell on the children — Clara in particular. The girl! Of course, he should have known it would be her! Who else would call the talisman, after all? His eyes burned as he saw it clasp itself onto her wrist. Leaping forward, he slashed out wildly with a sword that was now in such a blind rage that it would kill anybody or anything.

Lord Rothlan ducked swiftly as the sword all but beheaded him while Clara, full of joy at wearing the talisman once more, leapt nimbly to one side and watched Jezail carefully. As far as she was concerned, the worst was over. She had the talisman and, with rising excitement, felt its power. Now she just needed to catch Lord Jezail on his own. She didn't want anyone else getting in the way of her hexes.

Prince Kalman and Count Vassili hurriedly pushed Neil behind them and, hexes at the ready, faced up to the furious magician who stood before them, his sword still raised to strike.

With a dragon behind him and three powerful magicians in front of him, any reasonable man would have very quickly worked out that he didn't stand much of a chance. The sword, however, was beyond reason. It swung Jezail round on his heels and once more forced him to attack Arthur.

It was so unexpected that Arthur, totally taken aback, made no attempt to defend himself. Even the magicians were taken by surprise. Clara wasn't, however, for even as Jezail swung round, sword at the ready, she lifted her arm and, as she spoke the words of a hex, a brilliant flash of light flamed between her arm and the sword.

The sword, quivering in Lord Jezail's upraised hand, gave a deathly scream that echoed and re-echoed through the jagged peaks and pinnacles of the mountains. Everyone who heard it shivered. Even the magicians stiffened at its breath-taking cry of agony.

Taken aback, Lord Jezail crumpled to the ground, the sword slipping from his nerveless fingers.

All eyes then turned to Clara. Even the magicians had no idea what hex she had used but they knew it was from the *Book of Spells* for she had spoken in the language of ancient magic. "Wait," she said in a voice that was more than a bit shaky. Her eyes didn't leave the sword. Lord Jezail, however, rose to his knees and crawling over the ground, grasped its hilt and stroking the blade gently, crooned over the sword as though to ease its pain.

Clara raised her hand and shook her head, warning everyone to stand back. The spell had yet to work and as they watched in increasing amazement, the beautiful sword turned black in Lord Jezail's hands. There was a moment of silence as Jezail looked confusedly from the blackened sword to the stern faces of the magicians. Then, as his eyes dropped and he instinctively understood that Dragonslayer would kill no more dragons, his face convulsed suddenly. Madness shone in his eyes as, mouthing meaningless words, he struggled to his feet in a fearsome rage.

Prince Kalman, his eyes full of sudden pity, moved towards him. "It's all right, Lord Jezail," he said gently. "It's over now. Come, we will take you back to the citadel where you can rest."

"Rest?" Jezail snarled.

Vassili tried this time. "Milord ..."

But as Vassili moved forward, arm outstretched, Lord Jezail backed away. "Here," he snarled, "take the sword! What use is it to me now?" Raising his arm, he plunged it into the ground at the count's feet and then, with a cackle of what might have been laughter, strode off.

There was a moment's silence as, totally taken aback, they looked from Vassili to the black sword and back again.

"Wait!" Clara said, as the count made to grasp it.

Prince Kalman looked at Lord Rothlan with raised eyebrows and watched as Clara stepped forward and, holding both hands over the sword, recited the words of another hex in a clear, ringing voice. Nothing happened for a few moments and even Clara, glancing worriedly at Lord Rothlan, felt a sudden tinge of alarm. Why had nothing happened? Had she got the wording of the spell wrong?

"It's all right, Clara!" Prince Kalman said suddenly. "Whatever the spell is, it's working! Look! It's changing colour!" And they stared in astonishment as the sword suddenly shed its blackness and glowed gold.

Count Vassili laid his hand hesitantly on the hilt and then relaxed. "There's no evil in it," he said as they all crowded round. "Here, touch it yourselves," he said, pulling it from the ground and offering the hilt to Prince Kalman and Lord Rothlan in turn.

Clara sighed with relief. For a dreadful moment she thought she'd got the spell all wrong and, for a second, her mind winged back to the round room in the tower of the citadel where she'd copied the hexes with trembling fingers. It had been well worth it. The sword was still a magic sword but she had taken away its desire to kill dragons. Arthur and all of the dragons in the valley were safe.

Lord Jezail didn't see the sword's transformation. Eyes staring unseeingly, he shambled along, muttering to himself. Neil watched him go; a strange, pathetic figure whose scarlet robes trailed loosely in the dust behind him.

Circling interestedly, the grey dragons, too, watched the stumbling figure, their eyes sharpening as they saw their chance. Now, separated from the others, Lord Jezail was surely theirs for the taking.

# 40. Over the edge

Neil froze as he saw the grey dragons swooping in, ready for the kill. The great streams of fire belching from their nostrils told him that the dragons meant business as, indeed, they did.

Eyes shining with determination, Nestor led his troop in a deep dive towards the scarlet-clad magician who, unaware of his danger, still stumbled along, muttering to himself feverishly.

Everyone turned as Neil leapt into action, jumping onto his carpet with a loud yell of alarm.

"Jezail!" Lord Rothlan shouted a warning as he realized what was happening. "Jezail, look out!"

Lord Jezail started at his words and looking up, saw the approaching dragons. By that time, however, Neil's magic carpet was already speeding towards him, not only to save him from the dragons but to stop him from falling off the cliff edge which was dangerously close. There was a brief moment of total confusion. The grey dragons, seeing the approaching carpet, swerved wildly to avoid burning Neil to a cinder while Lord Jezail, suddenly realizing his danger, lifted his arm to hex the dragons out of the sky.

It was then that the cliff edge gave way beneath his feet.

Everyone watched in horror as he tried to regain his footing. The whole edge of the cliff, however, was slipping away from the side of the mountain and he slipped with it, disappearing with a shrieking cry amid the loose jumble of stones and falling rock that tumbled headlong into the valley below.

Prince Kalman ran to his carpet, forgetting that Neil had taken it. Where, he thought frantically, was the other one? Seconds were lost as Vassili's carpet sailed hastily up and dipped gently to allow him on board. "After them," he muttered, furious at the delay and seriously worried at what was going to happen; for he knew that Jezail might well be able to hex himself out of the avalanche and he certainly didn't want him to start killing off the dragons!

His carpet swooped down, following the billowing cloud of dust. It was so thick that he couldn't see a thing. Where was Jezail? And where had Neil disappeared to?

Neil, at that moment, was clinging to the edge of his carpet with one hand and holding his jacket over his head with the other, in the hope of protecting himself, however slightly, from the scatter of debris that surrounded him. The roar of the rockfall was loud in his ears and the choking cloud of dust made the carpet cough horribly. It was all he could do to stay on board as it rocked around like a boat on stormy seas.

"There he is," Neil gasped as a flash of red showed briefly through the debris.

The carpet gave something like a grunt as it, too, spotted the flash of colour. With a deft flick, it shot over and slid swiftly underneath the startled magician who thumped down beside Neil in a flurry of scarlet.

Neil hurriedly grasped the somewhat dazed figure as the carpet swung hastily out of the path of the falling rocks. "Are you alright, Lord Jezail?" he asked, releasing him when they were clear of the tumbling rubble.

He felt the thin, old bones move under the velvet and felt an unexpected pang of pity for the magician who now looked more like an old tramp than anything else. His long hair was tangled, his eyes were wild and dirt smeared his face. His robes, filthy and torn, were hanging off him but under the remains of his shirt, Neil glimpsed the shine of gold.

Still gasping for breath, Jezail didn't answer. He'd be all right, Neil thought, but it'd probably be some time before he recovered from the shock of his fall.

In this, however, he was quite mistaken. Magic gives great strength and, now safe on the magic carpet, Lord Jezail's mind was racing as he planned his next move. He couldn't believe his luck! Although his plans had come to nothing, he now, at least, had an ideal means of escape. All he had to do was get rid of the boy!

He continued to cough and, lifting his head, looked so piteously at Neil that the boy did, indeed, felt sorry for him. Jezail then threw out his hands, as if for comfort, but when the pawing fingers grasped Neil's arms, they tightened viciously and his pleading expression changed to one of sheer evil.

Neil gasped in surprise — surprise that quickly changed to fear as, with a venomous smile, Lord Jezail pulled him up and made to throw him off the carpet. Instinctively, Neil grabbed at the front of the magician's shirt. It was the only thing that was within reach of his fingers and he held on tightly. His mind was racing but he was quite determined that if he was going to go over the edge, then he was going to take Lord Jezail with him!

Jezail, conscious of his danger, gave a snarl of fury and, twisting Neil sharply, jerked him off balance with such force that the collar of his shirt ripped and came away in Neil's hand. So, too, did the gold chain round his neck!

Jezail, feeling the chain snap, shrieked in horror as he realized what had happened. He grabbed desperately at Neil but by then it was too late. Neil tottered on the edge of the carpet for barely a second before falling backwards into the void.

Screaming, crying and clutching at his throat, Lord Jezail knelt frantically at the edge of the carpet and saw his precious medallion flashing in the boy's fingers. *His* medallion! He *had* to get it back!

Then his carpet jerked violently as a grey dragon streaked past, diving downwards at great speed. He sighed with relief. The dragon had seen what had happened and was going to save the boy. There was still a chance! He might yet be able to get his medallion back!

Nestor had watched the struggle on the carpet and had been totally stunned when Jezail had thrown Neil off! Despite the magician's ruthlessness, he'd never for a moment believed that anything of the like might happen and, moments later, went into a dive that would have put a sparrowhawk to shame.

Claws outstretched, he managed to grasp the shoulders of Neil's jacket mere seconds before he hit the ground. Wings beating frantically, he then proceeded to make the most deplorable landing he'd ever made, hitting the floor of the valley sideways on, so that Neil wouldn't touch the ground.

Neil collapsed in a shivering heap beside the dragon as it loosened its claws. He felt sick. The ground had been so near, so very near. He'd felt it rushing up to meet him ...

Nestor, groaning with pain, his wing crumpled under him, was more of a nervous wreck than he cared to admit. Thank goodness, he thought, that he'd reached the boy in time. He knew perfectly well that he almost hadn't and shuddered in horror at the thought of what might have happened.

Gingerly, he heaved himself upright, his broken wing hanging uselessly by his side. The boy, stammering his thanks at being rescued, was unhurt, and that, he thought thankfully, was all that mattered. Dragon's injuries heal themselves in time but although he knew the damage wasn't lasting, a broken wing was the last thing Nestor needed! Especially here, on the valley floor where *she* was accustomed to roam ...

"What are we going to do?" Neil asked tentatively,

once they'd introduced themselves. He was still a bit nervous of this new dragon. Somehow he'd thought that all of the dragons in the valley would be the same as Arthur but this obviously wasn't the case, for although Nestor seemed friendly enough, he was nothing like Arthur. He was altogether much fiercer; thinner, sharper and jagged, his shiny grey scales gleaming threateningly, like the polished barrel of a gun.

"Well," Nestor shrugged, looking sourly at a huge tongue of rock that cut them off from the main valley, "if I hadn't broken my wing, we could have flown over that spur of rock in seconds. As it is, it looks as though we've a bit of a walk in front of us. Do you think you'll manage alright?" He looked at Neil shrewdly, for the boy still looked pale.

"I'll be fine," Neil grinned suddenly. It was true. He did feel a lot better. Just knowing he was alive acted as a tonic.

"Let's go then!" Nestor said with a sigh.

Neil had already started when the dragon's eyes caught the glint of gold. "I think you've dropped something, Neil," he said suddenly, nodding at the ground.

Neil glanced down and saw what looked like a gold coin lying in the dust. He looked at in some surprise and then, seeing the torn strip of shirt that lay beside it, realized that he'd must have been holding on to it when Lord Jezail had thrown him off the carpet. "It must belong to Lord Jezail," Neil said, picking it up and turning it over in his hand. "I noticed he had a chain round his neck when I was on the carpet." Looping it round his fingers, he stuffed it casually in his jacket pocket and, walking along by the dragon's side, promptly forgot about it as he scanned his new surroundings. What a fascinating place this was!

Nestor, too, was looking round sharply, his eyes missing nothing. He'd just worked out which part of the valley they were in and immediately felt uneasy. It was a place where the serpent sometimes lurked and although this wouldn't normally have bothered him that much, the present situation was hardly promising. Not only did he have a broken wing, he had the boy to look after.

Neil, knowing nothing of the dragon's worries, was gazing at the valley with interest. It was a strange place, he thought, a bit like the pictures of the moon that he'd seen on television. Outcrops of rock reared up here and there and between them, great cracks ran in jagged lines along the valley floor. Before Nestor could stop him, he ran across the dusty ground and peered down into one, drawing back abruptly, astonished at its depths.

"I wouldn't like to fall down there," he admitted, as Nestor's head reared worriedly.

"Best to keep away from them," Nestor agreed, keeping his voice calm with an effort. He knew that it was from just such a chasm that the serpent might appear and he quickened his step, grimacing slightly as he lifted his broken wing well clear of the ground.

Neil nodded and as he strode along he looked up at the dragon with an excited smile. He'd been a bit worried about its wing but, although clearly in pain, the dragon seemed otherwise okay. Despite its awkwardness, it was covering the ground at quite a speed. So much so that half the time he had to run to keep up with it!

"Look," he said, casually, "there's a track of sorts over there and it's heading in the right direction. It'll make it a lot easier for you if we follow it!"

Nestor followed his pointing finger and paled at the sight of the smooth, rounded track that wound gently among the scatter of jagged rocks that littered the valley floor. He knew at once who had made it and hissed in fear. *She* was nearby ...

It was as they reached the end of the outcrop and were about to move down into the main valley that they heard someone screaming.

Nestor lifted his head at the sound, wondering anxiously what was going on. He knew it wasn't one of his dragons for no dragon ever made a noise like that. The screams were dreadful and seemed to be coming closer. "Come on," he said urgently, "whoever it is, needs our help!"

As they rounded the corner, the main valley, wide and spacious, suddenly opened up before them and Neil gave a cry of joy as, pointing dramatically at the sky, a host of grey dragons suddenly appeared.

Nestor, although delighted to see them, drew his brows together in a frown for they were in no sort of order. Circling and swooping wildly in total confusion they drew ever closer; and it was as the sound of the screaming increased that they saw the reason why.

Neil froze and even Nestor drew back at the fearsome sight that met their eyes.

Lord Jezail appeared, still screaming frantically as he ran towards them. His robes were torn and filthy, his hair a tangled mess and his face totally and unmistakeably mad — for behind him a huge serpent reared, hissing viciously as it snaked swiftly after him. So huge was the serpent that Neil barely noticed Prince Kalman racing up behind on a magic carpet. Nestor did, however, and despite the urgency of the situation sighed with relief. At a time like this, a magician was just what was needed.

Neil clenched his fists so that his nails dug into the palm of his hands. His eyes were like saucers. What were they going to do? It was a huge snake, bigger than anything he'd ever seen in the zoo; its body, thick and powerful, was almost the same colour as the rocks in the valley, its black eyes gleamed and its great jaws were agape as it slithered swiftly after its prey, tongue flickering greedily, ready to strike.

Neil was never to know if Lord Jezail actually caught sight of him and perhaps lost his footing as a result. Maybe, as Prince Kalman told him afterwards, maybe the magician just tripped over his robes. Whatever the reason, Lord Jezail stumbled and fell heavily.

He didn't have a chance.

The serpent reared triumphantly and it was just as it was about to strike that both Neil and Prince Kalman threw a hex.

Prince Kalman jumped down from his carpet and rushed towards Lord Jezail who lay sprawled on the ground.

Neil, too, ran forward, shaking like a leaf. He'd thrown a hex! How he'd managed it, he didn't know, but he had! The power had flown automatically from his fingers and the words had sprung instinctively from his lips. He ran forward, anxiously, knowing that he'd hexed the serpent before it struck. Why then, wasn't Lord Jezail scrambling to his feet?

He knelt beside the prince as he bent over the still figure. One touch was enough. "I'm afraid he's dead, Neil," the prince frowned, looking decidedly puzzled as he slipped his arms underneath the limp body. It was only as he turned the magician over and lifted him to a sitting position that Neil saw the wound that scarred his forehead.

"It wasn't the serpent that killed him, Neil!" the prince muttered. He stretched out his hand, his fingers closing over a sharp stone that lay, half-hidden, in the dust. "It must have been this! He tripped and fell on it ..."

"But he had a protective shield round him," Neil argued, still shocked at what had happened. "Even Arthur's fire couldn't burn him ..." His voice drifted to a halt as his hand crept to his pocket where the gold coin lay and he swallowed hard as he realized what must have happened.

Prince Kalman looked at him thoughtfully but said nothing. Questions could come later.

"To be frank," he said gently, "it's a better death than he deserved. He was, truly, a vicious man."

It was then that the grey dragons swooped down from the sky and landed in a tangled heap of wings and claws beside them. Nostrils flaring, they hissed in relief at the sight of the serpent whose body lay sprawled in the dust. She was dead! Dead at last! They looked at Nestor, their eyes shining with relief. *She* would no longer terrorize the valley.

# 41. The gold medallion

The great castle at Trollsberg was a scene of bustling excitement. Never had it entertained so many visitors at one time. The kitchen staff had doubled overnight, working in shifts to cope with the new arrivals — they'd even set up special field kitchens in the meadows outside the town where the MacArthur's army was camped.

Sitting by the fire in the Blue Salon, Neil relaxed and watched Major Sallis and Clara idly. They had found a pack of cards and were playing some sort of Snap. He shifted slightly in his chair, feeling guiltier with every moment that passed, for he still hadn't told Clara about the magic coin — and the longer he left it, the harder it became. He hadn't mentioned it to the prince either and he knew that he should have handed it over to him straightaway while Lord Jezail was lying dead in the dust.

The prince, to give him his due, had coped with everything with his customary efficiency. He'd mended Nestor's wing with a hex and set a dragon guard round Lord Jezail's body until he could arrange for it to be transported to Trollsberg. As for the serpent, Neil shivered slightly at the thought — the dragons had taken care of it themselves. Strung out along its length, they'd lifted it in their claws, carried its heavy, lifeless body over one of the deep chasms that cracked the valley floor and dropped it into its depths. She would trouble them no more.

So many things had happened all at once that there hadn't really been time to say anything about the coin. It had all been *so* horrible and a million things had been crowding his mind. He surely couldn't be blamed for not mentioning it. And when Prince Kalman had brought him back to the top of the cliff on his magic carpet, he'd still been more or less in a state of shock. The magicians, although horrified at his appearance, had greeted him with relief and Clara had run forward with tears in her eyes — his magic carpet had returned without him and she'd obviously been thinking the worst! Even Arthur had surged forward, looking at him with concern.

And, once again, the moment had passed — for the prince barely had time to tell Lord Rothlan and Count Vassili of Lord Jezail's death when Nestor, once more in charge of the grey dragons, flapped out of the sky to land beside them. He bowed low to the magicians and to Arthur and hurriedly announced the arrival of the MacArthur's and Lord Onegin's armies.

And *that*, Neil smiled ruefully, had kept everyone busy for the rest of the day. Not that either he or Clara had known anything about it, for the prince had immediately instructed Arthur to take them both back to Trollsberg before the rest set off on their carpets. Perhaps a hex had accompanied his words, Neil thought, for once they'd arrived at Trollsberg on the dragon's back — to the stunned astonishment of the guards, who'd never seen a dragon before — all they could think of was hot baths and sleep. Worn out by the excitement of the day, they'd tumbled into bed and slept long and heavily, waking up sluggishly the next morning to the crowing of cocks.

It was Major Sallis who had told them over breakfast how the two armies had joined forces and between them had rounded up the scattered remainder of Lord Jezail's army. The black-clad Citadel Guard, he said, had put up no sort of fight but had surrendered immediately on hearing of their master's death. Then he described the return of Lord Onegin to Trollsberg, the arrival of the MacArthurs on a fleet of magic carpets and the burial of Lord Jezail in one of the vaults in the wall of the castle. It had been an exceedingly formal occasion, he said sombrely, and one that all of the magicians had attended. The death of a Dragon Seeker was always marked by special observances and Lord Jezail's body had been buried with all the honour and ceremony that was his due.

Clara's voice interrupted his thoughts. "What's the matter, Neil?" she asked, looking across at him as she pushed the cards towards the major, who'd won handsomely. "You've been very quiet since we got back."

Neil looked uncomfortable but was saved from answering by a murmur of voices as the high, double doors opened and Prince Kalman entered followed by Lord Rothlan, Count Vassili and the MacArthur.

The two children stood up respectfully, smiling a welcome as Amgarad flew over and landed on Clara's shoulder.

"Well," the MacArthur said once the initial greetings were over and they'd settled themselves in a group round the fire, "you seem to have had an exciting time. Prince Kalman's been telling me all about it!"

Clara smiled and raised her eyebrows. *"You've* been fighting battles," she pointed out. "That must have been exciting, too!"

Neil said nothing but looked at them warily for there was an air of seriousness about the four magicians that told him they'd been discussing him and his hex.

It was as the conversation petered out that Prince Kalman looked at Neil thoughtfully. "Before we go any further, I ... er, I think that you might have something to tell us, Neil? About Lord Jezail's medallion?"

Neil looked apprehensive for there was little warmth in the prince's voice.

Count Vassili, however, noticing the shocked surprise in Neil's eyes, intervened quickly. "What happened, Neil? Please ... just tell us. It *is* important, you know."

Neil by this time was sitting straight up in his chair. "You ... you don't think I stole it, do you?" he said, looking at them disbelievingly.

"Stole what?' Clara looked from Prince Kalman

to her brother and back again. "Neil never stole anything in his life!"

"I didn't say anything of the sort," the prince pointed out, slightly taken aback at Clara's hot defence of her brother, "but we didn't find the medallion on his body when we brought him here to Trollsberg," the prince continued," and Neil did throw a hex at the serpent."

"Serpent?" Clara echoed in bewilderment. "What serpent?"

Neil ignored her question. "A medallion? Is that what it's called?" He frowned but looked interested at the same time. "I thought it was a coin. No, he didn't give it to me," he answered. "You know that perfectly well! It's a magic coin. He'd never have given it to me."

"Then how did you get it?"

Neil didn't answer. The question brought back all of the dreadful memories he'd been trying to push to the back of his mind. His face reddened and he clenched his hands together as unexpected tears clouded his eyes. He looked at the ground so that no one would notice but stumbled over the words. "Actually, I wasn't going to say anything," he said, eyeing Clara sideways, "but ... well ..."

"Well what, Neil?" Lord Rothlan asked softly, throwing Kalman a warning glance.

"It was really quite horrible," Neil answered, lifting his eyes and looking straight at Prince Kalman. "Lord Jezail," he whispered, "I ... you see, I managed to catch him when he fell off the cliff. I thought he'd be grateful but he ... he grabbed me and threw me off my carpet."

"Lord... Jezail ... what?" The prince's voice cracked in disbelief as the others jumped to their feet. Whatever they had expected to hear, it hadn't been that!

Neil looked at the prince through a sudden blur of tears. "I caught hold of his shirt but it tore and I think that's when the chain broke ..." he swallowed and managed a feeble grin, "I didn't notice it at the time. By then I was falling and I'd more to worry about. Fortunately, Nestor saw the whole thing. That's when he swooped down and caught me just ... just before I hit the ground. That's ... that's how he broke his wing."

Prince Kalman took two steps forward and hugged Neil tightly. "Forgive me for doubting you, Neil," he said. "I never dreamt that such a thing could happen. None of us did," he added, stepping back and holding him by the shoulders. "You see, we just couldn't understand ..."

Clara had never seen the prince look so upset. He'd misjudged the situation completely and didn't know how to put things right.

Neil fished the coin out of his pocket and held it out to the prince. "It was Nestor who saw it lying in the dust," he explained." He thought I'd dropped it and maybe I did when I was falling. I can't remember, really. I just picked it up, shoved it in my pocket and more or less forgot about it. I was still a bit shaken, you see, and Nestor's wing was broken and ... anyway, he'll tell you if you ask him."

There was complete silence for a long moment as the magicians looked at one another very oddly indeed. Prince Kalman, however, barely heard what Neil had said; he'd stiffened abruptly as he felt the power of the coin that lay heavily in the palm of his hand.

It was the MacArthur who broke the silence. "Well, gentlemen," he said quietly, "it looks as though we have a brand new magician in our midst. I think we'd all agree that the medallion made a wise choice in Neil."

As Neil and Clara watched curiously, the coin passed from hand to hand. The MacArthur took it and, drawing a sharp breath, looked at the prince in disbelief before passing it on to Count Vassili, who shuddered as he held it and, with a horrified look on his face, passed it quickly to Lord Rothlan.

Pale with shock, Lord Rothlan's face was unreadable as he handed it back to the prince. "Well," he said heavily, "now we know why Lord Jezail acted the way he did. Whether or not *he* influenced the medallion or *it* influenced him, we'll never know but ..."

"No, Alasdair," Count Vassili interrupted. "There was nothing wrong with the medallion when Jezail inherited it from his father. *He's* the one who corrupted its magic!" He paused and looked at the two children. "And I don't need to tell you that there's no *way* Neil can wear it. Not in its present state, at any rate. It would control him within days."

Prince Kalman pressed his lips together in a thin line. "You're right, of course, Vassili," he said grimly, "except that it didn't take days. It controlled him from the start." He looked at them all in turn. "Neil's honest. We all know that. Yet he didn't tell me about the medallion when he hexed the serpent, did he?"

There was a silence as the magicians looked at one another, eyebrows raised.

"You mean ... it was the medallion that stopped me from telling you?" Neil said slowly.

Lord Rothlan nodded.

"Then I don't want it," Neil said sharply. "It made me lie!"

The MacArthur smiled wryly. "It's not as easy as that, Neil. It's a magic coin and ... well, the fact remains that *it* chose *you*."

"Only because I was there," Neil pointed out, biting his lip in disappointment as all thoughts of being a magician faded rapidly from his mind.

"No, no, you're wrong, Neil," Lord Rothlan said slowly. "First of all, the medallion would sense the magic in your firestone and secondly, *I* rather think it was looking for a new master. Lord Jezail was very old, remember, and in the end, went completely mad. And madness, you see, was the one thing the medallion couldn't control ..."

The MacArthur nodded. "Yes, I think Neil was a deliberate choice but as Vassili says, he can't wear it in its present state. It's much too dangerous!"

"I know it made me lie," Neil said hesitantly, "but otherwise, you know, I didn't feel all that different. Yet, you ... all of you, looked so horrified when you held it ..."

Count Vassili smiled and put an arm round his shoulders. "You must remember, Neil, that apart from the firestone, you have no real magic in you;

but we are magicians and when our magic met that of the medallion we immediately knew how evil it was."

"There *are* ways of removing the evil from the medallion," Prince Kalman said slowly, turning it over in his hand, "but quite frankly it's a job for the Lords of the North and ... it'll take time."

Neil looked anxiously from one to the other.

"What do you think, Neil?" Lord Rothlan asked. "If you agree, we could rid the medallion of evil and give it to you when you are older. You see ... the medallion *is* yours. You didn't take it from Lord Jezail. It chose to give itself to you."

"May ... may I hold it?" Neil asked, his spirits rising at the thought that one day he would wear it. "Just for a minute."

"Of course," Prince Kalman answered, smiling reassuringly as he handed it over.

Neil looked down at the circle of gold that was going to change his life. Lifting it closer, he looked at the strange symbols that curved round two intertwined crescent moons. It was beautifully made and his fingers closed over it protectively. It was his but he knew within himself that the magicians were right. It had to be cleansed of evil before he could wear it. Taking a deep breath, he gave it back to the prince. "Please keep it for me," he said.

"When you *do* wear it, Neil," Prince Kalman said, "you will be one of us. You know that, don't you? And your magic will be just as great as ours."

"But in the meantime, you'll be our pupil," Lord Rothlan said with a smile, as the others nodded in agreement, "for there's a lot more than magic tokens to being a magician, believe me! I'm afraid it'll be a bit like being at school all over again!"

Neil nodded, looking confused as Clara hugged him. Thank goodness for the medallion, she thought. It's really evened things out between us! I really wasn't happy at having the talisman when Neil only had a firestone. He wasn't jealous, exactly, but he must have felt a bit left out. She smiled happily at him.

"Now then ..." she said aloud, "I'm absolutely dying of curiosity. For goodness sake, tell me about the serpent!"

# 42. The citadel

Clara gasped and clutched at Maria as their magic carpet approached Stara Zargana. "Look!" she gasped, "look at the citadel. It isn't black anymore!" They looked at one another in amazement and Clara gestured to Neil and Colonel Strelitz who were travelling alongside them.

"Look at the citadel!" she called. "It's changed colour!"

"It must be because Lord Jezail is dead," Colonel Strelitz called back, looking in wonder at the shining white towers that rose, clean and shining, against the green backdrop of forest-clad mountains. His heart filled with hope. Life was going to be very different now that Lord Jezail had gone. He was going to marry Maria and, now a colonel and the newly appointed Commander of the Citadel Guard, he would never have to return to Dragonsgard and its lonely, rocky valley.

Soon they were flying over the red-roofed houses of the little town and in no time at all had landed in the deep courtyard of the citadel. Clara smiled at Maria, her eyes shining as she looked round. How different it all was from that dreadful night when they'd left for Dragonsgard!

Carpets landed all round them and it was Prince Kalman who led the way towards the rounded curve of shallow steps where Count Vassili, the new Governor of the Citadel, waited to receive them. The Citadel Guard, in smart, white uniforms, snapped to attention as they approached and it was a happy, chattering group that entered its halls.

"You should have seen it when *I* was here," Clara said to Neil. "It was awful; really dark and creepy." She looked up at the shining, vaulted ceiling and marvelled at the difference.

Count Vassili ushered them into the Great Hall of the citadel and it was then that they saw Dragonslayer. Hung against the glass of a tall window, it glowed golden with happiness.

"I asked it to choose where it would like to rest and it chose the window," Count Vassili explained. "After hundreds of years shut up in Sir Pendar's tomb, it wanted the light and the view. That's why it's so high up," he admitted. "The window overlooks the citadel garden but from that height it can see over the walls to the town and the mountains and forests beyond."

"Does it remember its past," Clara asked curiously.

"Only vaguely, I think," the count answered. "The hex you used from the *Book of Spells* blotted out all of its evil desires. It's now a very definite force for good."

Prince Kalman looked at him, knowing there was more.

"It was only after I had it placed in the window that the citadel started to change colour!"

"A good omen," Lord Rothlan smiled.

"And a powerful one," Prince Kalman added, looking at the sword speculatively.

The sword heard their words, for its hearing was sharp, and smiled to itself. It had no intention of revealing just how powerful its magic was or how, from its vantage point high in the windows of the citadel, it could use it to its best advantage. For the sword, as always, had its own agenda and cleansing the citadel of Jezail's warped personality was just the start ...

Lunch was a pleasant meal as they talked lazily over the happenings of the past days. It was as they rose from the table that Clara asked the count if she could show Neil her old rooms in the tower.

"Why, of course, Clara," he answered readily. "You can go where you like. Your room will be just as you left it."

Clara nodded, secretly glad that nothing had been changed and, beckoning to Neil, headed for the spiral staircase that wound its way up the tower, stopping every now and then to peer through the slit windows. "I was so miserable and unhappy here," she murmured, as she opened the door to her bedroom and looked round, "but there's no feeling of it left."

Neil walked over to the window and peered down at the red roofed houses and narrow, winding streets of Stara Zargana.

"I used to stand there," Clara said, sadly, "and look at the houses, wondering who lived in them and what their lives were like. I thought about Mum and Dad, too." She paused. "I can't believe we'll be seeing them tomorrow. They must be worried sick about us. I mean ... we've been here for ages when you think about it."

Neil shook his head. "Don't forget that magic time and our time are completely different," he pointed out. "When we do get back, we won't have been gone any time at all, as far as Mum and Dad are concerned. Anyway, Lady Ellen's there and even before we set off, she'd more or less convinced them that everything would be fine."

"Do you think we'll ever come back here?"

Neil looked at her ironically. "I'd say so," he grinned. "Didn't you hear Prince Kalman talking to Count Vassili about hunting wild boar? Not that I want to hunt wild boar," he added hurriedly, "but, well, I always liked Count Vassili, even when he taught us German at Netherfield ... " he tailed off as a sudden thought struck him. "Do you know, I'd forgotten all about school!"

"So had I!" Clara looked at him in horror. "I guess our holidays must be almost over!"

"I haven't looked at my holiday homework either," Neil groaned as they left the room and clattered down the dizzying spiral stairs.

"Hey! Neil! Clara!"

Clara beamed with delight as she saw Hamish and Jackie walking towards them. Both looked absolutely exhausted.

"Clara!" Jackie said in relief. "They told us you were here! Thank goodness you're safe!"

"We heard that Amgarad rescued you from some dragon's castle or other!" Hamish added. "Are you alright?"

Clara laughed. "I'm fine," she smiled, "but where's Archie?"

"He stayed in the Valley of the Dragons," Jaikie answered. "Arthur wanted to see that everything was sorted out before he left. I think the dragons are throwing a party for him."

"We wondered why you didn't turn up at Trollsberg." Neil looked at him enquiringly." All the MacArthur would tell us was that you were busy. Did you see any fighting?"

Jaikie shook his head, smothering a yawn. "Jezail's men were glad to surrender," he said, tiredly. "We stayed behind to round up the last of them."

"He'd sent scouts in to suss the place out," Hamish explained, "and we had to scour every nook and cranny to find them. By the time we'd rounded them all up, the carpets were pretty shattered, I can tell you!"

Clara looked concerned. "You *do* know we're leaving tomorrow morning, don't you?" she asked.

"We heard," Jaikie nodded, pushing his hair out of his eyes. "We could have done with another rest day, but what to do? The carpets are asleep already and we're heading for bed as soon as we've eaten. I can hardly believe that by this time tomorrow, we'll be home!"

"I can hardly believe it, either," Neil sighed. "*We've* got *school* next week!"

"I'm not going to say goodbye to you, Neil ... nor to you, Clara," Count Vassili smiled, taking their hands in his, "because I know you'll be back. We, the Onegin, are deeply in your debt and you will always be welcome here, you know that!"

Neil and Clara murmured their thanks, genuinely sorry to be leaving.

"And don't forget to work hard at your German grammar when you're back at Netherfield," the count urged with a twinkle in his eye. "It's spoken here and if you're going to go out exploring on your next visit, then it might help if you speak the language!"

As they thanked him again, a chill wind swirled round the shallow steps of the citadel blowing a scatter of brown leaves round their ankles. Autumn was setting in and despite the blankets they'd piled on their carpets, they knew it was going to be a cold journey home.

"I hope you put on that extra sweater I laid out for you," Maria fussed as she hugged Clara before seeing her safely onto her carpet. "I hadn't realized how bitterly cold it was up there until I flew back with you the other day!"

Clara smiled and waved as her carpet followed Neil's into the air and drifted towards those of Hamish and Jaikie. They'd fly home together, side by side, for company.

Prince Kalman, Lord Rothlan and the MacArthur then said their goodbyes and waved as their carpets lifted higher and higher until they soared over the high wall of the courtyard.

As they flew over Stara Zargana, Clara turned to look at the citadel one last time. Neil wasn't terribly bothered about it but now that it was free of Lord Jezail's menacing presence, she found that she was really going to miss it. I'll try and paint a picture of it when I get home, she thought, trying to memorize the shape of the slender turrets, the delicately crenellated battlements and the massive height of the great door. She kept her eyes on it for as long as she could and it was only when it faded to tiny, white speck that she sighed and turned her face towards Scotland and home.

# 43. Homecoming

It was a long journey and by the time they reached the border, night was falling. The waters of the North Sea gleamed in the moonlight as they passed over Holy Island, crossed the River Tweed and slipped over the dark slopes of the Lammermuir Hills. After that it was just a matter of following the coastline as, one after another, the lights of the many little fishing villages blinked peacefully beneath them as their carpets headed north.

"There's Edinburgh!" Clara called to Neil as the lights of the city glowed on the horizon. Soon, the outline of Arthur's Seat appeared, crouched like a protective dragon over the housetops; its massive bulk growing ever larger as they approached, rising darkly from the sprawl of glittering lights that marked the city. Although stiff and cold, they forgot their discomfort in the excitement of coming home as, one by one, the exhausted carpets swooped thankfully into the old familiar tunnel that led into the depths of the hill.

Lady Ellen gave a cry of pleasure as she saw the carpets soaring towards her across the dim vastness of the Great Hall. She'd been expecting them for the last half hour and had begun to get fidgety. "Look, they're here at last!" she said, leaping to her feet.

John and Janet MacLean joined her, eyes shining at the thought of seeing their children again. Really, Janet thought, the MacArthur had been as good as his word when he'd said he'd have Clara back in no time at all. Here they were, back already; only a few days later!

"Neil, Clara, it's lovely to have you back," Mrs MacLean cried, hugging Neil and clasping her daughter tightly as Clara stumbled tiredly off her carpet. "I hope that horrible Lord Jezail treated you well!"

"Of course he did," Clara reassured her with a smile, feeling that it was best not to go into too much detail.

"He won't be troubling us anymore," the MacArthur said reassuringly, greeting the MacLeans with a broad smile. "He died in the Valley of the Dragons!"

"The Valley of the Dragons?" John MacLean looked round, realizing for the first time that Arthur was nowhere to be seen. "Arthur's alright, isn't he?"

"He's flying back with Archie," Neil said, easing his aching bones. "You know, MacArthur, now that Count Vassili is Governor of the Citadel, I think it would be a marvellous idea if you were to give him a magic mirror as a present."

"I was thinking that myself," Prince Kalman smiled, looking at Lord Rothlan. "It'll make it much easier to get to Ashgar in future ... and we never did get to that old hunting lodge in the forest, did we?"

Amgarad spread his wings and gave an approving squawk. Although he was, perhaps, the only member of the party who wasn't tired — for he'd travelled back snuggled in the warmth of his master's cloak and had slept most of the way — he nevertheless agreed wholeheartedly. Magic mirrors were by far and away the easiest, and most comfortable, way to travel.

"I'd set one up right away then, Father," Lady Ellen advised, "for the Lords of the North will be inviting Count Vassili to Morven in a couple of days' time. They're planning to have a banquet to celebrate your safe return!"

Neil dug his elbow into Clara's ribs as she hid a yawn. Lady Ellen noticed, however, and smiled understandingly. "You must be exhausted," she said, putting an arm round them both. Although she'd said nothing to the MacLeans, she'd kept in touch with her husband through the crystal and Lord Rothlan had told her much of what had gone on. "Your parents have been keeping me company while you were away and I've given you rooms beside theirs."

Clara's eyes brightened. It wasn't often that they slept in the hill but she loved the huge rooms and the long, stone corridors with their suits of armour, ancient pictures and the displays of old-fashioned spears and claymores that decorated the walls. It was as if, at one time, an old castle had somehow been built into Arthur's Seat.

That night, curled up snuggly in the huge four-poster bed that dominated the bedroom, she sighed happily. The adventure was over, Lord Jezail was no more and the talisman was, once more, curled round her wrist where it belonged. It would never again leave her. She felt its content and relaxed, knowing that it, too, was happy to be safe and well in the heart of the hill.

In the bedroom next door, Neil blew out the flickering candles that lit the room and slipped between the sheets. Usually, he lay for a while, enjoying the richness of the room; the tapestried walls, the huge carved pieces of furniture and the silk carpets that felt so smooth under his bare feet. Not tonight, he thought, he was just *so* tired. A wave of comfort swept over him as he shut his eyes and let his mind drift as sleep overtook him. But his last thought was of the medallion and its magic and what it would be like to be a great magician ...

# 44. Celebrations

The blue and silver halls of the Lords of the North were ablaze with light as Neil and Clara stepped through the magic mirror into Morven, the great mountain in the Grampians that housed the Lords of the North. Clara smoothed her dress. Magic, she thought, was just so handy. Given that none of them had any clothes at all, far less anything suitable for such a grand occasion as a banquet in the halls of the Lords of the North, Lady Ellen had hexed up a whole new wardrobe for each of them and even her mother, who still wasn't at all sure if she approved of magic or not, was delighted with her beautiful new evening dress.

The Lords of the North were just as richly attired. Sitting proudly on their silver thrones in long robes of embroidered velvet they welcomed them graciously to Morven.

It was only after they'd paid their respects and Lord Rothlan was busily introducing Count Vassili to the lords that the hobgoblins moved tentatively forward on tiny hooves and clustered round the two children.

"We're so pleased that you got back safely, Neil," Rumblegudgeon said, his goat-like little face shining excitedly. "And you, too, Clara! We were really worried about you!"

Lady Ellan eyed the hobgoblins with an amused smile and then looked up as the magic mirrors shimmered suddenly to reveal two gorgeously robed magicians.

"The Sultan and Prince Casimir!" Neil gasped in surprise.

Prince Kalman strode forward, bowing low to both the Turkish Sultan and his father, Prince Casimir. "Father!" he said, delightedly. "How wonderful to see you!"

The Turkish Sultan smiled as the two embraced warmly and then bowed as Lord Alarid hastened forward to greet him. "Thank you for informing us of Jezail's death, Alarid," the Sultan said once he'd greeted all the lords in turn." We are well rid of him!"

"I still can't believe that he was so evil." Prince Casimir said, shaking his head. "He seemed so ... so *kindly*. And he always treated us with great respect."

Prince Kalman reached forward in his chair and laid his hand over his father's. "He was laughing at us all the time, Father," he said gently. "It made him feel powerful to hex us the way he did and he enjoyed our suffering." He paused and then added thoughtfully. "What he didn't, and couldn't realize, was that to do such a thing in the first place meant that his mind was diseased. I saw his true face," he grimaced distastefully at the thought, "and it wasn't pleasant, I assure you. The poor man was mad and he didn't know it. Don't you think so,

Alasdair?" he queried, looking up at Lord Rothlan, who, with Amgarad on his shoulder, was standing beside the Sultan's throne.

Lord Rothlan nodded." His medallion knew it, too," he observed. "That's why it latched onto Neil."

The Sultan looked at him sharply. "The *boy* has his medallion?"

"Actually, Lord Alban has it at the moment, Milord," Prince Kalman said seriously. "In fact, he'll probably be asking you for advice."

"Indeed?" the Sultan sounded curious.

The prince sighed. "The medallion's changed into a twisted, evil thing," he said, a frown crossing his face. "You'll be shocked when you hold it."

"There's very little goodness left in it," Lord Rothlan added, "and making it safe again will take some time. Years perhaps, depending on how deeply Jezail's magic penetrated."

"Anyway, there's no way the boy can wear the medallion as it is," the prince stated firmly. "Besides which, he's very young to wield such power."

"Quite," the Sultan said frowningly." This is a serious matter. Why, he will be one of us eventually!"

"We know that, Milord. And so does he."

"Is he suitable? I mean ... I know Neil as well as you do. He's a brave lad. But will he be able to cope? The responsibility ..."

"I saw his behaviour when Jezail died," Prince Kalman said briefly. "Jezail had just finished throwing him off his magic carpet — in mid-air,

I might add — and," he paused as they gasped in horror, "... and the boy saw him rushing towards him with a serpent on his tail, one of the Ugleira, I think ..."

"The Ugleira?" Lord Alarid looked amazed. "They still exist?"

The prince nodded. "A huge specimen," he agreed. "It must have been feeding off the young of the dragons for centuries."

"Go on," the Sultan said with an impatient wave of his hand, "never mind the Ugleira! What happened next?"

"It was a split-second decision for Neil," Kalman said slowly, "and he quite unhesitatingly hexed the serpent."

"Ah!" The Sultan relaxed. "That certainly bodes well for the future."

"Nobody, and no magic, killed Jezail," Prince Kalman pointed out. "He tripped and hit his head on one of the many rocks that litter the valley. He'd no protection, you see — for by then, Neil had his medallion — although, of course, I didn't realize it at the time."

"The boy will have a lot to learn ..." the Sultan said slowly.

Lord Rothlan and the prince looked at one another in relief. The Sultan had agreed!" He knows that," the prince said. "And we'll all teach him ..." he looked at the MacArthur, who nodded approvingly. If the medallion was going to go to anyone, then Neil was a good choice.

Catching her husband's eye, Lady Ellan brought Neil and Clara forward to greet the Sultan and

Prince Casimir. She squeezed Neil's shoulder warningly as they approached for she'd guessed what the huddled conversation had been about.

The Sultan, however, was gracious and Neil looked at Clara in relief. He knew there and then that he was going to work very hard to gain the approval of the magicians.

The banquet was followed by speeches from just about everyone for it wasn't only Lord Alarid who spoke. All of the Lords of the North had their say, thanking Prince Kalman, Lord Rothlan, Count Vassili, the MacArthur and the children for the success of their mission.

"We are, of course, sorry that Lord Jezail didn't see the error of his ways," Lord Alarid finished, "but we must be grateful for an accident that prevented further suffering. We are delighted, too, at the news that his medallion has found a new master." He looked at Neil and bowed. "A magician, approved by us all, who will one day join our ranks."

John MacLean raised his eyebrows at this while Janet turned and looked at Clara suspiciously. "Lord Alarid doesn't mean Neil, does he?" she whispered as her son rose somewhat guiltily to his feet and bowed to Lord Alarid.

Clara looked at her parents apprehensively. She'd urged Neil to tell them about the medallion but he'd been strangely reluctant to mention it. "Just leave it," he'd said. "You know what Mum's like about magic at the best of times. All she'll do is worry herself silly and, let's face it, they'll never know unless *you* tell them!" Well, she thought to herself, now the beans have been seriously spilled! She sat back and waited, wishing herself anywhere else but Morven! She hated rows and was afraid that one might be brewing.

She had, however, reckoned without Lady Ellan, who smiled quietly. "How wonderful, Neil," she whispered, with a warning flicker of her eyelashes, "it's such an amazing coincidence! You see, I'd already asked your mother if I could give you a magic token and now ... well," she said ruefully, "... it seems that you have a much nicer one than anything I could have given you!"

"That was really kind of you, Lady Ellan," Clara said warmly, one eye on her mother's face. "Lady Ellan is so thoughtful, isn't she, Mum!"

"Yes ... yes, of course she is," Mrs MacLean answered, looking doubtfully at her husband. "It was a very kind thought ..."

Clara hid a smile. Lady Ellan had obviously been busy!

Which was, more or less, the truth for, having heard the story of the medallion from her husband, Lady Ellan had quietly prepared the MacLeans' minds for just such an event. It hadn't been hard — she'd just mentioned in the course of conversation that she didn't think it was good that Clara had the magic of the talisman at her fingertips while Neil had nothing but his firestone. It was, she pointed out, the kind of thing that encouraged jealousy and it worried her. Would they mind, she'd asked shyly, if she gave Neil a magic token of some sort? Something small, perhaps, just to make them equal? For it wasn't fair that Clara should have all the magic, was it?

By the time she'd finished, Mrs MacLean had agreed with her wholeheartedly. When all was said and done, she wanted both her children to be happy.

So the evening ended on a high note and Neil, it must be said, walked back through the magic mirror with a more assured step. While Lady Ellan and Clara were saying goodnight to the little hobgoblins, the magicians had taken him to one side and talked to him seriously about the responsibilities of magicians. And, although they'd spoken to him kindly, they hadn't talked to him as a boy, but as one magician to another. He couldn't help but feel honoured.

# 45. And so to bed ...

When they arrived back in the hill, they found that Archie and Arthur had arrived in their absence. The air was almost too warm as Hamish and Jaikie had lit braziers round the cavern, knowing that Archie would be cold after his flight. And he was! Hugging a fur round him, he was warming his hands while Arthur blew bursts of flame everywhere.

They sat round the fire for a long time that evening, clutching hot drinks and revelling in the warmth. Nobody said very much. Arthur was tired after his long flight, but happy to be home; Hamish and Jaikie, who had just finished the monumental task of stacking armaments away in the store cupboards, relaxed gratefully and the magicians sat back in their chairs, pleased at the way things had gone and glad that Lord Jezail would never cause them any trouble, ever again. It was all very satisfying!

"We start school next week," Clara said suddenly into the comfortable silence. "It seems a bit tame after being kidnapped by an evil magician, doesn't it?"

Neil almost added that it seemed a bit tame after being thrown off a magic carpet by the same evil magician, but as he didn't want his mother to freak out, he said nothing.

"You'll have to call a meeting of the witches sometime soon, Clara," Lord Rothlan reminded her. "You have the talisman and you'll have to lay down some pretty firm rules to keep that little lot in order!"

"Where do they usually meet?" Mrs MacLean asked enquiringly.

The MacArthur paused and eyed Prince Kalman and Lord Rothlan with a twinkle in his eye. "In your house, I believe," he answered.

"Oh, that's alright then," Mrs MacLean said, "but ..." she added, turning to her husband, "I'll have to buy a lot more cups and saucers, John."

As everyone knew her opinion of witches — never high at the best of times — there was a somewhat stunned silence at this, only broken when Lady Ellan let out a sudden snort of laughter, which set them all off.

The party broke up after that, principally because Arthur had succeeded in filling the cavern with sparkling smoke that danced in swirling wreaths over the braziers. Goodnights were said as they made their way to their rooms but the MacArthur remained in his chair with Arthur and Archie at his feet.

"Well," he said, looking round the misty heights of the cavern, "that's a job well done, Archie! Who would have thought the old man had so much evil in him!"

"We didn't suspect him at all ..." Archie nodded, "that was what was so scary."

"Let's hope that life will be a lot quieter now that he's gone," the MacArthur said, rising to his feet. "Goodnight, Archie! Goodnight, Arthur!"

Archie climbed on Arthur's back. They were both tired after their long flight and Archie clung on grimly as the great dragon set off eagerly for his beautiful, treasure-filled den.

Arthur had already visited it, of course; it was the first thing he'd done when he got back. And it had all been there, his treasure; just as he'd left it. He sighed happily as he reached it and clambered contentedly to the top of the sparkling pile. The Valley of the Dragons had been wonderful and he'd made lots of good friends but there was nothing, absolutely nothing, to compare with a shiny, gleaming, glittering bed of precious treasure. *How* he had missed it.

Clara was just getting into bed when there was a quiet tap on her door. "Come in," she called. "Oh, it's you, Neil. I thought you'd be asleep by now ..."

Neil plonked himself on Clara's bed. "D'you know," he said, bouncing on it slightly, "I think your bed's bigger than mine and more comfortable, too."

Clara wrapped her arms round her knees and looked at him. "You didn't come here to tell me that, did you?"

"No," he confessed. "No, I didn't. I ... I was just wondering how you felt about me having Lord Jezail's medallion. I mean ... you don't mind, do you?"

"Mind?" Clara looked at him in surprise. "Why should I mind? I'm glad it went to you! I've always felt guilty that Auntie Muriel left me the talisman."

"I did feel a bit left out," he confessed.

"I know you did," she answered, honestly. "I'd have felt the same way, if it had been the other way round."

Neil grinned. "Now I've got the wizards to deal with and you've got the witches!"

Clara's eyes narrowed. "Don't worry," she said, "I'm going to be tough!" She looked suddenly thoughtful. "Do you remember when we first met the MacArthurs," she said quietly, "when we used to play on Arthur's Seat and didn't know they were magic?"

Neil shook his head. "Oh, I think we did, in a funny kind of way ..."

"Life's strange, isn't it?" she continued." It takes you along all sorts of paths. I mean, what would our lives be like now if Dad hadn't been a Park Ranger on Arthur's Seat? All this would never have happened to us! Scary, isn't it? You never know where you'll end up, really, do you?"

"Well, I'm glad it all happened the way it did — maybe it was meant to be this way for us, who knows?" Neil said with a huge yawn. "It'll be weird being a magician, though," he added as he slung his legs over the bed and stood up. "I'm glad you don't mind."

Clara grinned as he headed for the door. "Don't be daft!" she said sleepily." Night, Neil, and don't worry about being a magician. You'll be fine!"

Prince Kalman and Lord Rothlan were saying much the same thing as they sat on the slopes of Arthur's Seat enjoying the night air. Amgarad soared in the sky overhead, well content with his part in the proceedings. He'd done his bit, he'd rescued Clara and, as Count Vassili had invited them all to stay at the citadel whenever they cared to visit, he looked forward to many happy days soaring above the forests of Ashgar.

In the depths of Arthur's Seat, Arthur shifted on his pile of treasure. Thoughts of Gladrin and Nestor flickered through his dreams and he knew that one day he, too, would return to the Valley of the Dragons.

So if, by any chance, you're wandering the streets of Edinburgh in the early hours of the morning, and see a host of dragons flying over Arthur's Seat, it won't surprise you, will it? Nestor, Gladrin and many of Arthur's friends visit him quite often these days. And if you can see them, the chances are that you've probably picked up on some of their magic ... for, as you know, the power to see dragons isn't given to everyone ...

# Anne Forbes
# Author Interview

*Q: When did you start writing?*
Anne Forbes [AF]: I started writing in 2001. My first book was a history book which took a few years to research and write. Strangely enough, writing a history book is actually much easier than writing a novel which relies solely on the author's ideas and imagination.

*Q: What inspired you to start writing?*
AF: Once the history book was finished, I knew that I wanted to go on writing but knowing the amount of research another history book would involve, decided to write a children's novel instead. I then looked out a short story I'd written many years previously (called 'Sir James and the Dragon') and it formed the basis of my first novel, Dragonfire.

*Q: What was your favourite book when you were a child?*
AF: My favourite book was, and still is, *The Black Riders* by Violet Needham. Her books are out of print now but are possibly still available on Amazon. Great stories!

*Q: How do you come up for the ideas in your books?*
AF: Ideas are everywhere. You just have to look for them. A picture, a newspaper article or a snatch of conversation can trigger the idea for a story. The most important thing about writing is having a really good idea, preferably with a twist to it, which will make the book interesting and exciting rather than ordinary.

*Q: Do you plan your stories in advance?*
AF: Very much so! I spend most of the summer thinking of the plot for a new book. I write down ideas, try to get two or three different threads to the plot, work them into a story and then write down the personality of each character and how each one reacts to what is going on ... all this is almost another book in itself!

*Q: How long does it take you to write each book?*
AF: This is a tricky question! Once I have worked out the plot and everything is cut and dried, the first draft takes about four to five months to write.

*Q: Did you know when you were writing the first book in the series,* Dragonfire, *what would happen in the last book?*

AF: Only vaguely, however the seeds of the plot for the last book were sown in the first book.


*Q: What do you need to write well?*

AF: I need a computer, a quiet room and music, preferably classical. Music relaxes the brain, the rhythm helps you write good sentences and enhances the tone of the story. If I were writing about Christmas, for example, I'd play Christmas carols to put me in the mood.


*Q: Who is your favourite character in the* Dragonfire *series?*

AF: Quite frankly I love them all. I have a soft spot for Clara, however ... and my two magicians, Lord Rothlan and Prince Kalman ... and Arthur, of course!!


*Q: Have you ever based one of your characters on someone you know in real life?*

AF: No, not really but I must admit that Lady Ellan has a lot in common with my daughter!


*Q: Have your characters ever done anything you didn't expect them to?*

AF: Frequently! Characters often develop a life

of their own and do things you hadn't thought of. Sometimes this is helpful and improves the story but not always ...

*Q: You have written about a lot of magical creatures in your books. Which is your favourite magical creature and why?*
AF: Arthur the dragon is, of course, the main magical character in the series and I have always loved him but I must admit that I had a soft spot for poor Amgarad — especially when he was a monstrous bird.

*Q: How do you feel when you launch a new book?*
AF: Wonderful! The most exciting moment of all is when the publisher gives you the very first copy of your new book. I know it sounds strange, but the story in book form somehow looks completely different from the manuscript.

*Q: How do you think of the titles for your books?*
AF: Titles are very personal but it is actually the publisher who has the final decision. They have experience of the market and know the kind of title that will attract children.

*Q: Which is your favourite book in the series?*
AF: I think the first book will always be my favourite.

*Q: How do you decide what the covers of your books will look like?*
AF: The publisher decides what should appear on the cover and discusses ideas with an artist who then produces a choice of several pictures.

*Q:* Dragon Seeker *is the sixth and final book in the* Dragonfire *series. How do you feel now that the series is over?*
AF: I really feel quite sad ... I grew to love all my characters.

*Q: Are you planning to write any more children's books now that the series is finished?*
AF: I hope so. After finishing a series of books, however, it is quite difficult to dream up new ideas. It helps, too, if the ideas are lucky as well as good ... and perhaps lead to another series!

*Q: What is the best thing about being an author?*
AF: While writing, I become totally involved in the characters and the plot. It's like living in another world.

To learn more about Anne Forbes
and the *Dragonfire* series visit
DiscoverKelpies.co.uk.

Sign up for the Discover Kelpies eNewsletter
and receive the latest Kelpies news,
exclusive previews and competitions
direct to your inbox every month

# Have you discovered the Discover Kelpies website?

Adventure

Animals

Environment

Friendship

History

Laughs

Legends

Magic

Monsters

Secrets

Spooky

Thrills

Discover Kelpies is *the* website to visit if you love books!

- Read all about your favourite Kelpies books and authors
- Check what is happening on our blog
- Read exclusive extracts of new books
- Enter competitions
- Discover new books in your favourite subjects whether you love adventure, animals or magic!

## How can *you* get involved?

- Sign up to our Discover Kelpies eNewsletter

- Comment on our blog

- Send us reviews of your favourite Kelpies books

- Take a quiz, write your own story or make a wish with our Fun Stuff page (new fun things are being added all the time!)

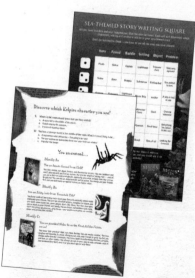

# Log on now at
# discoverkelpies.co.uk

# Lari Don

Helen and her fabled beast friends face
treacherous tasks and dangerous monsters in
three thrilling adventures.

*First Aid for Fairies and
Other Fabled Beasts*

*Wolf Notes and Other
Musical Mishaps*

*Storm Singing and
Other Tangled Tasks*

# Janis Mackay

Join half-selkie hero Magnus Fin on two exciting
underwater adventures as he struggles to save
the sea and his selkie family.

*Magnus Fin and
the Ocean Quest*

*Magnus Fin and
the Moonlight
Mission*